Dark Mountain Ambush

Dark Mountain Ambush

A Western Edge Mystery

Nicole Helm

TULE
PUBLISHING

Chapter One

T HINGS WERE BORING.
Samantha Price had been through enough *excitement* in her life to know that this was a good thing, for her mental well-being anyway. It wasn't exactly good for business though.

Private investigating required a certain level of not-so-boring to be profitable. She had all of *one* case here at the end of a particularly hot summer that had meant a lot of wildfire threats around the pretty little town of Marietta, Montana.

But fall was sweeping in. Cooling things off. Maybe the heat, the threat of loss, had kept cheating husbands, embezzling employees, and bored teens bent on destruction home and otherwise occupied.

Besides, the two biggest criminals of the area were currently behind bars. Two murderers.

Her father.

And the man walking through the front door's father.

It was what had brought Nate Bennet back to Marietta. Sam's quest to clear her father's name. And she might have—he hadn't committed that first murder—Benjamin Bennet had. But something about the time in jail for a

1

murder he didn't commit had broken her father. He'd committed his own, and framed Benjamin for it this spring.

Sam wasn't altogether sure if she'd *dealt with it* yet. But how did she deal with everything she'd believed and rested her reputation and hopes and dreams on being a lie? A tragic, pointless lie?

She shook her head and the past away with it. As much as she could. Nate barreling toward her helped.

"You sent me on a fake errand," he accused, as she'd known he would.

When Mrs. Cather had been their one and only case, Sam had pretended to hand it over to Nate to give him his first solo case, now that he was licensed.

In reality, she'd been desperate to pass off Mrs. Cather on someone else.

"It's not fake," Sam replied with a bland smile. "Mrs. Cather loves hiring Honor's Edge. She pays."

"No one dug up her damn sunflowers except her own dog. Maybe herself. I'm not altogether sure which." His scowl was fearsome, irritation roiling off him.

He made an impressive figure when angry. All windswept dark hair, no matter how little wind there was. He'd never gone back to the military short, but he didn't let it grow too long either. He'd returned to Marietta more soldier than the lanky, abused boy he'd slunk out of it as, but he'd still been recovering from an injury these past few months.

The limp was mostly gone now, and he was packing on more muscle. The gaunt look in his face had softened into chiseled. She couldn't deny that the changes made it harder to ignore the fact that he was … physically appealing.

She rolled her eyes at herself. *Physically appealing.* The guy was drop-dead gorgeous and she was hardly the only one in Marietta to notice. Ever since word had gotten out that he was working for Honor's Edge, she'd noticed an uptick in the female population walk by, necks craned to peer in her windows.

She scowled at her own thoughts, her own reaction. Pushed it away. Ignored it, because if there was anything Sam Price could do, it was ignore that which she didn't want to deal with. "She's old. She's alone. She's bored. Did you hear the part where she pays?"

This did not appease him. She hadn't really expected it to. "Then you take it," he said. "*You* deal with her."

"Nope. I'm the boss." She kicked up her heels on her desk and shot him a grin. "Finally, some perks."

His scowl lightened a bit, and she knew she'd amused him at least a little. "Should I ask the cops to arrest her dog then?" he grumbled.

"Present her with the facts. Act all apologetic like. She'll eat it up, make you some cookies—very good cookies, I might add—and then she'll leave you alone for a few weeks. Then next month she'll have a new mystery for you to solve. Remember, Nate, you're working partially on commission, and if she wants to pay you for a little attention, that's part in parcel with what we do here."

He sighed heavily. He didn't need money quite the same way she did. He was getting some kind of army compensation. For Nate, this job was something to do. Something to give him purpose. And yeah, Mrs. Cather wasn't much of a purpose, but Sam didn't have anything else to give him at the moment.

She understood it might be more difficult for a former Army Ranger to make sense of small-town nonsense, but he *had* grown up here. Even if he'd spent fifteen years off in the world doing *army* things. He should know how things worked. How people worked.

"Those out-of-town cases sure dried up fast." He stated this like it was just a casual observation and not a complaint.

Sam shrugged. It was true. After news that Honor's Edge had been involved in finding the truth of *two* murder cases—one fifteen years old—business had really picked up. She'd been slammed, and desperately waiting for Nate to finish his licensure so she could send him off on his own on occasion.

But the rush had turned to a trickle, and now there was nothing coming out of the tap. Sam had to believe it was just a hot summer. Fall would pick up. Besides. "The trial and sentencing will rile it all back up again."

"They said December for my dad's trial."

"Talking September for mine's sentencing." She smiled at him ruefully. "Aren't we a pair?"

He made a kind of grunting noise she'd taken to counting as a laugh, even if it was a little on the bitter side. The way she saw it, they both had some things to be bitter about. But if they let that eat at them…

She couldn't help but remember the way her father had tried to justify killing a woman in cold blood. Bitterness had done that to him. She wouldn't let it happen to her.

"Listen—" She was about to do something dumb, like invite him to dinner or suggest they go hit the bar.

Stupid because they spent too much time together as it was, and maybe they considered each other friends, after a fashion, but they didn't need to spend *all* their time together. That felt … risky. Especially when they were both feeling a little bored and antsy, because no cases and boredom might mean having to face their daddy issues.

We are a pair indeed.

Luckily Nate's phone ringing cut her off. He pulled the cell out of his back pocket. His expression changed from annoyed to something far more guarded. "It's Landon," he muttered.

She watched for another second as he only *looked* at his phone, didn't answer it. Maybe the brothers had made *some* inroads at repairing an incredibly broken relationship the past few months, but only some.

"Answer it, Nate," she said, in that gentle way Nate brought out in her that she still hadn't figured out what to do about yet.

Apparently hire him so you can be around him all the time.

"Hey," Nate greeted, phone to his ear. He listened, grunted a few times, then said, "Yeah, sure. Right now's good. Yeah, bye." His frown was back but puzzled as he pushed END on his phone screen, but then just kept staring at it, like he wasn't sure how it got in his hands. "He wants us to come up to the ranch."

Sam glanced at the clock on the wall. "You go ahead. I'll close up."

"*Us*, Sam." He looked up at her, worry and probably frustration *over* the worry in that dark gaze. "Not me. Honor's Edge Investigations. Something is wrong."

Sam sighed. This was all her fault.

She'd thought things were boring.

Chapter Two

The Bennet Ranch

Aly Cartwright frowned at Landon Bennet. Which she considered fair, because he was scowling at her.

"I told you not to call them," she said, trying to maintain her calm. "It's nothing."

"It's a *threat*," Landon insisted.

"It's a *prank*." One she wished she'd had the good sense to do something about before Landon had seen it. But someone had spray-painted a few colorful obscenities on the bed of her truck while she'd been running errands this morning. She'd walked out of the grocery store and there it had been.

Glaring and obvious in the pretty morning light. And okay. It had been jarring. A little concerning. But hardly a threat. It wasn't like the spray paint said, *Aly Cartwright, you are a bitch.*

No. It was just BITCH and a few other names she'd rather not think about.

"In the middle of the day? Who'd take that kind of chance without a reason to?"

"Some dumb kid, Landon. Or someone high and not at all concerned about consequences. I'll take it into the shop tomorrow and see if they can paint over it."

"Sure," Landon agreed. "After you talk to Sam and Nate."

She wanted to groan in frustration, but what would that do? Landon had already gone ahead and been his high-handed self and called Honor's Edge.

Once she got past her frustration with him not talking to her first, she might actually be okay with it. He was including Nate, and that felt like a step in the necessary continued repairing of their relationship. Aly desperately wanted all three Bennet brothers to find some common ground, some … friendship, amidst all the trauma their father had caused.

But right now she was mad. Because why would this be a threat? She didn't *want* it to be. Hadn't they been through enough?

Maybe it was wrong to want to bury her head in the sand, so to speak, but things were good. After almost a month of a lot of upheaval and worry and tragedy, things had evened out. Settled. It didn't make anything that had happened *right*, but a person couldn't fix the past.

They could only try to build a better future. And they'd been doing that.

Landon had asked her to move into the main house. It wasn't a marriage proposal, but considering she'd known Landon Bennet her whole life, she didn't expect different. Not yet. Eventually, yes. He was a traditional guy.

But he was the slowest man to accept change in the lower forty-eight.

He'd need time, and she'd give him time, because she always had. Always would. If she worried that made her pathetic, well…

Which one did she want to ignore more? Being pathetic or being scared?

"I reported it to the police. Why do we need to rope in Sam and Nate?" she demanded of Landon instead.

Because she hadn't *wanted* to call the police, but she'd known Landon wouldn't accept that. She thought she could get this by him.

She should have known better.

"They're going to do more than the police."

She could have argued more, but she'd get nowhere. He'd determined this was a threat, and Landon Bennet was the kind of man who had to save everyone from a threat.

Except himself.

Which she supposed was why she stayed by his side. *Someone* had to look out for *him* while he was so busy looking out for everyone else.

Besides, she loved him. She'd tried not to for most of her adult life, but it didn't work. And he might be a hard-headed pain in her ass, but he loved her too.

As if he could read her thoughts, he closed the distance between them, laid his arm over her shoulders. "Let's be cautious, Aly. Please. I need a little better safe than sorry right now."

Because he squeezed, she leaned into him. He smelled like horses and soap and home.

When she gave a slight nod, he pressed his mouth to her temple. "Thanks," he murmured. But he stiffened quickly, because they both heard the car coming before they saw it. The gravel drive that led up to the main house curved up a hill and then around to the flat plot of land much of the buildings had been built on years ago.

She didn't know what to expect from Sam and Nate. They'd investigated the Bennet murder, ripped apart the Bennet foundations, and in some ways, Aly still wanted to lay blame at Sam's feet for that.

They'd been friends once. Before loyalties had divided them as teens. And it hurt and twisted and *complicated* that Sam had been on the right side of all that.

Aly blew out a breath. Sam had nothing on the complication Nate had brought home, and Aly couldn't blame him for that. Not knowing his father had beaten him—had killed Marie Bennet all those years ago—had traumatized all three of his boys.

And she supposed her a little bit too.

She'd been born on this ranch, to the Bennet ranch foreman. She didn't know much about her mother, if the woman had ever been around or taken off the minute she'd given birth. No one had ever wanted to give her the details, and she supposed she'd learned not to ask for them.

Marie Bennet had been the closest thing she'd had to a mother, and then after her murder, Aly had tried to fashion herself into something of a mother as an orphaned ranch hand.

All things she hadn't spent much time thinking about as she'd grown up but had become impossible not to ruminate on since they'd discovered Benjamin Bennet *had* killed his wife all those years ago.

Sam was in the driver's seat of a junky old sedan, but it was Nate who got out of the car first.

Landon and Nate didn't look as much alike as Nate did to the oldest Bennet, Cal, who was back in Texas. But there were similarities. The Bennets were all lookers, as some of the older folks in town liked to say. Dark hair and eyes. Different builds, different ways those eyes settled into their faces, but the lines were often the same and the overall impact was very much the same. No one would deny the three were closely related.

Sam and Nate walked over to where Aly and Landon stood by Aly's truck. The offensive words painted all over it. Nate and Sam were clearly both surveying it as they approached.

"Not very artistic," Sam offered.

"Or personal," Aly replied, before Nate could.

She could tell he'd had the same thought when his gaze tracked to hers. Maybe it didn't register surprise, but he wouldn't look at her otherwise.

"I don't know," Sam said conversationally, working her way around the vehicle. "Maybe it's not your name, but it's clearly geared toward a woman. Bitch, whore ... and the rest. Those aren't generally words used against a man."

That didn't bring Aly any comfort. "Okay, so maybe they saw me get out of the truck or something."

"Can you think of anyone you've had a problem with recently?" Nate asked her.

She had no right to be angry. Not at them. They were doing their job. But panic was mounting, and that meant she used anger to keep it at bay. "You mean, anyone aside from the man we all helped put behind bars?"

"Yeah, besides him. Maybe one of the ranch hands

weren't too happy about that?"

"The ranch hands are behind me. Us," Landon said. "One hundred percent."

"Yeah, I'm sure if they weren't they'd let you know," Nate said. Sarcasm didn't drip from his tone, but it didn't need to.

"They would. And why would they take any of that out on Aly? Particularly *off* the ranch," Landon replied stubbornly. "Besides, it's been months."

"There's still a trial yet to go."

"It's a formality and everyone knows it."

Nate sighed, exhausted. "You called *us*, Landon. You said there's a threat. We're trying to determine where it could be coming from. It requires questions, whether you like them or not."

Aly knew it took a lot for Landon not to argue with that. And that his non-response amounted to being worried about *her*, because he cared about her.

"Why don't you both come on inside?" Aly offered, wanting to make some peace. "We'll have some coffee and see what we can come up with."

Nate looked up at the house. Sam looked at Nate. And Aly watched them both. Nate's reticence. Sam's concern.

But it was Nate who nodded, moving them all forward. "Sure, let's do that."

EVEN THOUGH ALMOST nothing was different in the house, Nate felt the years between the time he'd lived here and now as if they were plates of glass between him and everything around him.

He'd been here a few times since coming back to town. Always in the kitchen or the dining room with Aly bustling around, reminding him too much of his mother. Landon sitting at the table, a little dourly, just like their father.

Except, if Aly spoke to Landon, asked him to do something, Landon's face softened. Maybe Benjamin Bennet's face had softened once too, but Nate couldn't remember that ever being the case.

And considering he'd murdered his wife, beaten Nate to a bloody pulp when he'd been a kid, Nate probably didn't owe Benjamin Bennet any benefits of the doubt.

The strange note in this uncomfortable tableau wasn't the past though. He was getting used to the past haunting him at every turn. Months back in Marietta hadn't magically changed it into *home*.

Especially as they worked through the aftermath of learning their father had murdered their mother, and the things Cal had remembered after traumatically blocking them out.

Sam sat at the table. He didn't think she'd ever sat there. He didn't think she'd been welcomed into this house in something like fifteen years. *Maybe* back in high school when she had been friends with Aly, before Mom had died.

After that, supporting her father—who had been accused and convicted of killing Mom—had made her a direct enemy of the Bennets.

Everything that had happened since he'd been back had made her *less* of an enemy, but it sure hadn't made her a friend. He didn't know how she did it, but she didn't look uncomfortable. She sat at the table like she had every right to be there, like no one in this room had anything against her. Or that she hadn't earned some bitterness and some things held against *them*.

He could know it was an act and still be impressed she could do it so well.

Aly set a stack of coffee mugs on the table. He remembered his parents drinking out of the same mugs. Then she set a trivet down in the middle of the table and set the coffeepot on top. She followed this up with a little carton of cream and a folded-over bag of sugar mostly gone.

When Landon reached out and took her by the hand, she sighed and finally sat. Then, in the same silence, they all took turns pouring coffee into their mugs and doctoring it to their liking.

"On the surface, it looks like a prank," Sam said after she'd taken a sip of coffee with a little cream. "But surfaces can be deceiving."

Landon nodded at her.

Aly frowned. "I really don't know who would have done that on purpose," Aly replied. "In any kind of way that was meant to threaten me on a personal level. I've had hours to think about it, go back over the day." She cupped her hands around the mug, looking miserably down at it. "There's nothing that sticks out."

"We can ask around, see if anyone saw anything. The police will no doubt be doing the same, and I can see what they come up with on their report. If it *was* a prank, you'll have a culprit in a few days."

"And if it wasn't?" Landon demanded.

"My guess? You won't find the culprit. But something else will happen. An escalation."

Aly took in a sharp breath.

"I'm not saying you need to be scared, but you need to be aware," Sam continued, sounding professional and in charge. "Maybe a few months go by and nothing else happens. Maybe it really was just random. But the fact of the matter is, the murders brought a lot of attention to Marietta, and us, and you just never know who might have taken an interest in that."

"You think this is about the murders?" Aly looked torn between disbelief and horror.

"Not necessarily. I just think that's the thing that's changed lately. That's shifted how you might be perceived in town. Out of town. Unless you can think of some other interaction. But it's pretty well known you and Landon spend most of your time on the ranch. I'm pretty sure *interactions* of any kind would be the talk of the town. Just like the murders have been."

Aly smiled wryly while Landon frowned.

"Been pretty busy up here lately," he said, as if Sam had insulted him in some way.

Nate wanted to roll his eyes, but instead of rile up his brother, he focused on the problem at hand. Someone *had* vandalized Aly's truck.

"What about Sandy's family?" Nate asked, mulling over Sam's theory. "Did you have any contact with them?"

"Not in a while. After the murder, I talked to her mother a few times, but it was mostly just the woman sobbing. Not really a conversation. Right after they arrested Ben, her brother came by wanting any of her stuff that was left. I gave it to him. I wouldn't say he was *polite*, but he certainly wasn't threatening."

Nate shared a glance with Sam. She gave a little nod—a sign she wanted him to take the lead.

"Take us through the interaction with the brother. From the beginning."

"I don't think…"

Landon laid his hand over hers. "Go on, Al. It doesn't hurt to go through it."

LANDON LISTENED AS Aly recounted her one and only encounter with Brody McCoy. Brody had come to the house without warning a week after Ben had been arrested. Landon had been out dealing with calving, and Aly had only come back to the house for lunch.

"He'd just been sitting in his truck. He got out the minute my feet hit the porch. I remember because I hadn't noticed the unfamiliar truck. It had been mostly hidden behind Ben's, which we hadn't figured out what to do with yet."

"And you don't think that was on purpose?" Sam asked, a kind of gentleness that made it sound less like the accusation that would have no doubt come out of Landon's own mouth.

Habit born of fifteen years of hating the woman who couldn't let the past *be* meant he hated giving Sam credit where credit was due, but he understood, even if he didn't want to, that she was good at her job.

When it came to making sure Aly was safe and not some kind of target of something, Landon would admit whatever uncomfortable truths he had to.

"No. It was a natural place to park. Maybe he startled me a little, but he just kind of walked up to the porch. I didn't recognize him. He introduced himself, politely, asked if Sandy had any belongings left. I told him she did, that I'd packed them up myself, and offered them up."

"And he didn't seem angry?"

Aly took a moment, clearly thinking back to the moment. "I can't say he didn't seem *angry*, but it wasn't geared toward me. He didn't glare or curse or anything. He seemed to just … be mad his sister was dead. Or mad that this was an errand he had to do, you know? I told him to wait outside, and he did. I got the box. I took it to him. And that was pretty much that."

Nate's gaze moved from Aly to Landon. Landon tried not to tense, but sometimes it was just damn disorienting. How much Nate looked like Cal. Or, in certain lights, Dad. And, in those same lights, Landon himself. But Landon had no context for his baby brother looking like him or Dad or Cal. Landon had watched Dad and Cal get older. Nate had left a sixteen-year-old and returned a thirty-one-year-old man. Fully grown. Fully … someone Landon didn't know.

They'd shared dinners since Nate's return and Dad's arrest. There were attempts to be in each other's orbit, to treat each other like brothers—whatever the fuck that looked like. But nothing had really *gelled* yet. It was still damn weird.

Nate said nothing to him, just looked, then turned his

gaze back to Aly.

The trill of a phone interrupted the silence, and Aly looked at her phone screen. Then up at him. "It's Jill."

"You go on and take it," Sam said before Landon could offer anything. Sam pushed back from the table. "We've got enough to poke into it."

Aly answered the phone and walked out of the kitchen and into the living room. Nate stood and followed Sam out of the kitchen.

Landon walked Sam and Nate out of the house. It was a strange feeling. The woman he'd hated for fifteen years. The brother he'd thought dead for fifteen years. Now they were all connected.

Now, Landon figured he needed their help if he was going to keep Aly safe. Nothing was more important to him than that.

"You really think it could be the brother?" he asked, gearing the question more to Nate than Sam out of habit.

"If it's anything, I think looking into the McCoys is a good start," Sam answered.

But Landon was looking at his brother.

"You have to entertain that, Landon," Nate said, and Landon tried not to bristle at the lecture in his tone. "As much as this could be *something*, it could be *nothing*."

"But you'll figure it out. Either way."

Nate looked from Landon to Sam, then gave a nod. "We will."

The *we* was pointed, so Landon forced himself to look at Sam. He couldn't force himself to smile—that wasn't easy on a good day with someone he liked. But he tried not to scowl at her. "Thanks for coming out. We appreciate it."

"*You* appreciate it." Sam jerked her chin toward the house. "She doesn't."

Landon couldn't keep his neutral expression in place. It morphed into that scowl. "No shit?"

She let out a little laugh, that almost eased some of the jagged edges in his chest. "Okay, so you know that. We'll be in touch." She began to walk away, but Nate stood there for a few extra seconds.

"I appreciate the call, Landon."

Landon wasn't comfortable with the way Nate said things sometimes. There was a gravity to his baby brother Landon could handle when it was doused with stoicism. Hell, that was the Bennet way.

But Nate seemed perfectly comfortable to *verbalize* that gravity, in the sharpest ways, and Landon didn't know how to just accept the words.

He had to deflect them somehow. "It's for Aly."

"Yeah, which is why I know it means something that you called us. It wasn't just a gesture. You trust us."

"Trust is a hell of a word," Landon muttered. He shoved his hands into his pockets, knowing if the woman in question was standing out here, she'd nudge him to give more than that. And because he loved her in spite of himself, he made the effort. "But I guess I do."

Nate only nodded and then turned to follow Sam. Thank *God* he hadn't belabored the damn point. Landon practically jogged inside, just in case Nate might change his mind and want to have some kind of heart-to-heart.

When he returned to the kitchen, Aly was off the phone

and tidying up. He grabbed the rest of the mugs off the table and brought them over to the sink.

"How's Jill?"

Aly smiled, but it was tight. "Oh, just fine. I guess Glenda had a doctor's appointment this afternoon, so she heard about my truck while they were in town." She ran the water to hot. "It's all over. Everyone's gossiping about it apparently." Her smile completely died at that. "Even though I purposefully didn't go to Murphys because I don't like the way people ... *whisper* about us now."

"It's not such a bad thing in this case, Al. I know people love to talk and that's annoying, but it also means people will be on the lookout for anything off. Hell, if it *was* kids I bet someone at the store will have the culprit tagged in no time." He tried to adopt the low, gruff tone of the group of old men who liked to sit around town pretending they weren't just gossips. "That Hank's boy's cousin's brother bought four cans of yellow spray paint at the hardware store on August third."

Aly actually laughed, which made him feel less ridiculous for impersonating anyone. "I hope so." She looked back at the entry into the kitchen. "But you're still going to have them look into it."

"Yeah," he agreed, and he didn't bother to explain himself.

She knew him well enough to understand, and if she didn't like it, they just had to be in a stalemate.

"I don't think the McCoys had anything to do with it. I hate the idea Sam and Nate might go bother them. They lost their daughter, their sister. They've been through enough."

"So have you."

She shook her head. "No one I love is dead, Landon. No one I love was ... well, I did love your mother, and she was murdered, but ... That makes it all the more poignant. It's awful to lose someone that way. Don't you have any empathy for them?"

Maybe that was what was wrong with him. Empathy for people he didn't know felt like an expenditure of energy he couldn't muster when so much of his energy went to worry about and over the people he did know and love.

But how was he supposed to tell her that? She wanted him to have empathy, and he didn't. She wanted him to be someone he wasn't, and...

Well, that wasn't true. Aly had never asked more of him than he should give. In fact, she frequently asked for nothing at all. So he tried to give her something without her asking for it.

"It's hard to have empathy for whoever might be behind this. Whether it's a threat or just a dumb prank. Because it feels like a threat, and I know how fragile it all is." He'd lost his mother, and for fifteen years believed Gene Price had been the culprit, only to find out it had been his own father. To find out Dad had beaten Nate, and possibly Mom as well.

Only for *all* of that to lead to Gene Price *actually* killing Sandy McCoy.

So no, he didn't have empathy. He had fucking *terror* that something else horrible would happen. "It'd kill me, straight up, if anything happened to you, Aly."

She held his gaze, even though her pretty blue eyes filled.

"I know." She lifted to her toes, pressed her mouth to his. "That's why I put up with you."

He managed half a laugh. He didn't know how it was enough. He was a surly asshole most the time. But he held her against him, found comfort in someone putting up with him at all.

Chapter Three

Sam's apartment above Honor's Edge Investigations Office

S AM AND NATE had gone their separate ways last night after she'd dropped him off at his truck. They hadn't said much. A lot of times they didn't.

She'd wanted to though. Ask him how long he was going to keep renting that cabin. If he was ever going to sack up and put down roots. He'd bought his truck, but that and getting his PI license was about the only thing he'd done with any sense of permanence since moving to Marietta.

Not that she'd ever asked him about his *permanent* plans. She didn't poke into his private business. And he hadn't offered any information on it either.

Still, eventually renting a cabin from her aunt wasn't going to be financially feasible, even if Aunt Lisa was cutting him a break.

Since she didn't particularly want to think about her aunt right now, she reminded herself it was none of her damn business as she tossed and turned through the night, instead of sleeping peacefully like a woman *should*. Though she'd much rather ruminate over Nate and his future than the *other* thing that plagued her insomniac nights.

Her father. Murder. Jail. Aunt Lisa blaming her for the last bit.

Yeah, Nate was a better focus.

Eventually she gave up on sleep, made some coffee, ate some breakfast, and headed downstairs to the office to get started for the day.

She needed to hire a cleaner for the offices, she thought to herself with some frustration. It was a thought just about every day, only with gradually more frustration she hadn't sucked it up and done it yet.

Her father had done the job up until his subsequent arrest.

She could afford it, but dry times like these made her worry about money and affording it long-term. Sure Aly's case might bring in *some* money, but Nate would probably want to cut them a break cost wise. As he should.

And just like that, her thoughts were back to Nate. Which, in fairness, was better than thinking about her father.

He was an employee. Kind of a friend, in that weird coworker friend, connected pasts kind of way. If he wanted to tell her his plans, he would. If he didn't, he wouldn't.

And neither eventuality mattered.

So she focused on work.

She started with doing some research on Brody McCoy. Where he lived, what he did. Any comments he'd made publicly about Sandy's murder. She worked on that for maybe twenty minutes before she heard the sound of the back door opening.

She looked up. It was still dark out, but Nate stepped in from the back. He stopped short at her sitting there.

"You're down early," he commented.

"So are you."

They surveyed each other, neither giving reasons for why. Her reasons—crappy sleep and needing to do something instead of lying there and thinking about *him*—were hers. She didn't need to know his.

"I got a head start," she said looking back down at her laptop. "Brody McCoy lives in Livingston. Short drive. We could try to set up a meeting rather than have a conversation on the phone."

"Sure. You want to make the initial contact, or should I?"

"I'm going with you since Sandy's murderer happens to share my last name. Yours isn't much better, but it's some better. In fact, I think it's best if we keep my relationship to my father out of the equation as much as we can."

"Makes sense."

Sam sometimes wondered if she'd ever be used to this. She had a partner, essentially. After being mostly alone since her father had been arrested all those years ago it still struck her as *odd*. Aunt Lisa had been a parent figure. A soft-ish place to land—she was a tough Montana ranch woman after all.

But it wasn't like being in this together. Sam had been the kid. Lisa had been the adult. And now, Lisa wasn't talking to her at all.

But this, Nate, was just two adults working together, taking different elements of one case. She could sort of hide her identity from Brody McCoy, let Nate take the lead, and still get done what needed to be done.

It was a nice change of pace, having someone to share the work, especially considering the stress of the past few months. She felt less like she was constantly walking a tightrope.

Nate made the call once it was a decent hour, and Brody McCoy agreed to meet them at some hole-in-the-wall diner before he had to work his afternoon shift. Nate said he didn't sound happy about it, but he also hadn't refused.

Not the move of a guilty man.

Nate drove since Sam had driven last night. A habit they'd fallen into without ever really speaking about it. When they had to drive somewhere together, they took turns. When they were both in the office together around lunchtime or dinnertime, they usually walked over to get pizza or grab something at Main Street Diner.

"You don't think he's got anything to do with it, do you?" Nate asked, navigating the truck into Livingston.

"No," she replied, happy to get her mind geared toward the case. "If it had happened a few months ago? Sure. But unless he says something like he's been on a submarine since he took Sandy's things, the timing doesn't make much sense."

"Unless it was a crime of opportunity over a crime of passion."

"Stop reading detective stories, Nate."

She got a snort of a laugh out of him and tried not to grin. "The thing is, I just don't see words like those on Aly's truck being random," Sam said, thinking it through. There was just one thing she couldn't get over. "But Aly doesn't go around making enemies."

"Except you."

Sam shook her head. "Luckily I don't hold a grudge."

"My ass you don't, Sam."

"Okay. Fair enough." She would have laughed, but some of those grudges still stuck in her craw. "Sometimes I see your brother and I'd like to trip him and watch him fall face first into a puddle of mud."

"So violent," Nate said, amused.

Landon and Nate might be trying to make some inroads into being brothers again, but there were still some resentments that lingered.

And because there was, and she understood that all too well, she figured she might as well explain.

"And sure, I remember everyone who sniffed at me for fifteen years—thought I was stupid, delusional, or pathetic and made it clear to me. *But*, my point is, I don't have a grudge for Aly. Do I want to be best friends again? No. But I can't blame her for the way she acted. Your family was the closest thing she had to it. Why wouldn't she have protected that? Same goes for Landon, though I can't promise when I was younger and angrier I didn't *think* about keying his truck on occasion. The thing is, I didn't though. If I *had*, it would have been *early*. It would have been when I was mad, when I didn't have control over all that mad. What does Brody have to be mad about now?"

"Maybe he's more a fester and explode type person?"

She didn't think it was pointed at her father, but she tensed all the same. "Maybe, and that's why we're going to talk to him."

Brody McCoy was about what she'd expected. A rough-around-the-edges blue-collar guy, irritated his day was being upended by talking to *private investigators*, and not at all grateful that they'd been the ones to uncover his sister's killer because, hey, she was still dead.

"Do you know Aly Cartwright?"

His brow furrowed, and he seemed to think that over. "Sounds familiar, but I can't place it."

"She's a hand on the Bennet Ranch," Nate offered casually. "She said you picked up some of Sandy's things from her a while back."

"Oh right. Her." Brody's expression didn't darken, but it was already dark enough. Still, he shrugged. "That's the only interaction I ever had with her. Hope to keep it that way. What's this about? She got more of Sandy's things?"

Sam managed a friendly approximation of a smile. "Not that we're aware of. We're just investigating something separate and trying to get a handle on all the players, Mr. McCoy."

"Sandy's dead. Her murderer is in jail." Brody just sounded tired now. "That old bastard she just *had* to take up with is in jail too. As far as I'm concerned, as far as my family is concerned, it's over. It's all over. Dead and buried with her. We're not players in jack shit."

"Then I'm sorry to have taken up your time. We'll handle the bill."

Brody looked at Sam, then Nate, and then without another word got up and strode out of the restaurant. Sam watched him go, considering.

"Dead end," Nate offered.

"Yeah." She grabbed her credit card and the bill and gestured Nate to follow her up to the cash register.

"You don't sound convinced," he said.

It was a little uncomfortable that he could see through her. But maybe it was just informed by his own feelings on the matter. Maybe he wasn't convinced either.

Except it was more complicated than that.

"I am convinced Brody's got nothing to do with Aly's truck. But it's interesting, I think, that he'd bring up his whole family like he spoke for them. It's a protective kind of move. Leave us *all* alone."

"So you think someone in his family did it?"

"No, not necessarily." Sam considered what information she knew about the McCoys.

Sandy's mother and father were divorced and both remarried, her dad multiple times. She had a lot of siblings—full, half, and step. It was interesting Brody would collectively and proactively say they were *all* closing the book on Sandy's life.

"It's just another thread to pull," Sam said. "But first, I want to visit any hardware stores that might sell spray paint here." She signed the receipt the cashier gave her. "We're going to do some canvassing."

NATE HAD NEVER had any dreams of being an investigator, or even anything connected to law enforcement. He wasn't sure he'd really had dreams as a kid. Maybe some distant ones about playing pro baseball or heading to the Olympics for hurdles, but the Bennet Ranch had been so all encompassing he had never really thought leaving possible.

Until he'd had to do it. He'd gone into the army because

it had been something. It offered pay and housing and a family of sorts. He'd found he excelled in a rank structure. In superiors who weren't as uniform or upstanding as they pretended.

It had felt a lot like home on the Bennet Ranch.

Besides, he'd been broke, homeless, and alone. There'd been no real choice there. There'd been no real plan. He'd just kept stepping up the ranks because he was good.

So it was still disorienting to have been discharged, even though it had been almost two years. It was still disorienting to be delving into what his own dreams might be or look like.

He couldn't say getting his PI license had been a lark. Maybe the idea he could do this had been ... offhanded almost. Something to pass the time with. But he'd had to apply himself to get the license. And he'd had to really consider if this was what he wanted.

What any kind of future outside the army and being back home in Montana looked like.

Sometimes, like right now, he tagged along with Sam, watched her do her job, and felt a bit outside himself. Like it wasn't him who'd made any of those choices and now didn't know what to do with them.

She was damn good at her job. She was some kind of multifaceted prism, who could reflect whatever she needed to. And yet it didn't mean she didn't have personality. Sam was Sam, and he'd never met anyone else like her.

She could smile and charm and threaten and intimidate at any given turn. Her brain worked in fascinating ways when it came to a case. She told people what they wanted to hear, or the direct opposite, all depending on the situation. And despite all her prickly ways, she had what seemed like an endless well of patience and empathy for just about everyone.

Even the people who didn't deserve it.

Not that Sam should be his current focus. And she wasn't, because this was about learning how to do this job he'd fallen into.

They'd bounced around a few hardware stores that sold spray paint, but Sam hadn't gotten anything she felt was a lead. He'd stood back and watched, tried to absorb what she did and why she did it.

Maybe he'd never expected to have a dream outside escape, outside the army, outside himself. But he wanted to succeed at this in ways he wasn't fully comfortable with, so he kept it to himself.

How much he watched, studied, wanted.

"They probably bought it at one of the big box stores in Bozeman," Sam muttered irritably as they left yet another hardware store. "Good luck getting any answers there. We'll get frozen out by those slick corporations."

"Did you expect something different?"

"Expect and hope are two different things, Nate," Sam said as she strode in long strides for such short legs toward his truck.

He slid into the driver's seat as she climbed up into the passenger's. He started driving back toward Marietta, thinking about the questions Sam had asked.

A big box store made sense, but it required time and effort. Drive out to Bozeman. Drive back to Marietta. Paint Aly's truck. It was a lot of effort for a prank.

So what if it hadn't started as a prank at all? "Yellow spray paint is used on ranches a lot. Depending on the color of the machinery you use. I bet if you went into one of the sheds up at Landon's place, you'd find bottles of green and yellow. Maybe red."

He felt Sam's gaze on him even as he kept his on the highway.

"You think someone at the Bennet Ranch did it?" she asked, her tone devoid of any indication of what she thought about that.

It irritated him that he realized he'd been hoping for her approval, or her agreement, or being impressed he'd drawn such a connection.

"No, I'm not saying that," he replied, trying to shove his annoying reactions away. "Just that it'd be easy to get your hands on it. Claim it was for your ranch. If you're a rancher."

"Or pilfer some if you know where to look." Sam let out a gusty sigh. "That doesn't really help us any."

"No, I guess it doesn't."

She leaned back in her seat, frowning and tapping her fingers against her thigh. "We can't rule out the other McCoys, we need to look into them, and I know Landon said the ranch hands are behind him, but it wouldn't hurt to look into them too."

"I'll take the ranch hands," Nate said.

Sam didn't say anything for a few humming minutes of driving. "That's likely to piss off Landon."

"He's the one who hired us."

She nodded slowly, thoughtfully. "I guess so. All right.

Then it's settled. You've got the ranch hands, and I'll poke into the McCoys."

Yeah. Settled.

He highly doubted it.

Chapter Four

The Bennet Ranch

ALY WIPED HER sweaty forehead with the back of her hand. She shouldn't wish for cooler temperatures. Winter was long and brutal on a Montana ranch, but by God she was so damn tired of sweating.

She'd spent her afternoon working in the pens to start cleaning them out and getting them ready for winter. Landon was out with the other hands trimming some trees and fixing up some fence line on the north side of the property.

She'd cut out a little early to mulch the garden now that she'd harvested everything, but it was just too damn hot. She was going to get an early start on dinner, then maybe head back out later, but as she reached the porch, she noted a car she didn't recognize in the drive.

Worse, a woman standing next to it. Aly supposed it was better than a man, or anyone holding a can of spray paint, but unannounced visitors were concerning enough all on their own. Now that Landon had made her *paranoid*, she was extra concerned.

The woman was looking at her, but didn't approach. Aly was looking right back, but also didn't move for her.

After a minute of this strange standoff, the woman

pushed off the car and crossed the yard to stand in front of Aly. She gave a friendly kind of wave, but nerves rattled off the woman.

She said nothing.

Aly forced herself to talk around a too-tight throat. "Can I help you?" It wasn't just a stranger being in the yard that was unsettling now, it was the woman's appearance.

Aly wanted to pull her cell out of her pocket and call Landon but couldn't quite bring herself to.

The woman just stared at her with blue eyes that matched her own.

When she finally spoke, she cleared her throat first. "I'm, uh, looking for Tripp Cartwright."

Aly's dad's name immediately made this entire interaction even more unsettling. Aly shifted from one foot to the other. She glanced back at the house. Landon would be out with the trees and fences for at least another hour.

Which meant she had to handle this. Which she should, considering Tripp was *her* dad. It was just … she hated saying the words, no matter how long he'd been gone. "Tripp Cartwright passed away. Quite a few years ago."

The woman stood stock still, but Aly could see the color slowly but decidedly melt out of her face. "Oh," she said. Then she repeated the noise, blinking rapidly.

She reached out, almost toward Aly, like she needed balance. It went against everything Aly usually was. She liked to help. But she stepped away, because this woman was making her feel really, really uncomfortable.

When the woman had nothing to grab onto, she simply sank to the ground. Somewhat gracefully and in an upright position, but right there on the ground, looking pale and shaky.

A year ago, Aly would have rushed to help her. But with everything that had happened since Sandy's death, Aly could only stand stock still.

"You okay?" she asked hesitantly.

The woman nodded, waved a shaky hand. "Yeah. Yeah, I just … It didn't occur to me he could be…" She swallowed, looked up at Aly beseechingly. "How?"

Aly tried not to picture it. His still body. His open, life-less eyes. And for terrible moments, just her and him. Until Landon had come in. Apparently she'd been screaming and she hadn't known it.

Aly hated being thrust back into that ugly past. "Heart attack," she managed.

The woman nodded again, took a shaky deep breath. "I'm real sorry about that. He was a good man. A good…"

"He was." Aly knew he'd always felt out of his depth be-ing the single father to a young girl, trying to raise her on his own, on this ranch that wasn't his. But she'd always known he loved her. "How'd you know him?"

The woman slowly pushed back to her feet, then shoved some of her hair back. Red hair, though Aly figured it was red from a bottle—it was awfully close to the same shade as Aly's own hair.

It was that, and the way the woman looked at her like she was a drink of water in the middle of a desert, that had panic tickling the back of her throat. She didn't want to touch the unbidden thought poking at her, but it kept poking. Kept trying to get through.

"What's your name, sweetheart?" the woman asked, instead of answering Aly's question.

She shouldn't tell her. Aly *knew* that instinctually, and yet the thought poking at her made it real hard to listen to her reasonable self. "Aly. Aly Cartwright."

The woman's eyes filled. "That's what I thought."

"You know me?" Aly managed to ask, even though none of this was what she wanted.

The woman shook her head. "No, not really. Not the way you mean." The woman brought up a still shaking hand, pressed it to her own abdomen. "I can't imagine how you'll take this, sweetheart, but I ... my name is Janie Turner."

The woman waited, like Aly should recognize that name, but she didn't. And still, she thought she knew exactly who this woman was, as little as she wanted to.

The woman swallowed, took another little step forward. "I'm your mother."

LANDON WALKED BACK to the house, cursing the heat and just about every damn thing under the sun.

He wanted an ice-cold beer, something for dinner that wouldn't make him any hotter than he already was, and he wanted to hear Aly hum while she did some chore. He'd kept his hands and eyes and *thoughts* of Aly to himself for a lot of years, some misguided promise he'd made to his father. But life, even with all the external factors that had been god-awful, had been better once he'd stopped trying to pretend like he wasn't in love with her.

It was the kind of realization that made him uncomfortable, because he hadn't exactly learned to trust the *good* things in his life. They usually up and disappeared pretty damn quick.

Except Aly. She'd always been by his side. And he'd been thinking a lot lately about making that permanent. How much it made sense to wait—they hadn't been *together* that long, but in the grand scheme of things they…

Landon came to a stop before he made it to the porch. He was surprised and confused to see Aly standing out in the yard with a woman he didn't recognize. Though as he got closer, there was something weirdly familiar about the woman's features.

The woman saw him or heard him approach first. Her blue eyes flicked over him with a kind of dissatisfied survey, but this prompted Aly to turn around.

She greeted him with relief. Her entire face sagged with it, and she took a few steps toward him. Her clasped hands dropped and reached out to him for a second, before she awkwardly let them fall at her sides as she turned back to the woman.

"Landon." She turned her gaze back to him and she looked as lost as he'd ever seen her.

Which prompted him to reach out to her, put his hand on her shoulder.

"This is Janie Turner," she said.

Her voice was weird. Everything about her was off. She was pale. He didn't even bother to look at this Janie woman when Aly looked like she'd seen a ghost.

"What's wrong?" he said, keeping his voice as low as he

could so the woman wouldn't hear.

Aly shook her head, but there were tears in her eyes as she looked up at him. "She says she's my mother," Aly said on nothing more than a whisper.

He didn't think she spoke that quietly to keep it from the woman, but because she couldn't physically get the words out at a normal volume. Landon immediately moved in between Aly and the woman, even if there was no physical threat here. It was hard to deny the *familiar* he'd noted in her was a resemblance to Aly, but even if she *was* Aly's mother, that didn't mean she had any right to be here. Landon had always heard Aly's mother had given birth and then disappeared with little more than a very brief note addressed to Tripp.

Showing up almost thirty-two years later wasn't about to fly. Not when it had clearly upset Aly.

"Ms. Turner, I don't know who you are or why you're here—"

"I came to find Tripp. Aly told me he ... passed."

"A long time ago," he replied, squeezing Aly's hand that grabbed his. "Maybe it's best if you head on out of here for now. Leave your phone number if you'd like. Aly will be in touch if she wants to be."

The woman's expression radiated hurt, but Landon wouldn't be deterred. She shouldn't have ambushed Aly like this.

"I don't ... have anything to write with or..."

Landon pulled his phone out of his pocket, pulled up his contacts and hit the button to add a new contact. Then he held it out to her. "You go on and type it in there."

The woman looked at the outstretched phone, then Landon, then Aly standing there behind him. Her expression was inscrutable, which Landon didn't trust in the slightest, but she finally took the phone and typed in her number.

Along with the name. JANIE TURNER (ALY'S MOM).

Landon tried not to scowl. He slid his phone into his pocket, then turned his back on the woman and began to usher Aly up the stairs of the porch.

"I'd like to talk, Aly. About so many things," Janie called.

Landon opened the door, didn't look back. "She'll be in touch if she'd like to be." He led Aly inside.

He didn't bother to make sure the woman went to her car and left. He'd check that later.

"You didn't … you probably shouldn't have…" Landon moved Aly into the living room as she babbled.

He nudged her onto the couch.

She sagged into the cushions. "I should have been more polite. Invited her in. I…"

"Aly, honey." He sat next to her, sliding his arm around her shoulders and pulling her into an embrace. "You're shaking like a leaf."

For a few minutes, Aly didn't say anything. She just leaned into him, still shaking.

When she finally spoke, her voice was a bit of a squeak. "She looks like me."

"Yeah." He could hardly argue cold hard facts. He brushed a hand over her hair. "I guess she does."

She looked up at him. "It's got to be true then, doesn't it? Dad didn't talk about her much, but he never said

39

definitively that she was dead. He didn't like to talk about her, didn't let anyone else talk about her. It's ... true. Don't you think?"

The tears in her eyes that didn't fall just about killed him. The desperate need for an answer he couldn't give her. "Maybe. Maybe it is true." He kissed her temple, held her close, trying to will the shaking away. "We'll sort it out, but at your pace. She can't just show up and expect to be invited in. She's got to give you time and space."

"She's my mother."

"Maybe. We'll figure out if that's true. But you don't owe her anything, Al. Nothing you don't want to give." He held on tight, hating how much this had rattled her.

If it was true, Landon desperately wanted it to be a positive thing for her, but he didn't know how a random appearance after all this time could be *good*.

"Maybe she ... left for a good reason," Aly said, her voice a little muffled by his shoulder. "She said she didn't know Dad was dead, and she seemed really surprised. Really ... affected when I told her. Maybe she's back for a good reason. Maybe there's ... a good reason."

"Maybe," he agreed, because she needed some hope. Some possibility.

But he doubted it.

Chapter Five

The Harrington Cabin

JILL HARRINGTON SAT at the tiny, scarred table in her grandmother's little cabin and held Aly's hand while Aly relayed what had happened to her yesterday.

"She just came right out and said, I'm your mother?" Jill asked, trying to imagine the scene.

She had a pretty good imagination, her writing career could attest, but this seemed ... one of those *real* things no one would believe in a fictional book.

Aly nodded. Then she swallowed. "I didn't handle it very well."

"Why should you have?" Jill replied, giving her hand a squeeze.

Aly wasn't one for physical comforts, even though they'd been friends—increasingly close—since Jill came to live in Montana almost three years ago. So Jill wasn't about to let go until Aly did. "Some random woman pops up claiming to be your mom out of nowhere? That's messed up."

"But ... what was she supposed to do?" Aly asked, clearly desperate for answers that weren't going to be easy to come by. "Send a letter? Make a phone call? I don't think there's a good, right way to do this."

"Did you call her?"

Aly shook her head. "Not yet. I don't think Landon wants me to."

Jill tried to keep her expression neutral. "What do you want?"

Aly took her hand away, raked it through her hair. "I don't know. That's why I…" She looked up from the table to meet Jill's gaze.

Aly's blue eyes were a little wild. A lot had happened to her in the past few months, but this was the first time Jill thought she'd really seen Aly … *lost*.

"What do you think I should do?" Aly demanded.

"Aly. I can't tell you what to do."

"Why not? I'm asking. I'm *begging*. No one will tell me what to do. Even Landon. I know what he thinks, but he won't tell me. He's always happy to tell people what to do, but not this? Why won't anyone *help* me?"

Jill was never quite sure about Landon Bennet. She thought he did care about Aly, but she also thought he was kind of a jerk. Still, if he wasn't telling Aly what to do, Jill would give him some points.

Jill reached out to grab Aly's hand again, squeezed despite the resistance. "We can't tell you what to do because it's your choice. And I know that's hard because there's no right one, but it is yours. And you get to do whatever you want. Either way. I'll support it. And so will Landon."

"I don't know *what* I want, Jill."

Aly's distress caused a lump to form in Jill's throat. She wished she knew how to make this easier for Aly, but she had no experience, no … anything that could help in this moment.

Except support. "I know. I know that's hard. I'll listen to whatever ways you need to talk it out though."

Aly shook her head, pushed back from the table and stood, her tea untouched and no doubt cold by now. "I have to get back," she muttered, clearly unsatisfied.

Jill stood too, feeling impotent and like a bad friend. "Aly ... I'm sorry."

Aly shook her head, but she didn't meet Jill's gaze. "No, don't be sorry. I'm just twisted up. I know it's my choice, I just wish ... I just wish it wasn't." She finally lifted her gaze, gave Jill a wobbly smile. "I'll be back on Friday with your groceries."

Because this was one of the few times Aly had come out to the cabin not even pretending like she was helping Jill with errands. And Jill had blown it. She followed Aly to the door, trying to think of something to say, some better way to help.

But she came up with nothing, and Aly was out the door and into her truck and then gone. Jill stood in the doorway, a cold autumn breeze—a direct contrast to yesterday's heat— blowing in while the whisper of leaves getting more brittle by the day rustled the air.

On a sigh, Jill closed the door against the cold and turned back to the table to clear it. Grandma was standing there, scribbling something on her little pad of paper she used as a communication method when she didn't think Jill would understand her makeshift signing.

Jill walked over, glanced at the writing. Froze.

Don't trust her.

Jill looked from the paper to her grandmother. Mostly,

she was used to Grandma's ... unique behaviors. Jill had been here since Grandma had come home from the hospital after her stroke almost three years ago. Everything *odd* about her grandmother had eased into feeling normal for Jill. After all, she spent almost all her time in this isolated cabin with Grandma.

But the stroke wasn't why Glenda didn't speak. Whatever had caused that had happened before Jill was born. And Jill had been here long enough to accept that no amount of caring for the elderly woman was going to miraculously cure whatever brain issue kept her from speaking.

Or communicated rarely and mostly in riddles. Like this note. *Don't trust her.* Considering Aly had been coming up for visits weekly for years now, Jill didn't think this was about Aly.

"Grandma, did you know Aly's mom?"

Grandma just shook her head, turned away, and went outside. To her garden.

Leaving Jill confused and worried, because she didn't think the head shake meant *no*.

Chapter Six

Austin, Texas

CAL BENNET HATED therapy. He kept coming back, because it scared the shit out of him that there were entire parts of his childhood he'd repressed so deeply he hadn't even known they existed.

Sure, seeing his father toss his mother's murdered body into a barn and burn it down was traumatizing, but what was really traumatizing was knowing his father had walked free for fifteen years because Cal's mind couldn't hack a little trauma.

All therapy seemed to do was stir all those bad memories up, leaving him feeling like a wrung-out washcloth. It was starting to affect his work. His boss had even mentioned the word *sabbatical* in passing.

Cal had laughed it off, pretending like he thought his boss wasn't serious, but if he didn't get his shit together on his current case, he wouldn't be able to laugh his way out of the unemployment line.

He slid into his car, let out a long breath, and just sat in the seat with his eyes closed, counting down backward from twenty. One of his newly learned *coping* techniques.

It worked, but it irritated the hell out of him that something as simple as breathing and counting seemed to calm him down. Shouldn't it be more complicated?

His phone rang before he made it down to one. He glanced at the screen of his phone and noted his brother's name.

Landon's calls were few and far between, though more common than they'd been before this summer. They were trying to repair all the damage their father had done, but it wasn't easy.

Cal didn't dread Landon's calls anymore, but they still always seemed to land at a bad time. He could have waited. Landon would leave a message these days, and Cal would call him back.

Still, he answered.

"Cal. It's Landon."

Like the name wouldn't show up on his phone screen. Like he wouldn't recognize his brother's voice. "You don't say."

Landon sighed audibly over the line. "Are you busy?"

Cal looked at the steering wheel, then the suburban commercial block his therapist's office was in. He didn't know what the hell he was. "No, not busy."

"I've got a favor to ask."

"Dad's in jail and suddenly you're full of favors to ask."

He was hoping for another sigh, maybe a mean remark, but instead, Landon just explained his position, which was how Cal knew it was serious.

"A woman claiming to be Aly's mom showed up at the ranch yesterday. I want to make sure she is who she says she is, and if there's anything about her we should worry about. ASAP. I know this isn't criminal law, but I thought maybe you'd have some connections that could look into her for me. Some kind of background check or something."

Cal frowned, trying to think back to anything he might know about Aly's mom. Ranch lore was always that she'd disappeared right around the time Aly had been born. Cal would have been four. So while he had memories of being small, he wouldn't have had any insight into the adult lives around him.

He knew some people who could do background checks, and because Aly was like a sister to him, he'd certainly look into this unexpected appearance. He understood why Landon was suspicious. After everything that had happened this spring, it just made sense to be more cautious about *everyone*.

But since it was Landon asking, not Aly, Cal couldn't resist some needling.

"What about Nate with his big fancy PI license now? Couldn't he do this? And locally."

Landon's silences always spoke volumes. Cal already knew why not, and it had less to do with Nate and more to do with his partner.

"I would, but this is ... I don't want Sam involved in this. Not something so personal. Besides, I don't think Janie Turner has been the least bit local."

Cal couldn't say he agreed with his brother's continued distrust of Sam Price, but it was none of his business. He was down here in Texas. Not much that happened up in Marietta and the Bennet Ranch was his business.

"Are you saying you trust me, brother?" Cal asked, grinning to himself as he imagined the dark look on Landon's face.

Didn't even need to be back in Montana to see it in his mind's eye.

"Are you ever going to stop being an asshole?" Landon asked with a kind of resignation that had Cal chuckling.

"Nah, kind of in the DNA."

Landon sighed heavily. "Are you going to do it or not? For Aly."

"Yeah, I'll do it for Aly." *And you, you giant asshole.*

But he didn't add that part, because even with therapy, he wasn't there yet.

Chapter Seven

The Bennet Ranch

NATE KNEW HE should have called first. He should have let Landon know he was planning to be at the ranch, talk to the hands.

But he didn't.

Maybe if Sam had been with him, he would have, just to avoid any of the lingering awkwardness between her and Landon and Aly, all over a past he hadn't been around to experience. He would have felt honor bound, as much to Sam as to Landon, to warn all parties then.

But he was on his own today.

He still didn't know how he felt about this ranch that he'd grown up thinking was partly his legacy, whether he liked it or not. How he felt about the fact that he was back after coming to terms with never returning when he'd been deep in the Middle East, not at all certain he'd return anywhere.

Nate figured if there was anything he'd learned in the past year, it was that nothing was ever really certain.

Except death.

But he was alive, somehow, and Sam was off in Bozeman tracking down some of Sandy and Brody McCoy's half siblings. So it was his job to talk to some ranch hands, see if there might be any lingering resentment toward Landon or Aly.

He didn't know why, but he was getting the distinct feeling Sam was avoiding him. Or putting space between them or something. Not in an angry way. In his experience, if Sam was pissed, she let a person know up-front. She was, in fact, one of the most up-front people he knew.

Not hard when he'd grown up in the Bennet house, full of secrets and lies and manipulations.

Still, he couldn't make heads nor tails of what was going on with her lately, and he supposed he didn't really want to. Looking too deeply at Sam, why she was doing things or behaving certain ways, always left him feeling more confused than he wanted to be.

That was why he was focused on the vandalism of Aly's truck.

He was surprised to see the paint hadn't been taken care of when he drove by said truck in front of the Bennet house. It seemed like the kind of thing she, or Landon certainly, would have taken care of immediately. But now it was three days later, and the crude spray paint was still decorating the sides of the truck.

Maybe the cops had told them not to. Sam hadn't gotten very far talking to the officer in charge of the case, so it was hard to know if the police were following leads or chalking it up to petty vandalism and not looking into it at all.

Nate drove around the house, up the gravel lane that would lead to the bunkhouse. No doubt at this time of day the hands would be out doing whatever needed doing, but Nate had determined he'd park there and walk around, see who he ran into.

It didn't take long. There was a trio of hands working at something outside the horse stables. Two people had shovels and were taking turns digging a kind of trench, while another guy seemed to be instructing them what to do next.

Nate didn't recognize any of them, but he didn't think that meant these were all new hands since he'd left. The Bennet Ranch bred loyalty. Nate knew with a self-awareness he hadn't had at sixteen that he would have stayed, if his father hadn't snapped and beaten him after his mother's funeral. He would have stayed in this world, working the ranch, even though that had never been something he'd loved.

He hadn't hated it—not like Cal. Granted, looking back, Nate couldn't help but wonder if part of that hate had been what Cal had been repressing. That need to get out just being his mind's way of trying to protect him.

But Nate hadn't loved this place either, not like Landon had.

Or maybe it was all tied up in their father, the murder of their mother. Maybe whatever he'd felt growing up hadn't been real at all.

Nate still just stood watching, trying to stitch together memory and the passage of fifteen years to put a name to any of these men. They were starting to take note of his existence, throwing each other looks that no doubt communicated something, though Nate didn't know what.

Finally the hand who'd been instructing turned away from the trench and toward Nate. He took his time, ambling up to Nate.

It was something about the gait, about the way the man put his index finger in his pocket that finally had a memory shaking loose.

"Skinny," Nate said, without meaning to speak it out loud.

It was just amazing how the years sat on the man who'd once seemed like a young, careless beanpole.

The man patted his generous middle as he came to a stop in front of Nate. "Funny how that nickname still sticks around, huh?"

It was, and yet Nate could barely manage a smile. He couldn't manage words at all. He remembered his father laughing with Skinny and Tripp and a couple of the other hands. The way they'd all looked up to Benjamin Bennet as not just a boss, but a *friend*. A man they could depend on. A man who had their backs.

An abusive, murdering asshole. No remorse. No apologies for the lives he'd ruined. And yet he'd so easily duped so many people.

"Heard you're working with the Price girl now," Skinny said, breaking the awkward silence Nate didn't know how to.

Nate supposed much like a no-longer-apt nickname for Skinny, Sam would always be *the Price girl* to a lot of the older generation. Especially the members of the older generation she'd pissed off in her pursuit of the truth.

It struck Nate as patently unfair that they all seemed to hold it against her even though she'd been *right*.

But he wasn't here to defend Sam to anyone, and she certainly didn't need any defending, so he didn't know why the urge was always there.

"Yeah. We're looking into the vandalism on Aly's truck that happened in town the other day."

"Don't want to tell you how to do your job, Nate, but seems like kids being kids to me."

Nate nodded along. "Kids I knew didn't usually do their vandalism in broad daylight in a grocery store parking lot without anyone seeing them."

Skinny ran his tongue along his top teeth, another gesture that allowed Nate to see the familiar man he'd been under all the years hanging on him now.

"Aly's well liked around these parts. Can't imagine a soul who'd have anything against her." Skinny's gaze was careful, a sweep from head to toe, then back to Nate's eyes. "Except maybe that Price girl."

"You guys would have yellow spray paint somewhere around here, wouldn't you?" Nate asked, keeping his voice just as casual as Skinny had kept his. "I seem to recall a whole shelf in the back of the utility shed would have housed a lot of spray paint." Nate jerked his chin to where the other two men had stopped digging and were full-on spectating now.

And next to where one of the guys stood, there was a yellow line of spray paint on the grass. Marking something they were probably supposed to avoid in their digging.

Everything in Skinny's demeanor changed. The smile died and his dark eyes went hard. Some skepticism at being connected to Sam turned into full-out belligerence. "You tossing blame out?"

"No," Nate replied easily. "I'm crossing off possibilities."

"There ain't no possibility here."

"Because you said?"

"Because I know my men. Because Landon knows his men."

"You mean, Benjamin Bennnet's men."

"I mean your brother's men," Skinny replied, eyes blazing with that fevered loyalty Nate remembered.

It left a sick feeling in his stomach. If it was for his father, but passed on to Landon, what did that mean?

"You think you know anything about how this place ran after you ran off?" Skinny demanded, taking a threatening step forward. "Gallivanting around like you were somebody?"

Nate didn't feel the need to defend *himself* to anyone. Usually. But *gallivanting*? "Serving my country, actually. Army Ranger sniper, if you want to get exact. Probably still be out there in the Middle East if it weren't for the IED that blew my leg to hell."

Skinny blinked once, glanced down at Nate's leg, then had enough shame apparently to flush. But before he could say anything, Landon appeared.

"What the hell are you doing, Nate?" Landon demanded.

Skinny took the interruption as an opportunity to turn away, walk back to his hands digging the trench.

"What do you think I'm doing, Landon?" Nate returned, not sure why Skinny had pissed him off so much. Not sure why he wasn't handling this as well as he should. "I'm asking questions. The thing you asked me to do."

"You can ask *me* questions."

"I wanted to ask your guys."

"I told you—"

"I know what you told me." And because he didn't want to go in the same damn circles, he shifted the topic. "You haven't gotten Aly's car fixed."

"Something … came up." Landon shoved the cowboy hat off his head, raked a hand through his hair. From the state of his hair, it looked like he'd done that quite a lot today.

"Going to explain that something or just leave me in the dark?"

Landon shook his head. "I don't want Sam involved in it, so no. Not going to explain."

If it hadn't been for Skinny, Nate probably would have kept his mouth shut, but he was already a little irritable about the whole thing, so the words tumbled out. "Because she was right all those years, and it hurts your feelings?"

Landon's face went hard, but he didn't explode.

He spoke very calmly. "You weren't here. You don't know. Just because she was right about something, doesn't mean she was good."

"Were you *good*?"

Landon sighed heavily, settled the hat back on his head with a jerk. "This is why I'm not getting into it with you. You take her side." He started to walk away.

Nate could only follow. "There's no damn sides," Nate muttered, tired of having this same conversation with Landon. Sometimes roundabout. Sometimes direct. "Both men you two supported are murdering assholes. No winners here."

"Just collateral damage," Landon returned, as close to agreeing as Nate supposed they were going to get. Still…

"Some of us are tired of bleeding out. I've seen my fair share of collateral damage, Landon, I'd like to be done."

Landon stopped and studied him in that way that was new, because even with fifteen years' absence there wasn't a lot about how Landon treated him that was *new*, but this look was. Like Nate was some alien.

Nate supposed in a strange way, it was like he was. He'd left. Not just Montana. He'd fought in wars and conflicts and seen things Landon couldn't possibly imagine, and Landon knew that.

"It's not my problem to tell," Landon said very carefully.

A kind of careful that hadn't been in place when Nate had first returned. Nate might not know his brother anymore, not the man he'd become, but he understood this was Landon making an effort.

"It's Aly's. If she wants to tell you, ask for help, involve Sam, that's up to her. I'm leaving it up to her."

Nate noted the repetition of *up to her*. To his mind, it sounded like someone trying to convince themselves more than someone who really wanted to do it. Still, he had to give Landon points for leaving *anything* up to someone else, no matter how reluctant that might be.

"And this vandalism you asked us to look into—you going to leave that up to me?"

Landon scowled, shoved his hands in his pockets and rocked back on his heels. "You can't go around blaming my men."

"I wasn't blaming anybody. I was asking questions."

"I know you've been gone a long time, Nate, but you know better. You know whatever your questions were, they're insulting. Whether you like that or not, that's how it is. How it's always been."

Nate hated that Landon was right. Hated that he hadn't handled Skinny as well as he should have. Nate had felt insulted, both for himself and on Sam's behalf, and had done something he'd known would piss Skinny off, rather than ask questions in a way that might actually yield results.

Maybe that wasn't altogether unlike him, but he couldn't do that kind of thing when investigating a case. Even if said case was a favor for his brother's girlfriend.

"Guess you're right," Nate said, falling into step next to Landon, back toward his truck and the bunkhouse.

"Hey, say that again. Pretty sure that might be the first time anyone I'm related to has ever said that to me."

Nate snorted in some amusement. "Maybe my methods were flawed, but I'd keep an eye on anyone who takes an undue interest in the utility shed today."

They walked in silence for a few minutes, back toward the bunkhouse, but Landon didn't stop there or at Nate's truck. He kept walking like he didn't even see it. So Nate kept walking too.

"I've got a camera on the shed. Just like I do on the stables. All my men know where and how it works. Aly and I are the only ones with access to the footage though."

"You'd have video then from the days leading up to what happened to the truck."

"It only records if it detects movement, but yeah. The cops took all the footage. They haven't told us if they've seen anything."

"You'd have your own footage though, right?"

"Hell, if I know. I'm about as adept with computers as I am with complex human emotion."

Nate let out a surprised laugh. Landon must have been surprised too, because he let out a laugh of his own.

"You just made a joke poking fun at yourself, Landon. You might just be capable of evolving yet."

"Wouldn't bet on it." They were in sight of the house now. Landon squinted at it. "I'm just heading in to get some coffee. Which is an excuse to check on Aly. You want some coffee? She won't fuss at me if you're here. Besides, she'll be able to show you the footage if we've got any."

He didn't really want coffee, but Nate understood it wasn't about the coffee. It was an invitation inside. Into Landon's world. To refuse would be to refuse that.

So Nate nodded and followed Landon into their childhood home.

Chapter Eight

Marietta, Montana

CAL COULD HAVE delivered all this information over the phone. Even over email.

Instead, he'd booked a flight. Texas to Montana. Condo to … *home*. He didn't know why he still thought of Marietta and the Bennet Ranch as home considering how little he liked it, how actively he'd been running away for most of his adult life, but that was the truth of it.

Taking some vacation days from the firm was only delaying the inevitable, he understood. Getting taken off his current case meant his days were numbered in his job. A job he'd been good at. A job he'd *enjoyed*.

Before.

He'd run away rather than deal with it.

Kind of your MO, isn't it?

He drove up 89 and turned into Marietta on his way up to the ranch. He'd already spent more days in Montana this year than he had in the past ten years before it combined, and now he was adding onto that total.

It had been easier to rationalize back in Texas when he'd been making the plans, but now he knew he was only here to avoid what was going on there.

"Funny how the tables turn," he muttered aloud as he

maneuvered the rental car off Front Street and out toward the Bennet Ranch. Autumn was creeping in. A hint of colors on the trees. The way darkness was already settling in the sky even though it was late afternoon. That bite to the air he'd felt when he'd stepped out of the airport in Bozeman.

Back in Texas there was only heat and humidity. It'd been a dry summer and that persisted.

The cold felt good, and that surely wasn't anything to do with his tenuous mental health, his failing at work, or everything that had been unraveling since spring.

He drove up the winding drive and pulled his car next to Aly's truck, shoving it into park. He didn't see Landon's truck anywhere. It was getting to be about dinnertime, so that was a bit of a surprise, but Cal wouldn't mind easing in with just Aly. Someone who actually acted happy to see him most of the time.

He grabbed his bag, hopped out of his car, then stopped as he noted the crude words spray-painted all over Aly's truck. He circled the truck, frowning at the severity of the words chosen.

When he looked up to the house, Aly had opened the front door and was standing in its warm glow. It was a gray day so there was no sunset, just the encroaching threat of more darkness. The light of the house was welcoming.

He wanted something to be.

He walked across the yard, up the stairs. He couldn't quite work up a smile. "What happened to your truck?" he demanded by way of greeting.

"Oh." She waved it away like it wasn't covered in nasty obscenities. "Just some weird prank. We haven't had a chance to get it cleaned up just yet." She fisted her hands on his hips and glared at him, but there was a smile on her mouth. "Cal Bennet, what are you doing here?"

"Thought I was always welcome."

"You are and you know it." She pulled him inside as if to prove it. "But welcome doesn't mean we won't have some questions."

He had *assumed* Landon had told her about their phone call, but he suddenly worried that maybe Aly was completely in the dark. "You do know Landon called me and asked me to look into … the woman who came here."

"My mother. Yes, he told me." She scowled as she led Cal into the living room. "After the fact, but he told me."

"Progress?"

She gave a little chuckle. "Yeah, I guess it is for him." She surveyed him then smiled thinly. "You have news for me then?"

"Information," he corrected. "And only a little. I had a friend in law enforcement who was able to look into some basics. For more, you're going to have to…" He trailed off as he heard the back door shut and Landon's voice call out for Aly.

"In the living room," she returned, but her gaze stayed on Cal. "If the friend is in law enforcement, the information is related to … breaking the law."

Landon appeared from the back. He'd shed his outer gear. "Saw the rental car outside. You didn't need to come all this way."

A year ago, Cal would have taken that as an insult. A clear sign his brother didn't want him here. And maybe a year ago, that would have been true.

But Cal was starting to see things for what they were. Like Landon's desperate need to handle everything—and mostly on his own, if he could. Something Dad no doubt drilled into him, just like Dad had drilled into Cal that since he didn't want to ranch, he didn't belong. Not on said ranch, not even in the family.

"I had some time coming to me," Cal said carefully. "I didn't get much from the background check, but it's easier to talk it out, answer questions, and talk about next steps in person."

"It's bad news," Aly said, as Landon took a seat next to her on the couch.

"Not really bad or good news. Just information." Cal unzipped his bag, pulled out his laptop case. He opened the computer, even though he had the information mostly committed to memory. "Janie Anne Turner. Born in Livingston forty-nine years ago."

"Forty-nine? She was only … eighteen when she had me."

Cal nodded. "Appears so. I've got a basic sketch of her life. Even as a kid, by all accounts, she never stayed in one place long. No information on a father, just a mother, who she lived with until she lit out on her own when she was sixteen. Some evidence she lived in Marietta around the time you were born. Then she disappears for a bit. Right after you would have been born."

Aly nodded along, her hands clutched in her lap, her color off. She was too pale. She didn't look herself, but Cal knew he had to continue.

"She pops up in Idaho, Nevada, Washington after that. Never stayed in one place as an adult either. She's got a bit of a record, but mostly petty stuff. Theft. Minor assault." There was also a solicitation charge, but Cal didn't think he needed to bring that up just yet. "So, not a perfect citizen or anyone I'd trust wholesale, but there's nothing dangerous on her legal record."

"That she got caught doing," Landon supplied.

"Ever the optimist," Cal muttered.

"That's a sad life," Aly said very softly. "No stability. No family. It's sad."

Landon put his hand over Aly's. Cal found his gaze oddly hooked on that.

An easy and even friendly show of physical support. Where had Landon learned it? Not from Dad.

Maybe Mom. Maybe Aly herself. But mostly, life had been ... isolating. But somehow in all that, Landon and Aly had found each other. They'd always been a unit, and now there was more to it.

Cal was happy for them, but he didn't know how to fully accept it. Didn't know how to sit here and watch Landon be ... a supportive *partner*, in every sense of the word.

So, he focused on the reason Landon had even called him in the first place. "I know you guys don't want to hear this, but if you want to know more, especially what she's been up to lately, you're going to need to hire a private investigator, and it'd be plain stupid not to hire Nate or Sam or both."

Aly and Landon sent him matching frowns.

He held up his hands in mock surrender. "You could talk to the ranch hands who worked under your dad back then.

Enough of those guys are still around. You could see what they know about your mom, but it doesn't seem like she's been around Montana for a while. You're not likely to get more than what we already know from the background check from anyone local. At best, they'd know something from back then that you'd still then need to investigate."

Aly smiled ruefully. "I tried talking to the hands, even your father, after Dad died. My dad asked them not to speak about it, and they won't. They wouldn't even tell me her name, if they ever knew."

"Another reason to hire an outside party."

"Nate and Sam are hardly outside parties," Landon pointed out.

Cal shrugged. "So go further afield. I can get you some names."

"You said that would be stupid," Aly reminded him.

"It would be. Doesn't mean you can't do it."

Aly sighed, her eyes looking suspiciously shiny. She pushed to her feet, gave Landon a look that screamed even to Cal *don't follow*. "I'm going to go put together some dinner."

She left the living room, and Cal watched Landon watch her go. Landon was the most stoic man Cal had ever met, and that was saying something. But the naked worry on his face had Cal's stomach twisting into knots.

"Is there more to this that I don't understand?"

Landon shook his head. "No, not really. I just don't like the timing. Setting a date for Dad's trial. The truck. The mother. I'd be worried about her if one or the other happened, but I really don't like these things happening at once. Or the way it's weighing on her."

Cal liked to think he'd make this offer either way, but he knew in part it was happening because he didn't want to face what waited him in Austin. "I've got some vacation days. I can stay here for a bit, work with Nate on it. I'd keep you in the loop, if that's what you're worried about."

Landon shook his head. "It's not that I don't trust Nate…"

"Then what is it?"

"I don't know."

Cal could only stare at Landon. Had his brother ever admitted he didn't know something? Certainly not voluntarily.

"I just thought … Dad's in jail," Landon continued, looking at his hands. "The trial will stir things up, but we know he did it. We know. I thought we could move past it. Set it aside. Move on. I thought there'd be some rest. Some … moving *on*," he said again.

Landon sat there, looking as lost as Cal had ever seen him.

"What if this is all there is? Pain and suffering and old secrets that only hurt. What if this is all there ever is for us?"

Cal sat in the chair, the weight of those words holding him there like an anchor.

What if this is all there is?

It was horrible. Crushing.

"You've got Aly," Cal managed to say, though his throat felt scratchy and closed up. "This ranch. Things you love. It isn't all there is."

Landon looked up at him then. He didn't argue with Cal. In fact, Cal thought he might actually have agreed with him. If one silent question didn't hang between them.

What do you have, Cal?

ALY HAD MADE dinner for everyone and cleaned it all up. Landon had offered to help, but she'd wanted to do it on her own. Sometimes, she just needed to handle things on her own to remind herself that she could.

So she also got the guest room ready for Cal while Cal and Landon had a beer and talked about the damage to her truck.

She didn't want to think about her truck. Or her mother.

She knew, deep down, that Cal had given her a very sanitized version of her mother's life. She also knew that neither Landon nor Cal had thought to do the math.

If her mother had given birth to her at eighteen, she'd been conceived when her mother had been seventeen. Not crazy young, all things considered, but…

Her father would have turned fifty-five this year, if he hadn't died. Which made him six years older than Janie.

Which meant when she'd been seventeen, conceiving a child, he'd been twenty-five.

It left her feeling sick to her stomach. She'd loved her father. Idolized him. In the fourteen years she'd had him, she'd thought he was the best man in the world.

Yeah, you thought that about Benjamin Bennet too.

Was she that bad at understanding people? Was she that warped that all it took for her to believe in a man was for him to tell her that he was good?

Had her mother's sudden appearance ruined *everything*?

It felt like it, and Aly hadn't even decided what to do about it yet. Call the woman? Have a conversation? Ignore her existence?

Aly just didn't know.

The house was dark and quiet once she was done with her cleaning. Were Landon and Cal already upstairs? Seemed unlikely, but if they were…

Aly eyed the door to her old apartment off the kitchen. She'd moved all of her day-to-day stuff into Landon's room upstairs this summer, but there was still furniture and a few things she rarely used in her space. She could just go … sleep in there and not deal with … anything.

It was so tempting she actually took a few steps toward the door. The only thing that stopped her was the thought of facing Landon in the morning. Explaining why she'd slept downstairs instead of in his bed.

It felt like punishing him, when he hadn't done anything wrong. It would hurt his feelings. He would pretend it didn't. He would pretend he understood.

But she would know.

She sighed, flipping off the lights to the kitchen as she passed them. If she got up and ready for bed and fell asleep before he got there, though, she could avoid him without hurting his feelings.

But when she reached his room, he was inside. She was usually in bed long before he was, because he always had one last ranch thing to check on or worry over. But tonight, he was in his room, his hair was wet from the shower, and he was dressed in sweats for bed.

He looked up at her, presumably because she was just standing in the doorway staring at him.

"Everything okay?"

She managed a nod. "I just don't think you've ever been ready for bed before me."

He smiled at her, the movement crinkling the skin around his eyes, flashing that tiny dimple she was pretty sure only ever appeared for her. "First time for everything."

Love for him just *swamped* her. In all this turmoil and confusion and just depressing thoughts and worries, there was him. And he had his own turmoil, confusion and depressing things, half the threads that connected them were wrapped up in those.

But he had always been her rock, her anchor. She always known she was welcome when it came to him. Even before they'd acted on anything romantic, he'd been the most steady, dependable person in her life.

Even though she hadn't changed into her pajamas, she slid onto her side of the bed. He put his arm around her shoulders, drew her close and kissed her temple when she leaned against him.

She was doubly glad she'd come upstairs instead of wallowing. Maybe they wouldn't talk about everything, maybe they would, but having her rock to lean on made a difference.

"I didn't expect Cal to come all this way when I called him," Landon said.

"Do you think he's hiding something?" Aly asked, because she couldn't let that thought go. What he'd told her would have been easily relayed over the phone, and Cal had never been one for coming home all that often. "Something worse?"

"No. He'd have told us something worse. He wouldn't string you along."

No, she supposed Cal wouldn't. For the monster their father was, the Bennet boys were good men. Flawed, screwed-up, *good* men. Well, Cal and Landon. Aly thought Nate too, but she didn't know for sure, and since he seemed content to spend more time with Sam Price than his brothers, she still didn't fully trust him.

But the thought of Nate and Sam brought her back to her own troubles, and what Cal had suggested. She must have tensed, because Landon kissed her temple again, gave her shoulders a squeeze.

"What do you want to do about all this, Al?" he asked her gently.

"I don't know."

"Okay."

"Just *okay*?"

Landon sighed. "Yeah, this sucks. And I don't know what to do either."

She jerked her head off his shoulder to look at him. "Did you just say *you* don't know?"

"Yeah."

"You *never* admit you don't know."

"Sure I do," he replied, frowning.

"Literally never once, Landon. Even your mom used to tell the story about you as a toddler insisting *my will do it* about everything."

He pulled a face, but he didn't argue with her. "Well,

I'm admitting it now."

She remembered what Cal had said earlier when he'd arrived, and she'd been a little frustrated that Landon had told her about their phone call *after* it had happened.

Progress. Yeah, this was progress. And there was a hope in progress that lifted some of the dark cloud that had been around her since the truck incident.

She thought about Cal coming home, giving her information about her mother. Petty crimes and bouncing around. Too many holes to trust the woman. Too many questions not to ask them.

She thought about the Bennet boys being good in spite of their father. And she thought about Nate Bennet and Honor's Edge Investigations. If it was just Nate, she didn't think she or Landon would have heavy reservations.

It was the Sam of it all. And still, Sam had been right for those years when she'd been obsessive and a bit of a bully. She had been *right*.

Nate had told her after Benjamin had been arrested that Sam needed a friend. Aly didn't know how to be a friend to Sam again. Not after everything they'd said to each other in the ensuing years of Sam trying to prove her father wasn't a murderer.

But Sam had been right, and didn't that mean she was probably good at her job? Aly looked up at Landon. Studied his profile. He wouldn't like it, but … maybe Nate and even Sam were the answer here.

She wanted some kind of relationship with her mother, if there was one to be had, but first she had to know that Janie Turner wouldn't be a threat to the ranch. To the people Aly loved.

"I know how you feel about Sam…"

"This isn't about me, Aly," Landon said firmly, turning those intense brown eyes on her. "If you want to bring Nate and Sam into looking into your mother, I'll support it. It's your call."

She studied him, saw that he meant it. Her throat got a little tight. Landon had every right to hate Sam, to not want her to do this. And she couldn't help but think that even a year ago, Landon would have swept right over what she *wanted* and done what he thought was right.

Everything that had happened this spring was awful, but it *had* made some positive changes in all of them. She hoped.

"Maybe. Maybe. I'll think about it, anyway."

Landon nodded, then used his free hand to tilt her chin up. He pressed his mouth to hers.

"I love you."

He didn't say it often. He struggled with physical and verbal intimacies, but when he engaged in them, he said important words with the kind of gravity and meaning that had tears stinging her eyes.

"I love you too," she managed. And she had to hold onto that, that anchor. Because everything with her mother might feel kind of awful, but she had this. She had *him*.

Her anchor. Her rock. It was enough. No matter what happened, it was going to be enough.

Chapter Nine

Honor's Edge Investigations Office

S AM GOT BACK home late, a headache drumming at the base of her temples, which wasn't as bad as the throbbing in her cheek. If she'd thought Brody McCoy had been unhelpful and unwelcoming, he had nothing on his half brothers and sisters.

She had dealt with belligerence, theatrics, and in the case of the youngest McCoy, outrageous flirtation that might have amused her if the little asshole could take a hint.

Then, she'd been stupid enough to try to stop a fight between said asshole and a much bigger guy and gotten an elbow to the face for her trouble. Not even on purpose. At least she could have fought back against an actual attack.

"Figures," she muttered, pulling her car behind Honor's Edge. She hadn't expected Nate to be at the office this late, but his truck was parked around back in its usual spot.

She lifted a hand to her swollen cheek. Something told her this wouldn't go over well. Nate was typically the most even-keeled guy she'd ever known, at least this adult version of Nate. If things rattled him, he kept it well below the surface.

She just didn't trust that to hold forever. Was it because she'd known him when he'd been a somewhat volatile teenager? Was it because he was Benjamin Bennet's son? Or did she just sense underneath all those still waters were some really dangerous currents?

She didn't know. Was too tired and in too much pain to try and figure it out before she decided what to do.

She could go upstairs, but then he'd wonder why she'd purposefully avoided him once he saw her car when he left. And that would make the whole non-ordeal seem to have more importance than it did.

Still, she couldn't just ... *go in* there. Muttering curses under her breath, she pawed through the car until she found some tinted moisturizer and a little compact of foundation powder that might have been from high school for all she knew. But she used them both to do her best to hide the red mark on her face.

Tomorrow it would be a bruise, no doubt, but she'd have her full makeup arsenal to hide it. If she could just get through a few minutes of telling Nate all the nothing she'd found and that she was going to call it a night, she wouldn't have to tell him.

Or wonder why she so badly didn't want to tell him.

She pushed out of her car, went through the back entrance. They'd rearranged some since he'd gotten his license. The small room that had once been hers was now their *interrogation* room of sorts. They went in there for private meetings or calls, while the larger room now acted as an office for both of them, with their desks set up on either side of the room.

Nate was sitting at his desk when she entered. He didn't look up when she walked in, but he did greet her.

"Hey. Got you a hamburger if you're hungry."

She looked at her desk. Next to her keyboard was in fact a wrapped hamburger and a cup, that no doubt held a Coke. He knew what she liked. And she *was* starving.

Unfortunately, it meant sticking around for a few minutes, but she supposed if he was going to keep his attention on the computer, she'd be okay. "Yeah, thanks."

She slid into the seat, unwrapped the burger and took a bite. She winced a little at the pain in her cheek but soldiered on. "Figured you'd be done by now," she offered in between bites.

"Probably should have been, but I dug myself a bit of a hole I'm trying to get out of." He sighed, leaning back in his chair and looking up from the computer screen. "I went to the ranch today, to talk to the ranch hands, but instead of getting any answers from them, I just pissed Skinny Adams off and got nowhere." He shook his head. "Except with Landon, I guess. But only on a personal level. Pretty much shit the bed when it came to the case."

Sam studied him. She heard what she supposed was a kind of guilt in his tone. An acceptance of failure. But if he'd made some kind of inroads with his estranged brother?

"We get to be people too, Nate."

His gaze held hers, a reminder why she was trying to split them up on this case. He looked at her like that, like he understood, like she offered something no one else did, and her heart did fluttery things in her chest it had no business doing.

"Guess you learned that one the hard way," he said in that way he had, like he understood everything, always.

When she didn't understand *anything*.

"What the hell haven't we learned the hard way, Nate?" she muttered, taking another bite of the burger and washing it down with the Coke.

He didn't answer that. He changed gears. "You get anywhere with the McCoys?"

"Not really." And she could admit that was part of her bad mood. Feeling like she'd wasted a day with a bunch of people who probably hadn't thought of Sandy much before or after the murder. At least not in any way that didn't have to do with themselves. "Accusations. Tears. A dinner and drinks invite from Denver McCoy." She rolled her eyes and took another big bite of hamburger.

There was a pause.

"Hot date, huh?"

She didn't quite recognize Nate's tone, didn't know how to qualify it, since it didn't exactly land like a joke. She snorted at the idea of a date with Denver McCoy anyway. Any date really. "Oh yeah. Why wouldn't I jump at the chance to grab burgers with a twenty-two-year-old felon who can't take no for an answer?"

"Just how didn't he take no for an answer?"

Sam looked up at the hard edge to Nate's tone. His expression was blank, but she sensed something lurking underneath. A sharp edge of temper. Those rip currents she knew better than to get caught up in.

He reminded her in this moment of the man she'd first come across up on that Tennessee mountain. The soldier all over him. Leashed violence, hidden under a glaze of purpose.

Her heart didn't flutter this time around. Because her

physical reaction to that look wasn't at the heart level. It was a hell of a lot lower, and exactly why she was trying to put some distance between them by splitting them up on this case.

She had to clear her throat to answer his question. "Nothing I couldn't handle, Nate. He's a kid who's used to his charm doing his heavy lifting. Not a lot of brains *or* brawn behind it."

He frowned at her, dark gaze zeroing in on her cheek. "What's wrong with your face?"

She looked down at the hamburger, shoved the last bite into her mouth. "Nothing's wrong with my face," she said around the food.

But he'd gotten out of his chair, crossed the room and now stood over her. He reached out, put three fingers under her chin and applied pressure until she had to look up at him. She scowled at him as she swallowed her food.

His eyebrows were drawn together as he studied the swollen part of her cheek. When his eyes met hers again, his gaze was hot and hard. "I know what it looks like when someone's been punched in the face."

"I wasn't punched."

"Did you run into a wall?" he asked, his voice icy. That temper in his eyes. But his hands were gentle.

And still on her chin.

"It was an accident," she said, even though every part of her body was now fluttering around like a guy had never touched her before. Like this was somehow romantic when it was mostly just insulting. "Denver near cried when he realized he'd accidently clocked me with his elbow."

"And why did he do that?"

Sam knocked Nate's hand away, because it was doing a number on her insides that she certainly didn't appreciate. She got to her feet so she could control the distance between them.

She wasn't used to touchy-feely stuff. Her mom had died when she was ten, and since then she'd determined not to need it. Not to need anything she couldn't handle herself.

"He was tussling with some other guy. Apparently, he'd slept with that guy's wife. The kid's a real winner. Anyway, I had the bright idea to stop things, since I was still trying to talk to Denver about any trips he might have taken to Marietta. The guy pushes him, Denver rears back to punch, instead gets me. Elbow to face. I'd have been fine if I was a few inches taller."

Nate stood there, roiling anger he didn't voice pumping off of him. After a moment of tense silence, he turned on a heel and left.

Sam stood in her office, not at all sure what had just happened. He'd just ... left? But no, she heard him rummaging around in the little kitchenette back there, and when he returned it was with a towel, tied around what was no doubt ice.

She opened her mouth to tell him she didn't need ice or help or whatever this was, but he didn't hand her the ice pack, he placed it against her cheek himself. So they were standing facing each other, except she had to look up because he was so much damn taller than her.

"Why'd you try to hide it?" he asked, and even though she still saw all that tension in him, his voice was soft. Gentle.

"Because I didn't want looks and comments." *And whatever this is.*

She tried to take the ice pack from him, but he held firm, so that their hands were just ... touching over the towel.

"I can take care of myself," she said, frustrated when her voice came out sounding scratchy.

"So what?" he replied, enough edge to his voice that this didn't feel *wholly* ridiculous, even though it *was*. "Doesn't mean you have to twenty-four seven." He was scowling at her, but she saw it. The momentary hitch in his gaze, when it dropped to her mouth, then back up again.

He released the towel to her grip, stepped back, and shoved his hands into his pockets. And for a full minute or two of silence, they just looked at each other. Nate looked vaguely angry, and she kind of figured her expression was the same.

Someone who walked in might assume they were angry at each other, but Sam figured the only people they were angry at were themselves. And maybe Denver McCoy.

"Well, sounds like we both struck out today," Nate finally said. "What should we do tomorrow?"

Sam breathed out very slowly, very carefully. She refused to look away from him. She refused to let *anything* that was scrambling through her show on her face.

So he'd looked at her mouth? So what? He'd also asked a very practical question that she needed to answer.

"I guess we see if we can find anyone who saw something in the parking lot that day."

He nodded. "Sure. Sounds good. I'll be back here at eight."

"Yep."

"Keep the ice on it." Then he was gone.

NATE HADN'T SLEPT well. He was used to that, all things considered. Between his injury, which only pained him on occasion these days, and the nightmares, also rare anymore, interrupted sleep had been a way of life more than it hadn't been.

He was not used to losing sleep over a woman though. Samantha Price was a tangle, and not a wholly sexual one.

Not a wholly *un*sexual one either. Which he supposed was the problem. He knew how to deal with blacks and whites, rights and wrongs, yesses and nos. Stay. Leave. Fight. Run.

Not these weird-ass middle grounds.

He pulled up to Honor's Edge. This job was supposed to be a choice. A very non-middle-ground. The decision to stay, to see if he could put roots down in the place he'd once ran away from.

It wasn't supposed to be complicated. He laughed at himself as he got out of his truck. When had life ever not been complicated? Why did he think he could make it be now?

Sam had mentioned that guy asking her out, and while Nate understood that to her it was just a random, insulting offer, to Nate it had been a realization.

She existed in a world outside the job. Their time together. She very well could have a boyfriend. There'd been that cop she'd gotten information from that had been a little too insistent. He'd noticed the way that detective on her dad's case had given her a once-over. He'd *known* she drew male interest.

But he hadn't really thought about her … engaging in it. Because they were always so focused on whatever case.

He should be now. This was no different. But something about her relaying the story had *felt* different. Left a visual in his head. One he couldn't seem to get rid of, even though it was benign and shouldn't have a damn thing to do with him.

Why shouldn't she date? Have a boyfriend? Had absolutely fuck all to do with him.

He stalked up the back walk, shoved the key she'd given him in the lock. This was the job. Be at an office when necessary. Investigate. Question. Uncover.

She came down the stairs from her apartment just as he walked in the door. She was dressed the way she usually was for work. Jeans, long-sleeved T-shirt, and a jacket in a nod to the colder weather.

But instead of the usual ponytail or braid, her hair was down around her face. The dark strands had some wave to it, and it was different enough Nate came up short.

She was wearing makeup, too, and not that he was any great expert in *that*, but it was definitely more than usual. He scowled when he realized *why*.

"You think anyone's buying that?" he muttered, gesturing at where she'd clearly used the makeup to cover up what was no doubt a decent-sized bruise. That was why her hair was down, too. Trying to hide where she'd been hit.

"No one's looking that close, Nate."

Apparently I am. Which frustrated the hell out of him.

"I was thinking we'd head out to Waiths first thing, see if we can get anything that takes us to the next thing," she said, all business.

"Sure." Because he could be all damn business too. "I'm ready if you are."

So they headed right back out. It was Sam's turn to drive, and Nate tried not to pull a face. He folded himself into her passenger seat. He'd prefer driving himself and his truck, but taking turns was this unwritten rule they had—and he wasn't about to cross any rules or lines right now, written or unwritten.

She started to drive, talking as she did. "We'll talk to the manager of Waiths, see if we can get a list of everyone who was working the day of the vandalism. I know they've passed their security footage onto the police, but what I don't know and can't seem to get an answer on is if the police have actually watched it."

"I would assume if you can't get answers that means they've looked into it and have a lead."

"My thought too, but they're not sharing, and I haven't heard anything from Aly or Landon about answers. Have you?"

Nate shook his head. "I think Landon would have mentioned something if he'd heard. They had some security footage of their utility shed that they handed over to the cops, but Aly said none of their inventoried spray paint was missing."

"Could have used it and put it back, but I wouldn't put money on it connecting to the ranch." Sam tapped her fingers on the wheel as she drove. "So we'll see what we can find at the grocery, let it lead us to the next thing. I've still got some McCoy questions, but I should be able to get that sorted in short order."

Nate nodded along, but the thought of the McCoys had him thinking about the splitting up they'd been doing. How they should handle the way they dealt with people. "I think we should do this a little differently."

"Oh, the new guy's got ideas."

He ignored her snark because being *new* didn't matter to his way of thinking. "You should take the women. I should take the men."

She hit the brake a little hard at a red light, causing him to jerk forward.

She scowled over at him, and he scowled right back. "Take the... Excuse me?"

"That guy harassing you doesn't need to happen again. Getting in the middle of fights and all that. Unnecessary risks. I'll take the men."

For a full-on second or two, she simply stared at him openmouthed. Until he gestured at the now green light.

She returned her gaze to the road. "I've dealt with *unnecessary risks* and an unwanted advance or two simply because I exist as a woman in this world, Nate. I've never needed a man with a savior complex to swing in and stand between me and anything."

"I'm just saying, you shouldn't be going into situations where it's an issue. If there's a guy to interview, I should handle it. Consider it the perks of hiring a man."

"The perks of ... you think you can handle an overzealous guy better than I can? Because you've got a penis?"

Offended that she was simplifying it down to gender politics, Nate found himself saying things he rarely brought up. "I was an Army Ranger. I was a *sniper*. It doesn't have a damn thing to do with…" He was not about to say *penis* out loud in this shitty car with her glaring at him.

"*Was* being the operative word there." She jerked the wheel and tires squealed as she turned them into the parking lot. Then, with a lot more jerking and braking than needed, parked.

She got out of the car, and he followed, tense and irritable. Only more so when she smirked at him.

"Follow my lead, *Sergeant*."

He did just that, following her as she sauntered her way into the grocery store's customer service desk. She asked for a man by the name of Jim Gary, who Nate assumed was the manager of the store.

She'd done her homework, and what had he done? Been worked up about dumb shit that didn't matter.

We get to be people too, Nate.

He wondered if she'd still think that if he knew what *being a person* meant in relation to her.

A wiry man with a thick mustache appeared, walking straight for Sam with the kind of irritable look Nate was beginning to recognize. This guy no doubt already knew who they were, why they were here, and he wasn't looking to be cooperative.

"Mr. Gary." Sam held out a hand to shake.

The man looked at it, then back up to Sam. He didn't shake it. "If you're here about the vandalism to a customer's car, the police have already talked to everyone who was working," Jim said, folding his arms across his chest. "And the police will handle it."

"So you didn't see anything that day? No one with spray paint? No discarded cans in the dumpster? No evidence—"

"Detective Hayes is the one looking into the case. If you'll excuse me." He walked away without another word.

For a few seconds, Sam didn't move or say anything. Nate half expected her to march right after him. Start her own fight.

Instead she whirled on a heel and stalked out of the store. When Nate caught up with her, she wasn't walking toward where her car was parked. She was walking along the storefront, eyes up along the roof of the building. Nate realized she was eyeing the security cameras.

"Detective Hayes isn't going to give us anything before he lets Aly know," she muttered. She walked into the parking lot, but at the opposite side of where they'd parked. "Aly said she parked here, more or less." It was a spot toward the end of the lot, next to a cart stall.

Nate positioned himself where the truck would have been. It should have been visible. "If the cops have the footage, they'd have to have some leads."

"I wonder if Mr. Gary doesn't like those leads," Sam said. "Hence the bad attitude toward more people poking into it."

"Him?"

"Or anyone who works for him. It'd look bad on him, if one of his people is out in the parking lot vandalizing. Let's head back to the office. Maybe hit up Main Street Diner once it's lunchtime, see if we can't start some conversations about who might have been employed by the grocery store that isn't anymore."

"Or who might have been at the grocery store that day and seen something."

"Yeah. Yeah, it's a plan."

They got back in the car and drove back to the office in mostly companionable silence. Whatever awkwardness from the morning had faded and Nate could only be grateful for it.

Back at the office, Sam checked emails, and Nate went over the list of people Aly had seen at the grocery store that day. He kept going back to Sam thinking the words chosen were *personal*.

He'd watched the way Skinny had changed his entire demeanor when Nate had made any sort of insinuation it could be one of the hands. Sort of in the same vein Jim Gary had cut off any discussions about his workers. Everyone closing ranks.

But not *everyone* could be hiding something.

Could they?

Around noon, Sam stood from her desk, stretched.

Nate found himself watching, the way she moved, the stretch of fabric over skin, far too closely. He looked down at his keyboard.

"You ready for lunch?" Sam asked casually.

"Yeah. Sure." Lunch. Ready. Losing his damn mind. He got up, shoved his keys into his pocket. "I'm driving. Then we can head directly out from there."

"Sure, if you want, but I'm going to follow up on a few

things McCoy related in Livingston after lunch. You can head up to the ranch, though, see if you have better luck today."

"Thought you got everything sorted with the McCoys."

"Denver's attempt at a fight kind of got in my way." She waved it away like it was nothing. "I've got a few more questions for him."

Nate straightened. "You're going to go question that guy *again*? After yesterday?"

"I didn't get to ask him the last few questions." She sighed heavily. "I told you he didn't mean to elbow me, Nate. I'm not an idiot. I know the difference between someone hitting me because they mean it and an accident."

She no doubt did, but he still didn't like the idea of her going back. Of her dealing with the guy who'd asked her out. He didn't like the idea of a lot of things, and none of them should matter. He should let it go.

But he couldn't. "Why don't we focus on the McCoys tomorrow then? Split them up, like I said before. Or at the very least, I'll handle Denver."

"I can handle fucking Denver McCoy, Nate. Why the hell are you harping on this?"

"I'm not harping." Which was lame even to his own ears.

"My ass." She stalked out of the office and toward the back door. Nate trailed after her.

"It just doesn't make any sense. Why you'd want to have another sit-down with a guy who, your own words here, can't take no for an answer."

"Jesus, Nate." She whirled on him, stopping their progress, so they stood in front of the back door facing each other. "You're starting to sound jealous."

That landed between them. Spiky and awkward, like a flopping fish on the floor between them. Both waiting for the other to pick it up and throw it back in the water.

Instead, silence settled. Except the odd *flopping* inside his own chest. Like this was one of those now-or-never moments. Make a choice, one way or another.

"And since you're not," Sam said, but her voice was very soft. "You can just knock it off. Okay?"

He should nod and agree. Still, he said nothing.

And neither did she.

But then the bell on the front door jangled, and neither of them had to say anything, because when they looked into the front room, it was Landon and Aly walking into the office.

SAM HAD NEVER in her life been happy to see Landon Bennet. Particularly in her space. Now she was. She pushed passed Nate and walked into the front room to greet the unlikely visitors.

Nate's silence had unsettled her, and she was not one for being unsettled. Not like *that*. Not with some … hope.

Her own fault, she knew. She'd said it. She hadn't had to bring up the word *jealous*. But it was something building between them and if she didn't throw out the grenade it was going to … she didn't know. She'd wanted an answer, even if it was horrible embarrassment.

And now she didn't have to know instead. So that was

great. She could … set it aside. Push it down. Ignore everything. Just how she liked.

"Um, hi," Aly said when neither Sam nor Nate made any kind of greeting.

"Hey," Sam replied. "We haven't really gotten anywhere on the vandalism. Still working on it though."

"I'm sure you are," Aly said. Her smile was polite, but nervous around the edges. Sam didn't sense any of the usual hostility. "We were just in town to drop off my truck to get repainted. And I … I wanted to ask for more help. To hire you for something else."

Sam looked from Aly to Nate, who seemed just as out of the loop as Sam was.

"I can go, give you guys some privacy." It was her place, and usually Sam wouldn't offer, because they had a whole damn ranch for private conversations, but she was eager to put an end to whatever was going on with Nate.

Aly shook her head. "No, you don't need to do that. I'd like you two to look into someone for me. Unrelated to the truck."

"Two?"

"It doesn't have to be both of you," Aly qualified. "The point I'm trying to make is I'm happy to have either of you look into it. And pay whatever prices you usually charge."

Sam flicked another glance at Nate, about the same time he did to her. He gave an almost imperceptible shrug.

"Sure. Let's sit." Sam led them back into their office room, pulled some chairs together.

Aly perched on the edge of the seat, Landon scooted his closer to Aly and put a hand on her back.

Sam stared at them. They'd always been a unit. Even back when Sam had considered Aly her best friend in the world, she'd known that, for Aly, Landon held a position just a step ahead of Sam. He was a *boy*, so Sam could convince herself that her friendship meant more, but…

Landon had always been part of the unit that made up Aly. And Sam had always been a little bit the odd man out.

She'd been jealous back then, but she hadn't fully understood what that twisting, complicated feeling in her gut was. Now she did and it was … weird. Weird to look back and see herself more clearly in retrospect than she had in the moment.

She lowered herself to a seat as Aly began to talk.

"A woman came to the ranch the other day," Aly said. "She said her name is Janie Turner and that she's my mother."

Sam felt an odd pang. Back when they'd been friends, they'd shared all their feelings about not having a mother. In some ways, Sam thought that was what had bonded them in Mrs. Brown's fourth-grade class. Aly'd never had a mother. Sam had lost hers. It was like that lack had cemented them together.

At the time, Sam had figured it was forever. What could ever come between best friends?

Murder, apparently.

"Cal had a friend do a quick background check, but it's basics," Landon added. "We want to know a little bit more before Aly decides if she contacts her again."

"That should be easy enough and straightforward. Nate should be able to handle it on his own, and I can step in if need be."

"How long would it take?"

"Depends but shouldn't be too long," Sam assured Aly. "If you've already got a rap sheet, we can track down people who might have known her. Collect some stories, some background information."

"I'll just need some basics to get started, and it wouldn't hurt to have the information that Cal came up with." Nate moved to his desk and his computer.

Sam let him handle it. She went to her own computer and even though she listened, she didn't interject. Maybe Aly and Landon suddenly didn't care if she was involved in something, but she didn't need to stick her nose in either.

They were family, essentially. She wasn't. Once Nate had the information he needed, he stood to walk Landon and Aly out. Sam heard the words even though they'd left the room.

"Cal's home for a few days, he said," Aly told Nate. "You should come to dinner."

"Yeah. Sure. I can do that."

Sam looked down at her keyboard, surprised at the odd lump that formed in her throat. Nate could go off and have dinner with his family. And she ... was still the odd man out.

Why wasn't she used to it?

When he walked back into the office, Sam worked hard to get a hold of herself. To focus on the job. "You thinking what I'm thinking?"

Nate nodded grimly. "We see if Janie Turner has anything to do with the vandalism."

Sam got to her feet and nodded. "Let's head to the diner, huh?"

Chapter Ten

The Harrington Cabin

JILL DIDN'T OFTEN take walks solo to clear her mind. It worked wonders when she was dealing with a difficult scene, but she hated leaving her grandmother for any extended period of time.

Grandma hadn't wandered since before Benjamin Bennet had been arrested. She'd mostly been working in her garden, getting it ready for a long winter.

She hadn't communicated much of anything since Aly's visit and talk of her mother, but Jill was mostly used to bouts of her grandmother being rather ... isolated.

Which was what helped make it feel like a safe time to walk. Grandma likely wouldn't wander or need Jill for anything, and it felt ... necessary to get out of her grandmother's orbit for a little bit.

When it was just the two of them together in their own little world, Jill felt mostly good. She'd adapted to the isolation, the rustic living, far quicker and easier than she'd expected to.

Of course, her parents and brother had expected her to run screaming home to Boston in less than a week, so spite had been a part of that.

Still, she *liked* living in the cabin. She *loved* her grandmother, even if they never communicated easily. Jill had learned a lot of Grandma's rudimentary signs for things. Grandma could write if the idea was complex or important, and Jill's creativity was blooming out here in the middle of nowhere.

But when outside things happened, Jill was reminded how little she knew about her grandmother, and how little she understood, no matter how much love was there. She started to feel very *alone* in those moments.

These past few days, Jill had done more obsessing over what her grandmother might know about Aly's mom than she'd spent working, and that was frustrating *and* depressing.

So, she walked through the woods, trying to find some place of acceptance. Because until she accepted it, her book was stuck, and *she* was stuck.

She couldn't push Grandma. She'd tried. Three years she'd learned that stubborn had nothing on Grandma.

Dad *had* tried to warn her about that, but Jill felt—then and even now in the midst of being frustrated over it—a woman who'd been through some kind of trauma that had made her mute for *decades* deserved a little stubborn.

So, Jill walked off her lonely, tense feelings, or tried. All the way down to the creek. She was going to walk along it for a while yet, but she came up short at the sight of someone across the way.

She never ran into anyone on her walks. Well, almost never. A few months ago she'd come across the same man she saw now.

Cal Bennet.

This time, he was on the Bennet side of the creek, so he

wasn't trespassing like he'd been in the spring—wet and muddy and pale like he'd seen a ghost.

No, he looked perfectly with it today, if a little under-dressed for the chill in the air.

Technically, she could probably back away and pretend she'd never seen him, because he hadn't looked up at her. She didn't *have* to run into him if she didn't want to.

Of course, the second she took a step back with the thought to do just that, he looked up.

She managed a wry smile and lifted her hand in acknowledgement. "Hi."

"Hey. Jill, right?"

Jill nodded, feeling a little foolish standing on opposite sides of the creek with a man who apparently only barely remembered her name.

Which wasn't fair. The few times she'd talked to Cal Bennet he'd been in the midst of some serious trauma. Figuring out his father had killed his mother. Remembering the fact he'd seen it. Why should he be sure of her name?

"I'd apologize," he offered with a charming smile that seemed to scream *lawyer*. He pointed at the creek between them. "But I'm still on Bennet land."

She smiled back. "No need to apologize. I was just going for a walk to clear my head." She gestured vaguely behind her in the direction of the cabin. "I'm a writer."

"Yeah, Aly mentioned." He frowned a little. "You, uh, had some questions for me, didn't you?"

She had. And Aly had given her Cal's email, and she'd sent all her questions about criminal defense attorneys. She had *not* asked for details on his traumatic memory loss and considered it amazing restraint on her part.

Either way, he'd never responded to her email, and she hadn't followed up because she figured he was a busy guy. It didn't seem right to bring it up now, especially right here. She could still remember that night all the Bennets and Aly and Samantha Price had shown up at her cabin. Wet and traumatized, realizations about Benjamin Bennet breaking up all their foundations.

"Any news on Aly's mom?" she asked him instead.

His expression registered some surprise. "She told you about that?"

"Aly's my best friend. I'd say I'm hers too, but I guess Landon probably takes that spot. Still, we don't have too many other people out this way."

Cal looked down at the creek, toed at a fallen log. "Landon'd be a shitty best friend if you're looking for someone to talk to."

Jill's sense of loyalty warred between her suspicions about Landon Bennet. Problem was, she had suspicions about all the Bennets. Cal included.

She wrote too many mysteries not to.

Cal must have sensed *something*, because he looked up, smiled again. "But if there's anyone he'd listen for, it'd be Aly."

"They do seem ... devoted to each other."

"Yeah, devoted is a good word."

They stood there in an awkward silence for a minute, Jill wracking her brain for something to say. Especially since he hadn't answered her question.

"Nothing especially new," Cal said, as if reading her

mind. "Ran a background check and the woman's got some … issues, but nothing too alarming. Then again, my father's a murderer, and I repressed that knowledge for like fifteen years, so maybe my gauge is off."

He said it with just enough of a self-deprecating smile that she didn't feel awkward over it. Maybe in part because she'd been Aly's friend through the whole ordeal and a kind of observer to the whole thing.

But remembering how they'd all found out about Benjamin Bennet—her grandmother had been the one to unearth some damning evidence—made her wonder if Cal was back because of the thing with Aly's mom. Aly hadn't mentioned Cal coming home, but they hadn't talked via more than text in a few days.

Jill took a few steps down the bank. The creek was low, and as long as she didn't slip, she could get a little closer to him without getting wet. Something about the way he'd talked of his father, of Landon, of this whole thing…

She needed to tell someone, and she didn't want it to be Aly, so who else was there?

"I … I think my grandmother knew Aly's mother. She … I shouldn't be telling you this since I didn't want to tell Aly, but … Grandma wrote this note after Aly came by and told me about it."

"A note?"

"She wrote *don't trust her*. I tried to ask questions, but when Glenda is done communicating, she's done communicating."

Cal's frown deepened, he took a few steps closer to the creek too, watching the ground carefully so as not to slip.

"That's a warning."

"Yeah, I guess it is. I just … Aly was so messed up over it, I didn't want to add to it. I'll tell her if she decides to contact the woman, but I just…"

"Wanted to protect her?"

"Yeah."

"You might have more in common with Landon than you think."

"Ouch."

He chuckled. "I don't think there's much to worry about there. They're hiring Honor's Edge to investigate the woman. See if they can get a sense of her before Aly reaches out, but it might be something Nate should know."

"You could tell him then."

"He might want to come by, talk to Glenda."

"He could certainly try. Anyone's welcome to try."

Cal nodded thoughtfully. "Okay, then. I'll pass it along. You got a cell phone number I could give him?"

"Aly's got the landline number, which tends to work better. The Wi-Fi is patchy at best, and I usually only use it for work."

"Sure. Okay." He flashed a smile, lifted a hand in a wave. He started to leave, but then abruptly turned back around to face her. "Wait. You emailed me questions. About a book you're working on."

"Well, yes. Aly said you would answer them, but…"

"Sorry. Hit at a bad time."

"You don't have to be sorry."

"I can answer them now, if you want." He gestured toward the creek. "Walk and talk?"

Jill studied him. It seemed like a genuine offer, but she also wasn't a hundred percent comfortable. Still, it might help her work through the plot tangle to be able to ask an actual lawyer her questions.

Besides, just because Benjamin Bennet had murdered his wife didn't make his son a psychopathic killer, no matter what stories her imagination was starting to weave.

He was Aly's friend, and Jill trusted Aly.

Who was dead wrong about Benjamin Bennet.

And she was overreacting and freaking herself out. All reasons why she'd become a writer—so she'd have somewhere healthy to throw all her anxiety. She forced herself to smile at him.

"That'd be great, but I don't really want to shout them over the creek."

"I'll come over."

Jill Harrington was an interesting woman. Of course, Cal was pretty sure he'd find anyone interesting if it meant not having to walk back to the ranch.

He'd managed to get across the creek without falling in—unlike last time he'd crossed in a nightmare fueled hurry. He found it reassuring. He was in charge of his faculties this time around, and no new unsurfaced memories were going to jump out and give him a panic attack.

Yet.

They fell into step next to each other. Cal kept a respectable distance between them. He could feel the nerves waving off of her. No doubt she was wondering if he had the same murdering tendencies as his father. Hard to blame her. He figured the only saving grace he had was the fact he was connected to Aly, and he'd helped turn Dad in when he'd had the chance.

Jill gave him a quick rundown of the book she was working on, and some questions she had about a lawyer character she'd created.

She was pretty. Which was also reassuring. He hadn't completely lost his mind. He could still appreciate a beautiful woman.

She didn't have the same ruggedness most of the women carried around here like a badge. Including her grandmother. There was something … graceful about her that gave off an aura of fragile, but he wasn't fooled.

This woman wasn't fragile. She was much darker than her grandmother—skin, hair, eyes, but she had that same sense of purpose he'd always gotten from Glenda. She moved with quick, easy strides and spoke quickly, animatedly, with broad gestures that sent the occasional resting bird off into flight.

She pushed the sleeves of her baggy sweater up to her elbows when they hit a sunny spot that was warmer than under the trees. He noted a little tattoo on her wrist, small and colorful, but he wasn't close enough to make out what it was.

But the more she explained her book, at least the part in the courtroom, the more Cal shook his head.

"That just wouldn't happen."

"But *could* it happen?" she demanded.

He shook his head. "It doesn't matter if it could. It wouldn't."

She blew out a frustrated breath and made another broad gesture. "It's *fiction*. It's not about *wouldn'ts*."

"Then why are you asking me about reality?"

"Because fiction still needs to *could*. At least the kind I write."

"The only way a lawyer could wield that kind of evidence, legally, and have any judge listen, would be to rope the police in earlier in the process."

She made a considering noise. He realized she'd brought them in a kind of circle, so they were coming up on the Harrington cabin from the opposite direction she must have left in.

Cal had always thought the cabin too small for one old woman, even when he'd been a kid. Now it housed an even older woman and a young one, and he could only think it would be damn crowded.

"How long have you lived here?"

"Three years come Christmas. I brought Grandma home from the recovery center on Christmas Day."

"Recovery center?"

"She had a stroke three years ago. It was fairly mild, but she still needed some work to walk and move around on her own again. My father wanted to move her into an assisted living center in Boston." Jill blew out a breath. "Sometimes I wonder how he came out of her."

Since he felt the same about himself and his parents, he didn't have any response to that. He just stood outside the cabin that was the source of many a Halloween night story down at the high school.

"I know the rumors," Jill said, as if she could read his mind.

Hell, as Glenda's granddaughter, Cal wouldn't quite put it past her.

"I know kids like to think she's a witch or a ghost or something. She's none of that, but she is ... different. She belongs here. To ship her out to Boston? It would have been like ripping some lupine out of the ground and then trying to plant it in concrete."

Cal thought about his move to Texas. How he'd convinced himself Austin suited him to the ground. The firm, the condo, the nightlife.

But he related a little too much to a wildflower planted in concrete. Dying.

The door swung open, causing Cal to jump. Jill didn't though. Yeah, she was sturdier than she looked.

Glenda Harrington stepped out. She said nothing but stared at him with those creepy light green eyes. Almost translucent, like there was something mystical and magical behind them.

Luckily, he didn't believe in shit like that.

"Hi, Mrs. Harrington," he offered in a nod to be polite.

"You remember Cal Bennet, Grandma?" Jill said. "We happened upon each other in the woods. We talked about Aly's mom, and he helped me with my book." She gave him a kind of side-eye that spoke of disappointment in him. "Sort of."

He ignored the dig about his help. Since Jill brought it up, and he was here, he figured it didn't hurt to try. "Janie

Turner. That's Aly's mom apparently. Jill said you might have known her."

Glenda's preternatural gaze moved to Jill. Then back to Cal. She said nothing. Communicated nothing. She turned and went back inside, closing the door behind her.

Jill blew out a breath. "Sorry. She does that."

Cal shrugged. "I understand the impulse to leave a situation when you don't want to deal with something." Hell, he left entire states. "Speaking of places left, I better head back to the ranch."

But the door swung open again, Glenda moving out into the yard this time. She held something out. A piece of paper.

Cal took the outstretched paper, except it wasn't paper. It was a photograph. He looked down at it. He didn't recognize the two people, but the woman in the picture had curly red hair and had more than a passing resemblance to Aly. "This is Janie?" he asked.

But Glenda didn't confirm or deny. She was looking at Jill, who was staring at the photograph, her mouth hanging open. Jill looked up at her grandmother.

When she spoke, her voice was shaky. "The man in the picture. That's my dad."

Chapter Eleven

The Bennet Ranch

ALY WAS SURPRISED to feel a little better after the visit to Honor's Edge Investigations. Or maybe it was returning to the ranch with her truck freshly painted. No more obscenities. No more reminders.

And she didn't have to think about her mother for a while, because Nate and Sam were handling it.

Weird? Yeah. Really, *really* weird. But it allowed her to set it aside for a little while. She'd brought back pizza for dinner since Nate had agreed to come. They didn't get it often since it required driving down into town, but she put it in the fridge to reheat later once everyone got here.

She was considering going for a late afternoon ride, maybe see if Landon needed any help, even though he'd told her to take the afternoon for herself after she'd picked up her truck. But *herself* was just roundabout thoughts she couldn't seem to get rid of. Work would take her mind off things and—

Before she could make a full decision, she heard the front door open.

She went to see who it was, as she doubted Nate would be early. She smiled a greeting as Cal entered. She hadn't known he'd gone anywhere, but—

The smile died when Jill followed Cal inside.

Aly's heart stopped for a moment. "What's wrong?" she demanded.

There was simply no other reason except *wrong* for the two of them to be together.

Jill crossed to her, smiling reassuringly. "Nothing. Nothing is wrong. At least not like really wrong."

"What about Glenda?"

"She should be fine for a little while," Jill said, waving Aly's concern away, which also worried Aly because Jill almost never left Glenda alone. "She … she showed me and Cal this picture." Jill looked up at Cal. "Well, mostly Cal, but…"

She held out an old picture. Aly took it. She didn't have to ask who the woman with red hair was. Maybe the years sat heavy on Janie Turner when Aly had seen her, but there were just too many similarities between this old picture and the woman Aly had met to discount.

The man next to Janie wasn't Aly's dad, she'd seen enough pictures of Tripp as a young man to know that for sure. Still, the man did look vaguely familiar. Something about those light green eyes…

"Aly. That is my dad," Jill said urgently. "Grandma didn't explain, but she had this picture of your mom and my dad."

Aly flipped the picture over. In looping script written in faded pencil, it said *Janie and Shawn.*

"I … don't understand."

"Neither do I. I tried to call Dad, but my mom said he had a few surgeries to handle today and won't be home until late. He'll call me when he can. And we're two hours behind Boston, so it shouldn't be too much longer."

"Tell her the other thing," Cal urged.

Jill looked up at Cal, and it was like they had a nonverbal discussion when they didn't even know each other. Not really. They'd met briefly a handful of times this spring, but that was it.

Or so Aly had thought. "How did you two…"

But Jill was too worked up to listen to Aly's question. "Should we take this to Nate?"

Aly looked from Jill to Cal. Who had to have told Jill about taking things with her mother to Honor's Edge. Which was just … it was all just beyond weird. "Can someone explain to me why you two are suddenly a pair who tell each other everything that's going on?"

They looked at each other, then back at Aly.

"It just kind of happened that way, I guess," Jill said, as if now that Aly brought it up, she wasn't really sure how it had happened either.

"I was out for a walk," Cal explained in that lawyer way he had. Laying out the facts. "Clearing my head. She was doing the same. I offered to answer those book questions, since I was a shitty friend and didn't do it back when you asked me to, Al. One thing led to another, and we got to talking about everything going on here."

"What should I ask my dad when he calls back?" Jill demanded. "What do we need to know?"

"I don't … know." Aly shook her head.

The *we* made her feel weepy. Like this wasn't just *her* problem. She had Landon looking after her. Cal helping.

Now Jill. Even Nate and Sam and… It was just a lot of help. A lot of … care.

She looked helplessly at Cal.

"You'll want to just get a sense of what he remembers about Janie. What their relationship might have been to have led to a picture your grandmother kept all these years. Don't lead him. Let him tell you what he remembers. If we have follow-up questions, we can always ask later. First, we want his unfiltered response, memories, whatever."

Jill moved forward, tucked Aly's arm into hers. "This is good, right? Someone who knew your mom around the time she had you. It'll give you some answers. And I know you don't know him, but you can trust my dad. I promise."

Aly felt like everything was spinning out of control. All these years, she'd hoped that maybe someday she might be able to know her mother, but she had never stopped to think about all the things that would be a part of that.

"Aly?"

It was Jill's voice, but Aly couldn't quite register she was supposed to talk. All she could think about was how she didn't have a handle on this. No grip. She couldn't make anything line up right and work out. Just when life started to settle, something jumbled it all up.

"Aly, breathe." Cal's order was sharp, and a rare instance where he actually reminded her of Landon. "I think she's having a panic attack."

"No. No. I'm fine." She thought she sounded fairly normal, though it was hard to tell with the ringing in her ears. "Everything is fine."

"No, it's not," Cal replied. "It's shit."

She managed to laugh at that. It was indeed shit, but what could she do except keep moving?

Jill was rubbing a hand up and down her back, urging her to sit down, but the doorbell rang, and Aly moved to answer it.

Cal beat her to it.

Nate stood on the stoop. Right on time.

"You don't have to ring the bell," Cal told him.

"It's not your house, last time I checked," Nate replied, but he stepped inside. He nodded at Jill. "Hi. Jill, right?"

Jill nodded. "Yeah, good to see you, Nate." She turned her attention back to Aly.

Shoved the picture at her. A nonverbal kind of *tell him*.

Aly didn't want to take the picture though. She didn't know why, but touching it felt … something bad. Still, Jill was right about bringing Nate into this. She'd asked for his help to look into her mother. This was a piece of that.

"Nate, Glenda Harrington gave Jill this picture," Aly said carefully. She didn't take the picture. She gestured at it still in Jill's hand. "It's obviously old, but it's my mother."

"And my father," Jill added, handing it over to Nate.

He took the picture, studied it. Like Aly, he flipped it over and read the back. "How did your dad know Janie?"

"I'm not sure. We're going to find out though."

Nate looked up from the picture to Aly. There was a calm about him that felt reassuring. Jill was excited to find a link. Landon was worried about her. Cal was, well, Aly thought he was still struggling with everything that he had blocked out all those years.

But Nate seemed calm. Detached. It was like a lifeline.

She untangled herself from Jill, smiled at Nate. "Come on. Let's eat."

LANDON WASN'T SURPRISED to walk into the dining room to find everyone already eating. He'd texted Aly to eat without him after all. But the presence of Jill Harrington was a surprise.

Though Aly went up to the Harrington cabin just about every week, Landon didn't know much about Jill except she was a good friend to Aly. And to Landon's mind, Glenda Harrington had always been a bit unfairly maligned down in town. Obviously something terrible had happened to her somewhere along the line. Didn't make her a witch or a ghost.

So, Landon thought it was nice she had a granddaughter who'd move more than halfway across the country and live in that tiny, isolated cabin with her.

Still, he knew when someone didn't trust him, didn't like him, and Jill Harrington might try to hide it, but Landon saw both those things in her.

Jill and Nate flanked Aly at the table, so Landon had to take a seat next to Jill. She offered a tight, polite kind of smile, but there was nothing warm about it.

"Sorry I'm late," Landon said to Aly.

She smiled at him—warm, love, but there was something in her expression. An exhaustion, a wariness. All that tension she'd been holding, just like after Sandy's murder. He wished there was some way to take it away for her, and he realized he'd been hoping the trip to Honor's Edge this morning would accomplish that.

"You were only late because I took the afternoon off," she reminded him. "There's been some … development in finding some things out about my mom." She nodded towards Jill. "Glenda had a picture of Janie. With Jill's dad."

Landon didn't really remember Shawn Harrington. As the stories went, Glenda's only child had gotten out of Marietta the second he could and made very infrequent visits. Before Glenda's stroke, she'd more often go out to Boston than the family Shawn had made would come out here.

"We're just waiting for my dad to call me back so we can ask him some questions about her." Jill tapped her phone, looked at the time. She frowned a little. "I don't know how much longer I should leave Grandma on her own."

"You don't have to—"

But before Aly could get out the words, the screen on Jill's phone turned to a picture. A family deal. The word DAD across it. She swiped across the screen to answer it, and only then did Landon realize it was a video call. He wasn't in the shot, but he could clearly see the man on Jill's screen.

"Heya, peanut."

Jill pulled a face, but she didn't correct her father. "Hi, Dad. Surgeries went well?"

"More or less. Mom said you had some important questions, and she won't let me eat until I talked to you." He squinted at the screen. "Where are you?"

"I'm at the Bennet place. Having dinner with Aly." Jill looked over at Aly, smiled a little ruefully. "I'll make it quick and blunt. Aly never knew her mother."

"I suppose I knew that."

"You did?"

The expression on Shawn's face had moved toward un-comfortable, but he didn't try to talk his way out of the subject. "Janie Turner, right?"

"Right. Grandma gave us a picture of you two together today. I didn't realize you'd known each other. How did you know each other?"

Shawn was quiet for a moment. "Janie and I were … uh … friendly, one summer."

"Ew." Landon heard Jill mutter under her breath. But she shook her head, leaned in. "What do you remember about her?"

The man scratched a hand through his salt-and-pepper hair. "We worked together at the rec center. The summer before I graduated high school. She was a few years older than me, so…" Shawn trailed off. "Why exactly do you want to know all this?"

"Janie contacted Aly recently, and Aly just wants to make sure … well, she just wants to protect herself. The more information we have about Janie Turner, the better she can do that."

"I'm not sure anything I know could help with that. It was a long time ago."

"I'm an adult, Dad. I can handle whatever you did in your misspent youth."

He sighed, but with a kind of rueful smile. "Don't say I didn't warn you," he muttered, before launching into his recollections. "Janie was older, so she was a coveted party invitee. A group of friends would get together, have a bonfire or a party or whatever, Janie would usually bring the beer."

"Underage drinking, Dad? For *shame*." Jill grinned at the screen though, and in the way Shawn Harrington shook his head, Landon saw something he'd never seen with his own father. Affection despite the exasperation.

"Is that why Grandma wrote down that we shouldn't trust her?"

Shawn again shifted in the frame, continuing to look uncomfortable. "I suppose Mom would say that. Janie … had a nose for trouble. She liked drama. The last drama I remember before she took off was, uh, well … she said she was pregnant."

"With Aly?"

"Yes. Tripp…"

Jill and Aly shared a look over the phone. Aly looked patently miserable, but she was trying to hide it. Landon couldn't seem to take another bite of food. Something about this just settled … all wrong.

"So you knew Aly's dad too?" Jill pressed.

"I didn't know Tripp well but knew him. Back then, Bennet and Harrington hands tended to hang out. But…" Shawn cleared his throat. "When Janie started telling people she was pregnant, she didn't immediately name Tripp as the father. She wasn't exactly…" Again the man looked uncomfortable.

But Jill wasn't giving up. Landon had to appreciate that. Aly might look miserable, but they needed to know. They needed to understand why after thirty-plus years of abandonment, Janie Turner thought she could waltz back into

Aly's life. Landon had to know it wasn't going to hurt Aly more than it already did.

"Dad, it isn't like you to hedge around the truth," Jill said gently.

"No, but I know Aly's been a good friend to you out there in that godforsaken place," Shawn said. His bitterness on the word *place* was there, but not heavy and ugly like the kinds of bitterness Landon was used to. From Cal mostly. "I don't want to cause her any … upset."

Aly moved closer to Jill, into the frame of the phone's camera. "It's all right, Dr. Harrington. I'd like to know. No matter how ugly the truth is, I'd like to know."

Jill grabbed Aly's hand under the table.

Shawn sighed, looked somewhere away from the phone for a moment, then gave a short nod. "All right. Like I said, Janie and I were … friendly that summer. She told me the baby was mine, at first. Then I heard from a few other guys, she'd told them it was *theirs*. Kinda like she was shopping around, seeing who would bite. I was young enough not to have realized she was … playing the field, shall we say."

Aly didn't react any, but Landon could tell Jill was squeezing her hand tighter.

"That was back when Mom still talked. Still helped Dad with our ranch. I told my parents, expecting the wrath of God, but I guess they'd heard enough rumors to know Janie … well, that it might *not* be mine."

Silence settled around the table, heavy and awkward.

"I don't know if they got involved," he continued. "But soon enough, Janie wasn't claiming anything about me anymore. She'd settled on Tripp."

"Who else?" Landon cleared his throat when all eyes at the table turned to him. "It just might help us to know who else she said was the father. Besides Tripp."

Cal and Nate nodded. Aly didn't look at him. Shawn took a moment before he spoke.

"A friend of mine. Guy by the name of Brad Johnson. I lost touch with him after we graduated high school. I remember he went to Montana State, but that was about it. His folks had a place over near Cowboy Point, but he was a lot like me. Young. Naïve. Scared shitless after she told us. Relieved beyond the telling when she settled on Tripp."

"So it was just you, this Brad, and Tripp?"

Shawn frowned, as if thinking back. "There was another guy we worked with at the rec center. Older. Name's escaping me. Jim, maybe?" He shook his head. "I haven't thought of this in years. And this guy wasn't my friend. He didn't really come to the parties. I just knew him from work. Jim … I can't think of a last name, but I'm almost certain the first name was Jim. Your grandmother might know, if she'd tell you. I'll see if I can figure it out and get back to you."

Jill nodded. "Thanks, Dad, and if you think of anything else…"

"I'll let you know." Shawn sighed. "Aly, you've been a good friend to my girl, something her mother and I greatly appreciate being so far away. I know this can't be easy to hear, especially with everything you've had going on out there. If there's any other ways we can help, you just let Jill know."

Aly's smile was small and sad, but she thanked Shawn for

his help. Jill ended the call.

Dinner after that was subdued. No one tried to make small talk. Jill ducked out early to get back to Glenda, and then Cal suggested he and Nate go have a drink on the porch. No doubt to give Landon some time alone with Aly.

"Do you mind cleaning up?" she asked, for the first time maybe in their entire lives. "I think I'll just go to bed."

"Al..." He tried to reach for her, but she sidestepped him.

"I just need to be alone for a bit."

It just about broke his heart in two, but he let her go and cleaned up the mess of dinner.

NATE STOOD OUT on the porch on an increasingly cold night, while the stars and moon shone bright and pretty above his head. He stood next to Cal. They hadn't spoken a word in about ten minutes. Just silently sipped beers Cal had found in the fridge.

Dinner had certainly been weirder than usual, and that was saying something.

Still, it was something to go on when it came to Aly's mother, and Nate couldn't deny that ... well, there were some timing issues to keep an eye on here.

Especially when he'd dealt with a *Jim* earlier today. A Jim who would have been a few years older than Jill's dad. A Jim who'd behaved as though he might be protecting someone, maybe even himself.

It was a leap, a big leap. Jim was a common name. But

what if … just what if Janie Turner had some connection to grocery store manager Jim Gary?

Something to look into anyway. On his own. No use bringing his brothers into that just yet.

The front door opened, and Landon stepped out, holding a can of beer himself. He came to stand next to Nate, so the three Bennet brothers stood on the porch of their childhood home, beers in hand.

The silence continued for a few more minutes. Nate had left town at sixteen, expecting to never be here or see these people again, and now he was back. His brothers were in his life. And sometimes it felt like some strange nightmare. Not because it was bad, just because the specter of what-ifs haunted him.

What if he'd never come back? What if they'd never uncovered Dad's abuse and murder? Where would they all be?

Not here. Not together. Not friendly … ish.

Of course, he wasn't really here tonight to be a friend. He was kind of here for work, more or less. So, that was what he led with.

"Have you ever seen Janie Turner before the day she showed up here? I don't just mean recently. I mean ever."

Cal and Landon exchanged a look.

"I certainly don't remember her." Landon was the first to reply.

"She would have stood out, right?" Cal said. "Red hair. Looking like Aly. If she'd been around at any point, I think someone would have noticed, discussed."

"I think so. But … Aly's right. After Tripp died, she tried to get any information about her mom. From hands who would have been there, who would have at least known *of* Janie. No one would give her anything. They'd made a promise to Tripp not to say anything, and even in death … well."

"Have you thought about the timing?" Nate asked.

Because the fact of the matter was, Tripp had been Dad's foreman. They'd been friends. A few of the men who worked for the Bennet Ranch now had once worked for the Harrington ranch before they'd sold to Dad.

Janie hadn't returned when Tripp had died. She'd returned not too long after Benjamin Bennet would have been in the news for his arrest.

"What about the timing?" Cal asked, but the way Cal said it, Nate thought he might be drawing the same conclusions.

"Aly's truck is defaced. Janie Turner shows up."

"Seems weird she'd deface Aly's truck, then follow it up with a visit. Not to mention, why should she be mad at Aly?" Landon asked before taking a long drink of his beer.

Nate shrugged, took a sip of his own. "I'm not saying she did or she is. I'm just commenting on the timing of it all."

"Because it's only been a few months since Dad's arrest," Cal said. "Big news here, but nationally maybe not so much. Last whereabouts for Janie Turner were Nevada. What if she stumbled upon news of Dad's arrest more recently? Then makes her way up here now that Dad's out of the picture?"

"What's Dad got to do with it?" Landon demanded.

"We don't know," Nate said equitably.

"But we could find out," Cal added. "I think we need to see what Dad knows about Janie Turner."

Landon swore, but there was no denying Cal was right.

Chapter Twelve

Honor's Edge Investigations Office

WHEN SAM WENT down into the office, it didn't really surprise her to find Nate already there. He'd taken off a few hours early yesterday to go have dinner up at the ranch and talk to Aly more about her mother.

Sam was grateful for the separation. She felt more … in control of things. The problem was simply too much time together. When they got some time apart, she thought clearly again.

Maybe she'd felt like shit last night, especially when Aunt Lisa had rebuffed any attempts at having a meal together. Aunt Lisa hadn't wanted to talk to her just yet. And sure, that hurt.

The only person she had left in this world thought she'd done something wrong by telling the truth. A truth both her and the man in jail had raised her to value.

But even that was illuminating.

She was on her own. And accepting that was freeing. Purpose had gotten her through the past fifteen years. Sheer force of will and certainty her father had been innocent.

She hadn't been *wrong*—at least for most of those years.

She had been focused and determined and alone and *fine* with it. She was simply missing that focus, that mission.

That driving force, since he'd gone ahead and proven her wrong fifteen years after the fact.

Once she found a new purpose, everything would go back the way it had been. She'd be right on track. No more getting hot and bothered over Nate Bennet and obsessing over it. No more reaching out to Aunt Lisa only to be rebuffed.

She just had to find the new mission.

"Morning," Nate greeted. "We've got some movement on Aly's mom if nothing else."

She could tell he was revved. He didn't often let it show, but over the past few months, when a case got kind of moving, he'd let it slip. How much he wanted to move forward. How much he liked this job, even if he'd never meant to end up in it.

He was a good investigator. It gave her a pang. Maybe she'd taught him some procedural stuff, but mostly he was just good at this. It fit him, like it fit her.

But being apart was definitely better for her mental health. She moved to go sit at her desk. "You know, you can move on it without me. I can stick to the vandalism end of things. You can handle the more personal thing. I think it works best for everyone that way."

He glanced up at her. She noticed the way his eyes immediately went to her cheek. She'd covered the bruise up with makeup again this morning, but he didn't comment on it this time.

"I think it's best if we keep working on this together," he said, instead of agreeing with her like she'd expected.

"Nate, you're fully licensed and fully capable of—"

"I'm very aware of what I'm capable of, Sam, and if I thought these were two different cases, I might agree with you, but I'm starting to think they connect."

"Connect?" *Shit.*

"Timing. Cal agreed with me. Kind of." He waved a hand in a restless gesture. "Let me fill you in." Nate relayed the conversation Jill Harrington had with her father over the Bennet dinner table last night.

Sam let him get it all out, taking some mental notes on where she'd have the investigation go with this new information. Except she was bound and determined to leave this to him. She didn't need to get wrapped up in Aly's personal parental business. Maybe Aly had said it was okay, but Sam figured they'd all be a lot more comfortable if Nate handled things.

And she'd be a lot more comfortable if she let him do the handling, without her anywhere near him.

Still, the mystery was intriguing. Complicated. She couldn't help but think of some questions, some angles, some possibilities.

One that Nate didn't verbalize, and Sam wondered if Aly had considered, was that Tripp Cartwright might not be Aly's biological father at all. If Janie had lied to multiple men, it actually meant *any* of them could be Aly's father.

None of Sam's business though.

"Cal and I got to talking about the timing of it all. Why did Janie decide on now? Sure, we don't know much about her just yet. Maybe there's some internal reason, but it's odd, isn't it? That Dad's story would have filtered through national news sometime this summer, and then out of the blue Janie comes looking for Tripp."

Sam nodded along, because her thoughts were following the same line. "It is odd. Definitely something to look into, but how?"

"Cal's working out a visit. See if Dad will tell us anything about Janie. He would have been there. He was Tripp's employer. My parents always treated Aly like a member of the family. He has to have some information we don't have."

"Think he'll give it to you?"

"If he knows we want it? No. But Cal's got a way about him. I think he can find a way to get the information we need."

"On his own?"

Nate stared hard at his computer. "He's a lawyer."

"Yeah, and good at it, no doubt." And this was none of her business, but that had never stopped her before. Even if she was trying to be Ms. Alone and Independent, she couldn't seem to deny her true nature. "You should go. The three of you should go."

"Why?"

"Because…" This wasn't keeping her nose out of his business.

This definitely wasn't keeping her distance. Still … she just couldn't help herself. Something about those damn Bennet brothers—one of whom she'd spent a lot of the past few years hating—made her soft.

"Your dad spent your whole lives trying to keep you three separate. Hating each other. He mostly succeeded. Why let him keep succeeding?"

Nate didn't look at her, and when he spoke it was quietly. "I don't hate them."

"I know you don't, and I don't think they hate you. Not really anyway. Bitterness and baggage is a lot different than hate. But it's ... it's like a symbol. Going to see him together. There's strength in numbers. In a united front against everything he is."

And yet you're so happy being alone.

"Maybe you're right," Nate said after a while. "But if I go do that with them, can you work on a ... really weird angle for me?"

"Sure."

He finally looked up at her. "It's going to sound crazy."

She shrugged. "What else is new?"

His mouth curved a little at that. That little hint of humor. That little hint of the man underneath all the layers of protective stoicism. And the damn heart flutter she just couldn't seem to get rid of.

There was something seriously wrong with her.

"One of the potential fathers was a man by the name of Jim, who was older than Shawn Harrington by a few years. The summer before Shawn graduated high school, they worked together at the rec center here in Marietta, with Shawn and Janie. Shawn couldn't remember a last name, though he was going to try to figure it out."

"You want me to see if I can track him down? Jim's not *much* to go on, but rec center and the time frame make it possible to narrow down some contenders."

"Eventually, if we need to. But first I want to rule something out. Jim Gary. I want you to see if he worked at the rec center thirty-two years ago."

"That's a leap." But Sam's heart rate picked up. An interesting leap. A connecting leap.

"Yeah, it is. That's why I want to rule it out."

"All right. I'm on it." And if he went to the jail to talk to his dad with his brothers, that kept them apart. *Hallelujah.*

"Sam…" He didn't say anything until she looked up at him. "I can't charge them for this. Aly … it's wrecked her, not that she'd admit it, but it's obvious. I know there's bad blood there…"

"I'm not going to charge Aly for this," Sam grumbled. And it wasn't some long-lost best friends thing. It wasn't about *Aly*. It was just … the right thing to do.

He got up from his desk, crossed over to hers. She kept her gaze studiously on her keyboard. Still, she felt him get close.

Too close.

Then his hands were on her shoulders. He gave them a friendly if kind of awkward squeeze as he leaned in close. "You're a big softy."

She snorted. She wanted to shrug his hands off her shoulders, but it was just a friendly gesture. *Friendly.*

Instead, it made her ache for something nebulous. A warmth, a contentment, something she didn't know how to express.

Or maybe it wasn't nebulous at all.

Maybe it was just him.

Chapter Thirteen

The Bennet Ranch

"I SHOULD COME."

Landon looked in the mirror at Aly's reflection. She stood behind him as he changed from the clothes he'd done chores in into something more suitable for a trip to town. A concerned frown was settled onto her face.

He turned to her and dropped a quick kiss on her mouth. Both to smooth over what he was going to say, and because he needed a reminder that whatever bad might still lay in front of them, Benjamin Bennet wasn't one of those things. Dad was the past now.

"No, you shouldn't. Cal and I are going to handle this."

"The *this* being *my* problem."

"I thought we didn't have individual problems anymore. I thought we just shared them now." Those were *her* words she'd tossed at him a few months back. He had to admit it felt pretty good to be able to use them against her now.

She wrinkled her nose, no doubt at her own words being used against her. "She's my mother."

"And I'm going to talk to *my* father." He framed her face with his hands.

It got easier, this ... whole *love* thing. If it soothed her, helped her in some way, showing it didn't feel like he was exposing some weak underbelly. Something no doubt his father had taught him and reinforced his entire childhood.

But his mother and Aly had taught him different, and he was working on accepting that—for Aly—though that was a more complex endeavor. Reassuring her wasn't.

"I think we both know that if Dad knows how badly we want this information, he's not going to give it. It sends a message if you're not there. That it's not that important. That he can give us information and it does matter."

She let out a sigh, placed her hands over his. "What if he refuses to see you? To talk?"

"He agreed to the meeting, so I don't see why he'd refuse to see us now. He might not talk or give us anything, that's true. Maybe we get nowhere, but it's worth a shot. And we're going to give it our best shot."

He tucked one of her hands into his, drew her out of the bedroom and toward the stairs. He needed to get going or they'd be late.

"What about Nate?" Aly asked.

Landon *had* considered texting Nate his plans to join Cal but had talked himself out of it. "Three might feel like an ambush."

"Or it's a symbol."

Landon didn't know how to argue that, but Cal was waiting for them when they got downstairs.

"We better get going," he said, looking up from his phone screen. "They might not let us see him if we're late."

Landon nodded and followed Cal outside, Aly trailing after them.

Landon's attention was on Cal though. Cal had wanted

to handle this himself. Use all that *lawyer expertise*, but Landon had insisted and, in the end, Cal hadn't fought too hard.

Cal wasn't right. Landon knew that, even if he didn't know what to do about it. Cal being here, staying here, it spoke to something bigger going on in his life back in Austin. And he just looked … sickly wasn't the right word, but it was close.

Cal had been seeing a therapist back in Austin, but Landon had yet to see it doing any wonders for his big brother.

But now wasn't the time to bring it up, if he ever found himself wanting to butt into Cal's business. Which felt like a bit of a leap. So he followed Cal out onto the porch.

"You know, Aly suggested that Nate should come with us. Maybe we should…" But before he could say it, a truck pulled up over the rise.

Nate's truck.

"I guess we don't have to ask," Cal said.

They both stood on the porch, Aly behind them, as Nate parked his truck and got out, walking across the yard to greet them.

"You're coming?" Cal asked.

Nate nodded. "Figured I should. Admittedly it was Sam's idea. But she's right. Seems like … if nothing else, any time we face him, it should be together. A … symbol."

Landon looked back at Aly, who'd said the exact same thing. Her gaze met his, then went back to Nate.

"It's a good symbol," she said reassuringly. "And I want you all to know you don't have to do this for me." She held up a hand before anyone could argue with her, like they were all gearing up to do. "But I appreciate that you all would."

"All right. Let's get this over with before we miss our window," Cal grumbled.

Before Landon could move with Cal off the porch, Aly grabbed him, pressed her mouth to his. "Good luck," she murmured against his lips, where he would have much preferred to linger ... if he didn't have a brotherly audience. "Don't let him get to you," she added.

"I won't."

When Landon pulled back and stepped away, Cal moved in.

"Do I get one?" Cal grinned at Aly who rolled her eyes.

Landon elbowed him down the stairs. "Find your own."

And then the three Bennet brothers walked to Nate's truck without needing to discuss who'd drive. Like they were a team. Going to face their dad. Again.

Like they'd never quite be done with that.

But Aly waved from the porch after he'd gotten into the passenger seat of Nate's truck. A porch where they lived, shared a room, a life. And Benjamin Bennet might have his fingerprints all over that house and that life, but he wasn't here anymore.

It was just Landon's and Aly's now.

"Why don't you just marry her already?" Cal asked from where he was sprawled out in the back.

Landon tried not to stiffen, because he knew Cal was poking at him to keep all their minds off what they were about to do. "It's been a few months," he muttered.

"It's been your whole lives," Nate replied awfully confidently for a man who'd disappeared from their lives for fifteen years.

But he wasn't wrong.

Chapter Fourteen

C AL HAD SUFFERED a few panic attacks in his lifetime. Namely over things his father had done. For a time, he hadn't always recognized them as panic attacks. He'd written them off as stress or lack of sleep or whatever.

His therapist said it was likely he'd suffered from them mostly when his memories and dissociative amnesia were fighting against each other. Which explained his constant need to get away from Marietta, and stay away, even before Mom had died.

But there was nothing dissociative about the panic fluttering in his chest right now. It was just straight up this moment.

He did not want to deal with his father. Ever again. He knew he'd have to. Maybe he'd never visit Dad for a good time in jail, where he'd likely spend the rest of his life once the trial was over, but he'd known there'd be a trial and maybe the occasional legal related issue he'd have to see his father for.

He supposed this could fit under *legal issue*, sort of. He had to be here. Not just for Aly, and he'd do a lot for Aly. But for his brothers, because they weren't involved in the law at all. They didn't know what they were doing. Maybe Nate was learning how to be an investigator or whatever, but he didn't know how to handle a difficult criminal. Not like this.

This was Cal's entire job—even if he hadn't been doing that great a job of it back in Texas lately.

Still, he was glad to have them here. At first, he'd thought it weak, needing backup, but hearing what Nate said about it being a symbol … that resonated. Maybe he was reaching, but it felt right.

Especially when Dad was led into the visitor's room in his restraints. A guard sat him at a table, then moved to the side to give the four of them the illusion of privacy.

No Bennet brother offered a greeting.

But Dad did. "A visit from my sons. Lucky me." He smiled at all of them in a way that Cal might have believed once.

It *seemed* warm. The guards might even buy it, though they'd likely seen enough of people to know warmth could be faked. And Benjamin Bennet's hard dark gaze was the key.

Jail had not been kind to dear old Dad. He looked sallow and like he'd lost considerable weight, but his face was puffy and that larger-than-life aura that had once enveloped him like a second skin didn't work here in a jail's visiting room.

Besides, the sheer *hate* in his eyes hadn't dissipated any since their last visit a few months ago.

"Consider it more business than social call," Cal said, his own fake smile in place. "We've had a woman show up at the ranch asking us about Tripp Cartwright."

"We? You suddenly ranching?"

Cal ignored the question. "You and Tripp were friends. I

thought you could give us some information on Janie Turner."

Dad took a few moments, no doubt to draw the moment out, enjoy being asked a question he could withhold information about. His smile even seemed genuine. "Why should I do that?"

Nate shrugged. "What's it to you if you do?" It was just the right note of casual.

No tension. No urgency. Maybe Nate was better at this than Cal would have wanted to give him credit for.

"Tripp was a good man," Dad said, tapping his fingers against the table. He studied each of them in turn, like he was sniffing out weaknesses. "Janie Turner, on the other hand, was a bitch."

The last word was delivered with venom. The kind of venom that spoke to some kind of personal interaction. A negative one.

Cal was careful not to show his cards. While Nate and Landon stood, Cal moved forward and took the seat across from Dad. He affected all the nonchalance he could muster. Put on the lawyer mask that had once felt like a second skin.

Not here. Here it felt heavy and awkward, but he worked to slide it into place all the same. He'd worked up an angle to protect Aly and the truth from Dad's venom and vindictiveness.

"Tripp's last will and testament listed you as executor. Is there anything he left behind that'd still be at the ranch that Janie should have since she's here?"

Dad's drumming fingers increased in tempo. "Your mother gave Aly everything of her father's. Even set her up her own little bank account with whatever was left." Benjamin rolled his eyes. "Aly has everything, but even if there was something, it wouldn't be Janie's to have. She got plenty."

"What's that mean?" Landon demanded.

At Cal's sharp look he shoved his hands in his pockets and shut his mouth.

Dad studied each of them, but he stopped at Landon, no doubt sensing the weakest link. Aly would always be his soft spot. Even Dad knew that. But Dad didn't clam up, he considered Landon, starting to look a little eager.

That panic that had been fluttering into Cal's throat earlier took a stronger hold, and Cal had to close his hand into a fist under the table in order to feel strong enough to breathe evenly.

"Aly should be thanking me," Dad said, his eyes never leaving Landon.

"For what?" Cal asked, trying to get Dad's attention back on him.

It didn't work. He delivered the next to and for Landon. "For getting rid of her bitch of a mother."

Cal struggled with an inhale, then an exhale. Just because he'd remembered everything he'd seen his father do to his mother didn't mean he wanted the images in his head, and the way his father said that reminded him too much of...

"Well, you didn't murder her since she's still around. So what did you do? Threaten her? Pay her?" Nate asked, with a kind of flat detachment Cal didn't think he had in him, and he knew Landon didn't.

Cal's ears were ringing. He was managing to breathe only out of spite.

Fuck it if he'd let his father see this reaction.

"Don't know why it matters to any of you, but she was trouble and Tripp didn't see it. Couldn't lose a good foreman over a vindictive slut. It didn't take much money to get her to move along once the baby was born."

"She was a teenager," Landon said, disgusted and not doing nearly a good enough job of hiding it.

"Told everyone around she was twenty-five," Dad replied, as if that made it all fine. "Her real age didn't come clean until she wanted to tie Tripp up in a marriage he didn't want. So I took care of it." He used some more disgusting words to describe Janie Turner, and Cal couldn't take it anymore.

He got to his feet. But in the back of his head, he noted Dad used some of the same words that had been spraypainted across Aly's truck. And he'd have to poke into that when he could breathe.

"You're expecting us to believe that out of some great loyalty to Tripp Cartwright, you paid off a woman he'd impregnated so she wouldn't stick around and make *his* life hard? *You?*" Landon said.

And he was calm now. Collected. At least on the outside.

Cal doubted very much on the inside.

"She told a bunch of guys they were the father. She was a slut. Spread her legs for just about anyone. I did him and Aly a damn favor. She was a cancer on that ranch, and *I* got rid of her." His gaze finally moved to Cal. "Quite legally, in fact."

"You sound awfully … jilted and bitter about it, Dad," Nate said, earning Dad's attention.

Cal looked at Nate, who stood there with every appearance of being relaxed, borderline uninterested. But the next words were delivered carefully, with the skill of any good lawyer. Almost like being a Bennet had prepared them all for a life of courtroom arguments.

"Almost as if she *spread her legs* for *just about everyone* but not you. And not for your lack of trying."

Dad jerked against his restraints, rage leapt into his face quick and easy. "Boy, you better watch your mouth."

Nate laughed. A bitterness so sharp and deep Cal nearly shuddered. "Or what?"

Dad was on his feet quickly, but not as quickly as the guards were to move on him. Cal noted that not he nor either of his brothers moved in reaction to Dad's violent turn. They all stood still, watching Dad as the guards dragged him away.

Then they were ushered out as well. Once they stepped outside, they all lifted their faces to the sun, like it could shine away all the ugliness of that encounter, of what their father was.

"Do you think he's telling the truth?" Landon asked, a weariness in his tone that he'd hidden quite well back there.

Cal kept his face to the sun, trying to put some order to his thoughts to answer Landon's question, but Nate spoke first.

"I think he's telling parts of the truth. Isn't that how he fooled everyone for so long? He wasn't a flat-out liar. Wasn't a flat-out abuser. He skirted lines. Manipulated truths. Gaslit the hell out of all his victims. So there's some truth in there, and it corroborates a lot of what Shawn Harrington told us.

Is it the whole truth though? I doubt it."

Cal glanced at Nate. He didn't understand his baby brother at all. The reckless man who'd disappeared and come back a stoic soldier with more emotional intelligence than Cal and Landon combined—or maybe just a willingness to show it.

"I think you were right on the money. He was bitter about Janie, and that speaks to something deeper." Cal glanced over at Landon. "Because you were right too. Whyever he decided to pay off Janie Turner to get her to leave, it wasn't to protect his friend or out of the goodness of his heart."

"He'll never tell us," Landon replied. "Or if he would, we'd never know for sure what was truth and what was lie."

"Maybe one of us should talk to her," Cal suggested as they walked toward Nate's truck. "She's probably the only one in this whole situation who knows the truth."

"Aly wouldn't go for it."

Cal looked at Landon, surprised. "Since when did that stop you from doing something to protect her?"

Landon shrugged, clearly uncomfortable. "She's been hurt enough by all this. I'm not adding to it."

"Besides," Nate added, unlocking his truck with the fob and climbing inside. "We don't know enough about Janie to determine that whatever she might tell us *would* be the truth. She's not exactly a model citizen."

They all sat with that for a minute before Nate turned his key in the ignition.

"Did we just waste our time and ruin our day in the process?" Landon said into the silence that had fallen.

"No," Nate said firmly. "We collected more information. It might seem small now, but it'll add up. You just keep adding it all up until you get the truth."

"I'm not sure the truth is ever going to exist for the Bennets," Landon muttered, with a lot of that same bitterness Cal had heard slip out just once in Nate's voice back in the jail.

Cal knew how easy bitterness was. He also knew it would drown them all, and he wasn't about to let Benjamin Bennet win again. "Maybe not, but the only way the truth can exist is if we fight for it."

Landon met his gaze in the rearview mirror. He gave an almost imperceptible nod. "Well, brothers, let's fight like hell."

Chapter Fifteen

Mountain Memorial Cemetery

ALY HADN'T MEANT to wind up at the cemetery where her father was buried. She had planned on diving into chores until Landon and Cal got back. Keep her mind off what they might be talking about.

But that hadn't worked. She'd started inventory over at least five times before giving up on having the kind of focus required of her for her duties.

So she'd gone to the kitchen and made some coffee cake. For a small period of time, that had worked. Baking was one of those tasks that calmed her mind, that brought her some joy. So she'd decided to follow that up with something intricate for dinner.

Which required a trip to a grocery store, which reminded her of the obscenities on her truck, though it was freshly painted now, and she would go to Murphys instead of Wraiths.

But the entire line of thinking brought her back to the topic of her mother.

She wanted to *scream*.

Instead, she'd marched outside and gotten in her truck. She wasn't going to let whatever was going on ruin her life, her day. She still had to go to the grocery store sometimes.

She still had to drive off the ranch. People would talk. Janie would lurk.

Such was life. And she had to live it.

So that was just what she did. But on the drive into town, she noted the sign to the cemetery. Without fully thinking the move through, she'd turned into the drive. She'd parked, got out into the windy but sunny fall day, and unerringly walked to her father's grave, even though she didn't visit often.

She'd never seen much reason to look at a name carved in stone when the things that made her feel her father's presence were back at the ranch.

The huff of a horse's breath on a quiet winter morning, the smell of leather and animal, the way the birds settled as day moved into night. Sometimes, in the right, quiet moments, those things felt like little beyond-the-grave hugs from the man she'd loved so much.

Marie Bennet had been the one to encourage her to believe that. *What's the harm?* She used to say. *If you feel him here, that's all that matters.*

So Aly had never had much reason to visit where he was actually buried.

But it had been a while, and she found in the turmoil of the current situation, she didn't feel her father on the ranch. So, she sought him here.

Not for those pseudo signs that he might be with her. No, she wasn't feeling particularly *loving* about him right now. And worse, the thing about what Jill's dad had relayed that she couldn't get over, no matter how hard she tried, was that Tripp Cartwright might not be her father at all. If Janie

Turner had been *having fun* with all those different men that summer, her father could be any one of them.

Including Jill's own.

Aly came to a stop in front of his grave. It was simple, paid for by the Bennets. Just his name and the years of his birth and death. Nothing fancy. He hadn't been a fancy guy.

Had he been a liar? Someone who took advantage of a young girl? Had he been just like Benjamin Bennet? A horrible man hiding under layers of pretending to be good?

A tear fell over her cheek, and then another. All those walls she'd tried to build, protections, all the things she'd tried to keep bottled up just started ... leaking out of her. Her vision wavered as she stared at his name.

"I don't want to think you were bad. I don't want you to have been awful," she said, as sobs began to break free. "You should have told me about her. You should have told me everything. You shouldn't have left me with this." It was so pointless, sobbing here in front of her father's grave, but there was some kind of release in it.

All the things she'd been white knuckled holding onto these past few days let go.

But even if she somehow made it through this still thinking he'd been a good man, she'd know he messed this up. He'd left nothing but secrets, and now Aly had to live with the repercussions of that.

When she'd started to get herself a little bit under control, she heard the tell-tale sounds of footsteps. She furiously wiped at her cheeks before she turned around to see if she knew the other cemetery visitor.

Shock hit her. "Sam."

The woman in question offered a sheepish smile. "Hey." She had a small clutch of flowers cradled in one arm. "Didn't mean to interrupt. My mom's up that way." She gestured up the hill, and Aly could tell it was the truth. Sam was just following a little footpath up to the higher ground of the cemetery.

"You didn't interrupt," Aly replied.

She remembered when Sam's mom had died. They'd been in the fourth grade. Sam had missed a few days of school, and Aly had been miffed she didn't have her recess partner.

And then Dad had taken her out of school one morning to go to the funeral. Sam and Sam's father hadn't cried. Aly could still remember in perfect detail the way they'd stood at the gravesite, clutching hands, looking pale and lost. But they didn't cry.

Aly had. And Dad had wiped her eyes. And for those first few months after it had happened, Dad and Mrs. Bennet had always encouraged Aly to invite Sam over, bring her an extra cookie for her lunch.

It hadn't been a hardship on Aly's part, they'd been like two little motherless magnets. But she looked back and saw now that part of that connection had been forged by the adults in Aly's life who'd had some compassion for a young girl who'd lost her mother.

Surely that compassion meant her father hadn't been … all bad. She wanted to hold onto that thought, that feeling.

Aly cleared her throat. "I'm really grateful you and Nate are looking into Janie Turner for me," she said, wanting to prolong the connection to something positive with her father.

"It's the job. Besides, it seems to me…" She stopped herself, then shook her head. "Never mind."

Aly took a few steps toward her. "No, I want to hear what you have to say."

Sam glanced at her then, but only for a second. A flash of a past Aly wasn't sure she recognized herself in anymore. Where they'd looked at each other and known what the other was thinking.

"Secrets caused all this. Secrets and lies and manipulations." Sam gestured around them. "Which means the only antidote to it is finding the truth. No matter the cost."

The idea of *cost* rankled. Sam's ferocious defense of her father had been what had come between them back then. Maybe Aly could look back and understand it better now, but that didn't mean it didn't hurt, that Sam had considered losing her friendship as just some cost to be weathered.

"I think that's easy for you to say."

Sam laughed, bitterly. "Maybe. Maybe cost is all I've got."

"That's not what…" But Aly didn't know how to explain what she meant.

Didn't know how to explain she both hurt and understood, both mistrusted and trusted Sam. Saw her somehow as both the girl who'd been her friend and the woman who'd been her enemy.

"Hell, maybe I'm wrong about it, all of it," Sam said, gesturing with her free hand again as if to encompass *everything*. "I haven't been met with much except opposition all these years of searching for a simple truth." She blew out a breath, straightened her shoulders. "But the only way I think anything gets better is if we have the truth. Leaving things buried, secret, it just means they're going to sprout up sometime. I'd rather rip them out at the roots. I'd rather know, even if it's shitty and painful. I'd rather know on my timeline." She shook her head, let out another bitter chuckle. "But so far all the truth has gotten me is a lot of fucking alone time."

"Nate seems to be with you an awful lot." Aly hadn't meant it to come out sounding snotty, but old habits died hard.

Sam's smile was wry, and it didn't reach her eyes. "He's a good investigator. A good employee." Her smile faded into a bit of a frown. "A good guy."

They sat in the silent truth of that for a few moments, and Aly sat in her guilt for being a bitch for no good reason, before Sam spoke again.

"But he's your brother, more or less. They're all yours, more or less. They'll get you answers." Sam inhaled deeply, lifted the arm cradling the flowers. "I've got to lay these, get back. I'll see you around, Aly."

She moved away, a slow, steady march, and Aly felt something she hadn't felt for Samantha Price in a long, long time.

Sympathy.

And the desire to do something about it.

SAM HAD VISITED her mother's grave the first of the month

every month pretty much since Mom had died. It had been a tradition for her and Dad. They'd never said much, but they'd always laid flowers. Then, Sam had maintained the tradition with Aunt Lisa until she was old enough to drive herself. Then she'd done it alone. All this time.

She'd been visiting this grave more years than she'd seen her mother in person.

Sam had always wondered, what might be different if her mother hadn't died. If she'd somehow beaten the cancer back then, would her father have still been a suspect in Marie Bennet's murder?

But thinking like that never did any good for anyone. She couldn't change what had already happened, or the choices—and non-choices—other people had made.

She couldn't even change her own choices, or the costs she'd been willing to pay to find the truth.

Like losing friends.

Sam laid the little clutch of flowers across her mother's gravestone. The older she got, the more she realized she didn't actually know this woman. Sam only had the most basic, childish understanding of her. Mother to young child.

She still loved her, loved the fuzzy memories of the woman she'd been, but it was a distant kind of grief. The loss of what could have been, not the loss of what had been.

Which was a little too on the nose when it came to about the entirety of her life right now. Handling a case for Aly Cartwright landing smack dab in the middle of the list.

"Sam."

Sam turned to find Aly walking up the path towards her. She was surprised, she could admit. She figured Aly would have had her fill of Sam's presence and gotten the hell out.

Certainly not follow her for more.

Aly's gaze dropped to the gravestone, the flowers, then back up to Sam. The traces of the tears she'd shed over her father's grave were in the splotchy red spots on her cheeks, the puffy eyes, but the tears themselves were gone.

Sam remembered going to Tripp's funeral. It had only been a year or so before the murder, before the end. But in that moment, they'd been best friends. And Sam knew, looking back, that even though Aly had been closer with Landon—if only because they lived and worked on the same ranch—in the aftermath of her father's sudden death, Sam had been the one she'd looked to for comfort.

Because Sam had known what it was like to lose. Sam had wrapped Aly in a hug, and they'd held onto each other through the whole service. Oh, Landon had been right there behind them, but it was Sam who understood the depths of loss, of grief.

It hadn't taken Landon long after that to learn about both, and more.

Hell, maybe they were all cursed.

"I want to…" Aly cleared her throat, her eyebrows drawing together. "I'd like to talk to you about some things, but maybe we could go back to the ranch?" She hugged herself, Sam presumed against the chill in the air. She wasn't dressed for the temperature. "Or somewhere in town? This place gives me the creeps."

"Still afraid of ghosts, Al?"

Aly's mouth quirked a little, and they shared that tiny little remembrance. A moment, where that childhood comradery stretched out between them, like a thread Sam could almost see. She'd once confided all her secrets to Aly, and vice versa. They'd passed notes in school about how mean their dads were for not getting them cell phones. About Keith Jones's *perfect* hair, Mr. Dalton being a creep, and the like. They'd whispered in school hallways, run through town, the mountains, wherever they could escape to. They'd dreamed and planned and imagined.

None of their current reality reflected any of that.

Well, Aly had Landon now, so maybe it wasn't all hopeless.

"Come by the ranch, if you've got time," Aly said, more firmly this time. "I've got some coffee cake I made this morning. We could have some coffee and talk. The guys are…"

"Yeah, Nate told me." Sam didn't want to go to the ranch.

She really didn't want to sink into more awkward discomfort. Having coffee with Aly felt fraught and raw and scary. Being alone was better, safer, easier.

And fucking lonely. "All right. I'll, uh, follow you there."

"Good. Good." She nodded for good measure, then turned and began to walk down.

When Sam didn't immediately follow, she looked over her shoulder, and didn't stop until Sam fell into step behind her.

Sam had no idea what she was doing, but Aly seemed determined, and … well, talking to Aly might give her some new information—on the vandalism, on what she knew about Janie Turner. It was essentially work.

It would be easy. It would be fine. Fifteen minutes, tops. An act of ... something. A peace offering, sure. She wanted peace. Rekindling a dead friendship wasn't on the table, but maybe a truce was.

They got in their respective vehicles without saying anything, and Sam followed Aly's truck the short drive to the Bennet Ranch. Aly pulled to a stop at the top of the drive, and Sam pulled her car onto the gravel patch next to her, where another car in even worse shape than hers was parked.

It clearly belonged to the older woman sitting on the porch of the Bennet house. An older woman with red hair who stood when she saw Aly get out of her truck.

Sam glanced at Aly, whose expression was ... not scared, exactly, but something close to it. Which prompted Sam to get out of her car, cross over to stand next to Aly. "That Janie Turner?"

Aly didn't move toward the woman, even as the woman took some steps toward them. "Yeah."

"You want me to leave?"

"No." Aly shook her head. "No, I'd really prefer not to be alone with her. Not yet."

But that didn't mean Aly wanted *Sam* here. "I can call Jill for you. Call Nate and see if they're done at the jail. I can—"

"Jesus, Sam," Aly muttered as Janie approached. "Just back me up."

"Right. Sure." She didn't mind backing anyone up, but this felt all those things she'd already worried about times a million.

Fraught. Tense. Not her place.

"Hi," Janie greeted as she approached. She smiled at Aly with what looked like hope in her eyes and didn't much acknowledge Sam's presence. "I saw the Bennet boy's truck in town and I just … I wanted a chance to talk to you. Without someone stepping in between us." She eyed Sam now. "Hello. I don't think I know you."

Aly shifted her body, so Janie looked back at her rather than at Sam. She didn't make any attempt to introduce them. "The problem with you being here is I'm not ready to talk to you. So, you should go. I have your number when I'm ready. As you already know."

Sam figured it was nice of her to use *when* instead of *if*.

"You mean that Bennet has my number," Janie said, a hint of venom at the edges of her tone.

"Landon has it in his phone, yes, and I'll get it from him when I'm ready. Now, please go."

Sam had to give Aly credit. She kept her calm composure, walked past Janie and toward the house.

Janie made a move to follow her. Maybe Sam would have let her, but she didn't like the belligerent cast to Janie's mouth, so she stepped in her way, bodily stopping Janie from following Aly.

Maybe this was none of her business, but Aly had told the woman point-blank what she wanted. "She said she didn't want to talk," Sam said to Janie. "So I think you should go."

Janie looked from Aly to Sam. "She's got a lot of body-guards."

Sam didn't reply to that, just stood in Janie's path hoping this didn't turn into a fight she got on the wrong side of.

Janie looked her up and down then turned on a heel, stalking for her car.

Sam watched her the whole way, not convinced she was just going to go.

But she opened the driver's side door, then paused, glaring at Aly who was over by the porch now. "There's not always going to be someone here to save you from the truth," she called out, then got in her car and slammed the door.

She peeled out of the gravel spot and flew down the hill.

When Sam looked back at Aly, she sank onto the porch stairs, like her legs couldn't hold her any longer. She covered her face with her hands. But she didn't sob like she had been back at the cemetery. She just breathed.

Not knowing what else to do, Sam walked over, then awkwardly took a seat next to her on the stairs. Their hips touched, reminding Sam of a childhood that was long gone.

Aly dropped her hands from her face, squinted at where Janie had disappeared. "I owe you one, Sam."

"I didn't do anything," Sam replied.

"You did. If you weren't here, she would have kept pushing. And I could have handled that, but I'm glad I didn't have to." She blew out a breath. "I guess it's simple all in all. I don't want the truth. I want to run away from it."

"You've got a right. By all accounts, she ran away from you."

"By all accounts," Aly agreed, still looking out at the drive. Her mouth firmed. "But ... you weren't wrong at the cemetery. All the bad that's happened lately was built on secrets and lies, and letting those stand only makes things worse. Maybe I should have talked to her."

"Not alone you shouldn't."

Aly looked over at her now. "Why not?"

It was an honest question, not a recrimination, so Sam answered it with as much honest as she could muster. "It's not a secret Landon and I don't see eye to eye."

Aly snorted.

"But if she really cared, if she really … if she was here for honest reasons, she wouldn't stand there trying to act like Landon is the one standing between you two when he's not. Trying to twist the story to suit her narrative is a little too…"

"Benjamin Bennet?" Aly supplied.

Sam looked around the ranch. One Benjamin Bennet had inherited, run, made a profit from. The ranch where he'd killed his wife, beat his youngest son, and created his own little kingdom of lies and pain.

"Maybe the boys will have something on that front."

"Maybe, but I won't hold my breath." Aly shook her head. "You know, you can leave if you want. I didn't mean to like, force you here."

"I don't force easy," Sam replied. "I can stay if you want. Till they get back."

"Since when did you get to be a martyr?"

She wasn't one. Not in the least, but … maybe underneath all the secrets, lies, costs, and pain of the past fifteen years, she still had this soft spot for her childhood best friend. "I guess fifteen years changes a person," Sam said, instead of trying to argue the point.

"Yeah, it does."

But before either of them decided what to do with that, a truck rumbled up the drive.

Chapter Sixteen

The Bennet Ranch

NATE FELT EDGY. Sick to his stomach. It was the usual reaction to being around his father. Maybe about *fighting*, when that's all he'd been doing, and he was bone tired of it.

They didn't speak the entire drive back to the ranch. Maybe they were all dealing with their post-visit nausea. Maybe they were all going over the prospect of Dad paying Janie off. What it meant that he'd forced her to leave.

Nate was seriously considering dropping his brothers off, then heading to the Wolf Den. It was early, but damn, he could use a drink.

He negotiated the truck up the drive to the Bennet house. Just about the time Nate recognized Sam's car of all things being in the yard, Landon leaned forward.

"What the hell is Sam doing here?" Landon demanded of Nate, like Nate had special tabs on everything Sam did.

"I don't know," Nate replied, keeping the bite out of his tone. "I'm not her keeper."

Sam and Aly were standing at the bottom of the porch steps. They both shaded their eyes and looked toward his truck in a similar movement. Aly with her red braid and fair skin dressed in jeans and a thermal for ranch work. Sam with her dark hair pulled ruthlessly back, dressed in all black.

Landon was out of the truck before Nate had gotten it into park.

Nate wasn't far behind, a strange blend of nerves and worry dancing along his skin. Why was Sam here? How would Landon react? What side would he take?

Because he didn't want there to be any sides, but he wasn't so sure Landon and Sam could agree.

"How'd it go?" Nate heard Aly ask Landon.

He was frowning at Sam as he put his arm around Aly's shoulders. "About like how you'd expect. Sam," he said by way of greeting, if anyone could call the way he said her name in that flat, terse manner a *greeting*.

"Sam and I ran into each other ... in town," Aly explained. "We had a little conversation I wanted to continue so I invited her to come on up for some coffee cake."

"There's cake?" Cal asked from behind Nate. "Then what are we doing out here?"

It was odd to Nate how Cal seemed to be able to do that. Switch off the trauma and the panic Nate had seen in his eyes in the jail. But it wasn't as smooth as it had been last spring. There were fractures in that façade. Cal didn't stop trying to put it on though.

"I guess you should all hear this first," Aly said before Cal could head up the porch and inside. "Janie was here. When we got back. Just sitting on the porch." Aly looked up at Landon, her hand wrapped around his on her shoulder. "She said she'd seen you in town, so she thought I'd be alone." Aly's expression was stiff, but she smiled at Sam. "I wasn't."

"She wanted to talk to Aly alone." Sam looked at Aly.

"Aly didn't want to, so I stuck around until she took off. It wasn't that long ago. You guys must have just missed her."

"She would have stayed, pushed, but Sam stopped her from trying to. I appreciate it, Sam, really." Aly smiled at Sam and clearly meant it.

Maybe there was some discomfort here, but it seemed something positive had happened with Sam and Aly while they'd been gone.

"I'm glad you were here then," Landon said, his tone gruff, but he looked right at Sam when he said it. Meant it.

It was as close to a white flag as Nate figured Landon would ever get.

Then the five of them stood there, no one saying anything, not quite sure what to do with the turn of events.

"You know what? I need a drink," Aly announced, clearly shocking just about everyone.

Especially Landon, who looked down at her with some concern. "Al, it's like three in the afternoon."

Aly looked at Landon, shrugged, then turned her gaze around the group. "Anyone else? I'm sure there's a bottle of whiskey around here somewhere." She slipped out from under Landon's arm and started marching up the stairs toward the front door.

Cal was on her heels and Landon quickly followed.

Nate moved to do the same, but noted Sam was still rooted to the spot. "You coming?"

Sam looked at him, a million heartbreaks in her eyes. He knew she was about to say no, to refuse, but he also saw something that looked a lot like yearning. Like she *wanted* to accept the invitation, rather than leave.

Before he could decide what to do with that, Aly stepped around him and grabbed Sam's arm, pulling her forward.

"She's coming," Aly said forcefully, not giving Sam a say in the matter.

When Sam looked back at him helplessly, he only smiled and followed them inside.

Aly marched them all to the kitchen, instructing them to sit at the dining room table. She collected mismatched glasses, a half-empty bottle of whiskey, a two-liter of some kind of cherry flavored soda and then set it all down at the center of the table.

"Cal, you're the bartender. I'm going to cut up the coffee cake."

Cal rubbed his hands together, eyeing the odd conglomeration of items. "Whiskey and coffee cake. What a woman. All right, Sam, you're up first. Pick your poison. Straight up, or mixed with this shit?"

Sam hesitated. Nate realized he'd never seen her quite so uncomfortable, so off her game, so ... vulnerable. And he'd seen some hints at the vulnerability, but that was wrapped up in finding out her dad was a murderer too. It had been more something that anyone would feel.

Her discomfort here, and those little hints of clearly *wishing* she had something like this in her life, was just ... Sam.

"Surprise us, Cal. Just make it strong," Nate answered for her, leaning toward Sam in some thought that it would be like support. Reassurance she should be here. She leaned toward him too, and he was gratified that maybe it had worked.

"I don't think I should be here," she whispered to him.

"Why not, Sam?"

She looked at him, clear distress written all over her face, but he was determined. She was going to stay. They'd catch everyone up on what had happened today. And they'd all work together to find the necessary answers.

Progress. Hope.

Together.

"You're a part of this," he said, when she didn't come up with an answer. "No backing out now."

CAL WAS PLEASANTLY buzzed on a ridiculous concoction he'd made of the whiskey and generic brand pop. Looking around the room, he thought they all were.

Maybe alcohol wasn't the healthiest coping mechanism, but there was something nice about this. All of them eating cake and getting a little drunk, rehashing what Dad had said at the jail, what little Janie'd had a chance to say to Aly with Sam there.

They were all drunk enough to make a few jokes, have a few laughs, not be so fucking serious about all the shit they were going through or had gone through.

Yeah, it was nice. But damn, it was hot in here. He shoved to his feet, realizing maybe he was more than a *little buzzed* as he swayed a bit on his way out to the porch to get some air.

If anyone noticed, they didn't follow. He fumbled his way outside for that cold fresh air, but stopped short, surprised to find Sam out on the porch by herself.

For a moment, they just regarded each other.

Then Sam fisted her free hand on her hip "All right, law-yer guy." Sam eyed him, maybe closer to drunk than buzzed too, she pointed with her hand curled around her glass. "What's your take?"

He moved fully out to the porch, closer to where she was leaning against the porch post. "My take on what?"

There was an intensity to her, even under all that drunk. "Either of them going to walk?"

He didn't need to be a mind reader to understand what she was referring to. Her dad. His dad. Murderers. It tensed inside of him. His understanding of the law, the system. He had concerns, still ... he couldn't voice them. "Your dad's sentencing might go a little easier since he confessed, and he's already served some time, but at his age? It's not likely either he sees life outside a cell."

"And your dad?"

"He's refusing to confess, but there's an awful lot of evi-dence against him. The trial will be messy, but it should be a slam dunk." He didn't mention *should* never mattered in a criminal trial.

"I'll drink to that." She clinked her glass to his, then drank deeply. He saw some of the same things he felt in her expression.

Relief, regret, and enough understanding that the *slam dunk* wasn't guaranteed.

"So, what's your take?" he asked her.

"On what? I don't know shit about law."

"Not murder." Cal gestured his cup toward where Nate

stood inside the big picture window they were standing on the other side of, talking to Aly and Landon. "Baby brother."

He watched carefully as Sam's gaze moved over Nate. It was shadowy dark out here, with just the lone porch light illuminating them. So it could be the low light that made it look like Sam's expression softened.

Particularly when Nate seemed to sense someone looking at him and looked through the glass and their way, meeting Sam's gaze.

She held it for a second, then looked back at Cal. "You Bennet brothers aren't so bad. 'Course your dad's the comparison, so not hard to come out looking all right."

"I wasn't asking about all of us. I was asking about your employee."

She shrugged, her shoulder jerking denoting clear discomfort, even as her gaze tracked back to the window, but Nate wasn't there anymore. "He's good at it." She looked down at her drink. "Natural aptitude. I can't say he's *good* with people, but there's something about all that calm that gets 'em to talk, you know?"

"Yeah, I know."

Nate stepped out onto the porch, as if summoned by people talking about him. Sam looked over at him, then shifted her gaze back to her glass. She took a long drink.

Nate just stood there, stoic and impenetrable.

"Not planning on going anywhere, are you?" Cal asked, gesturing at the glass in Nate's hand. "Don't think anyone should be driving after this."

"No." Nate kept his attention on Sam. "I forgot earlier what with the ... whole Dad thing. Did you find anything out about Jim?"

"Got a little waylaid with all this." She gestured at the house. "I'll get to researching him first thing in the morning."

"First thing in the morning you're going to feel like death."

"Who says?" Sam replied, hand on cocked hip. "I can handle my liquor."

Nate's mouth curved in response. The closest thing Cal had seen to a smile on Nate's face in a long time.

Interesting.

Cal watched them talk about some guy named Jim. He paid less attention to the content of the conversation and more to the *way* they spoke. Something there. Like boxers fake-swinging at each other, trying to get the other to land the blow first. Except Cal didn't get the impression either one of them wanted to land a *blow*.

Yeah, it was interesting all right.

Aly popped her head out of the door. "I know you guys won't want to, but since everyone has been drinking, I think it's best of everyone crashes here tonight."

Nate and Sam shared a glance. Clearly Aly was right and neither of them *wanted* it, but they seemed to come to a nonverbal agreement that they were going to do it.

"Come on, Sam. I'll show you which room you can sleep in," Aly said, waving Sam inside.

Even drunk, Sam's discomfort was clear, but she didn't argue. She gave Nate a long, quiet look, then followed Aly inside.

Which left Cal and Nate on the porch, and when Nate's

steady gaze landed on Cal, he knew he had to go on the offensive. Because Nate was a little too … *aware*, and a lot too willing to poke into things Cal didn't want to touch.

Cal settled himself onto the old porch swing, casually gave it a push so he swung back. Forward. "Never saw her in this light, but Sam's kind of hot, you know?"

Nate didn't react exactly, but the look he shot Cal wasn't *kind*. There was an intensity to it, before it shuttered into stoicism.

He said nothing.

Cal found himself cheered. Nothing like irritating his brothers. Maybe he could flirt with Aly later and really piss Landon off. But before he could entertain himself with that idea, Nate pulled out a pin and pushed it into whatever little bubble of enjoyment he'd created.

"How's life in Austin, Cal?" Nate asked.

Still, he smiled at his baby brother, despite the deflation and the twisting reminder that life in Austin *sucked*, and he was currently hiding from it. "It's life, Nate."

Nate settled himself onto the swing next to Cal. Cal didn't know why tension was winding in his gut.

"I get real philosophical when I drink," Nate said casually, lifting his glass.

Cal was less and less convinced Nate had drunk enough to feel a buzz let alone be too impaired to drive.

"So, I can wonder aloud why you're suddenly staying home even though you don't need to. Or I can think about how many people I killed and if it makes me any different than dear old dad that I did it for love and country."

"Shit, Nate." Cal had to rub a hand over his face.

Hard to play the role of distant oldest brother when Nate said stuff like that. So bald and straight to the point and *awful*.

Still, he tried. "Get a therapist."

"Had one. Army supplied." Nate shrugged, leaned back in the swing and downed the rest of his drink. Maybe he was closer to drunk than Cal had given him credit for. "Besides, yours doesn't seem to be working any wonders."

"She's a genius," Cal returned. "One must mine the depths of your horror to heal. So here I am. Ass deep in horror. I'll let you know when the healing starts."

Nate laughed at that, an actual laugh, without all the bitterness from the afternoon. Oh, there was still plenty of bitterness all around them, but this was commiseration over bitterness.

It was oddly nice. This whole night had been a weird bit of *nice* after all the awful of talking to Dad.

"He paid her to leave, if that's the truth," Nate said, clearly changing gears back to Dad. "She's back the minute he's in jail, or at least close enough. I don't think the timing is coincidental."

"Agree."

Nate turned to him then, eyes direct and intense. Cal really couldn't decide if he was drunk or not.

"Someone's got to talk to Janie Turner. One on one."

"Landon said no. Not behind Aly's back."

"Landon's not the boss."

"You want to go around him?" Cal said, determined not to rub at his chest where a band of tension squeezed tight. "Just when we're … starting to make some inroads?"

"I don't want to, but we may have to."

"Let's save it as a last resort, huh?" Cal said, glancing behind him at the window. No one was in view, but the house glowed with warmth. "I'm enjoying the peace."

"You got a fucked-up definition of peace."

Cal laughed in spite of himself. "Gee, wonder why."

Chapter Seventeen

The Bennet Ranch

S AM WOKE UP when it was still pitch black. Her stomach roiled, her head pounded, and when she sat up to figure out what the hell had happened, the room seemed to sway.

Somehow both still a little drunk *and* hungover at the same time. Yeah, that seemed about right. How had she ended up here? She groaned, tried to roll over, but her bladder had other ideas.

Grumbling curses to herself, she got out of bed, had to steady herself against the wall before she walked across the small room Aly had shown her to. Complete with a pair of Aly's pajamas to borrow, a bottle of water, and toothpaste.

It had been surreal then when she'd been fuzzy with alcohol, even more so now with some sense running through her brain.

She opened the door and stepped into the hall and realized she had no idea which closed door was the bathroom. She'd never been on the second floor of the Bennet ranch house. She'd never spent the night here.

Maybe the one with the light shining from under it? But that meant someone was *in* there, and she did not especially want to have any late-night hallway conversations with ... literally anyone under this roof.

She took a step back toward the room, but the door with the light on behind it opened, light spilling into the hallway and backlighting … Nate.

He wore sweatpants, low on the hips. He'd put the flannel he'd been wearing earlier on, but it was unbuttoned, nothing underneath. His hair was in disarray, and he must not have shaved in a few days because the scruff along his jaw kept getting darker.

Uh oh.

She could not stand here and stare at his *bare chest*, but there was the whole *alcohol* factor, and she was curious. Because she would have thought the massive injury that had landed him in a VA hospital for the better part of three months might have some effect on him physically, beyond wherever the scars on his legs were. Like some atrophy, some softening of muscles, *something*.

Whatever he'd done in his recovery on that mountain in Tennessee, the past few months here, certainly did not give way to any soft.

Look up, Sam, some sensible voice insisted inside of her. She managed, though it took way longer than it should have. He was watching her, his usual stoicism firmly in place. Or maybe that was shadows and wishful thinking, because *something* buzzed along her skin like a kind of exciting portent.

Her pajamas weren't all that different than what clothes she usually wore would cover, but she wasn't wearing a bra. Feeling unaccountably self-conscious, Sam folded her arms over her chest.

"Sneaking out?" he asked, his voice a rumbled whisper.

He reached up, raked a hand through his hair, making it messier, also allowing his shirt to fall open a little more.

Sam's chest was full of jitters she wished she could blame on the mix of booze and coffee cake and the spaghetti Aly had made later and insisted they all eat before bed.

But it was him, the sight of him. All this annoying *attraction* she certainly didn't want and resented the fact it was there. Some immovable reaction inside of her.

"I just needed to use the bathroom, wasn't sure which door," Sam replied, though sneaking out sounded like a hell of a plan right about now.

Nate pointed at the lit room behind him. "Have at."

"Thanks."

She stepped inside, closed the door behind her, and near-ly sank to the ground in some sort of weird relief. He'd go back to his room, and she could go back to hers. Or she could grab her clothes, her phone, and sneak out.

Yeah, that seemed like the right option. Once she was done, she washed her hands, flipped off the light and then stepped out into the hall.

Only to find Nate still in the hallway. Like he was wait-ing for her.

Uh. Oh.

Because she'd flipped the bathroom switch off, the only light was the faint glow of the smoke detector above them, and a little sliver of moonlight shining through the window at the end of the hall, in a line along the pretty if worn carpet runner.

They stood on either side of that line, facing each other. It felt way too symbolic.

"I could leave now. I think I'm good enough to drive," she told him. "You can tell Aly thanks for me."

"I could," Nate agreed, but in that way he had that wasn't agreement, but more an invitation for her to think about what she'd just said and change her own mind before he did it for her.

Nate looked down the hall. Sam had never been up here before tonight. She didn't know whose room was whose, but she couldn't help but wonder if he was looking toward whatever door Landon and Aly slept behind.

"I was talking to Cal earlier," he said, as if weighing each word spoken in a careful near-whisper. "I told him I think someone needs to talk to Janie Turner."

"Okay, so have at."

"I would. Or Cal would. Landon didn't want to go behind Aly's back. He's probably not wrong there, but … it got me thinking. I think it should be Aly."

"She didn't seem too keen to do that today. She was pretty clear, in fact, that she wanted Janie to leave and not have a discussion at all." Sam still saw the way the woman's face had hardened. Heard that threatening way she'd spoken about secrets.

No, Sam didn't like Janie Turner, or the idea of Aly sitting down with her considering Aly had been desperate enough to use *Sam* as a shield.

But maybe that wasn't fair. Aly had invited Sam back for coffee *before* Janie's appearance. It wasn't a truce, exactly, but it was something along those lines.

Still, Sam didn't trust Janie Turner as far as she could throw her, and Sam might have a lot of complicated feelings about Aly and the past fifteen years, but she didn't think it was right for a mother who'd abandoned her daughter, regardless of the circumstances, to waltz right back in with no warning and expect an audience.

Especially sneaking up to the ranch when Landon wasn't there, like she wanted Aly alone and vulnerable.

"She needs to, though," Nate said, with a determined insistence.

He took a step closer to Sam, his foot stepping right on that line of moonlight. Sam found herself staring at the piece of sock illuminated by it.

Then she shook herself and tried to focus. "Is that our business?"

Nate's expression was hard. Determined. "Maybe it should be." He took another step, so there wasn't much hallway floor between them at all. "If you stay tonight, we can convince Aly in the morning. It should be her, if she's up for it. But if she's not, maybe it could be you. With Aly's support."

All of this spoke to getting way more involved in Bennet business, and that was not why she was here. That was not what she'd signed up for.

"Look, maybe Aly and I made kind of a truce today, but that's it. All's not forgiven—on either side. We're not just magically best friends again."

"You don't need to be best friends to offer to help, Sam. It'd mean something coming from you. She can dismiss us—especially Landon the overprotective boyfriend and Cal the pseudo-older brother. But you? I think she'll listen to you, especially with my weight behind it."

"Why don't you include yourself?" she demanded and then blamed the liquor for loosening her tongue. Because it was none of her business the way he held himself apart from his family. "You're a Bennet brother," she muttered.

"I was gone. I'm not as ... attached to the ranch, this life."

"You could be."

"Like you said, I'm not just magically attached again. I was gone a long time."

She didn't know what to say to that. Fifteen years *was* a long time. He was back now, but no ... nothing took away those years. Nothing fully could. Regardless of how right he'd been to leave.

"Stay," he said, not urgently exactly, but maybe as urgent as a stoic man like Nate ever got.

He was standing close. There was absolutely no reason for him to stand this close. No reason for him to look down at her like that, the moonlight illuminating just a little line of light across his scruffy jaw.

She actually lifted her hand, like she was going to reach out and touch him there, feel that scrape against her palm. Just curiosity. Just...

"Sam." His voice was low, charged with something.

He didn't say anything else, or maybe her heart was just hammering too hard in her ears to hear anything else.

Then a door creaked, and more light spilled out into the hallway. Cal shuffled out on a big yawn, stopped at the sight of them.

"What is this? A party?"

"Yeah, the drank too much and need a bathroom party,"

Nate said, easily enough, backing away from Sam.

She used the distraction and the distance to move swiftly to the door to her room. "Bathroom is all yours, Cal," she offered, hoping she sounded casual and breezy instead of twisted up.

But as she stepped into the room, she gave one quick backwards glance.

And found Nate watching her.

Her heart did that fluttery thing, harder this time, because she was starting to realize this whole *attraction* thing wasn't exactly one-sided.

And she didn't know what the hell to do about that.

ALY DEFINITELY FELT a little worse for the wear in the morning. She was not a drinker, at *all*, but it had felt right. *Been* right. A night to blow off a little of the tension that had done nothing but build and build.

To have kind of a full house again. To act like a family. Even with Sam, who wasn't family at all, but was … tied up in all this.

It had been easy to paint Sam the villain when there'd been no evidence she had been right about her father's initial innocence. About Ben. Sam hadn't been *kind* about it, so Aly couldn't beat herself up for being … hesitant about Sam's involvement in anything.

But with both men in jail, both murders solved, Aly was starting to be able to look back and realize they'd all made mistakes born of loyalty. And made worse by the secrets other people had kept.

Secrets that could sprout any time. Maybe Sam was right. Maybe … maybe Aly needed to start being the one to decide when they got uprooted so they could stop blind-siding her.

But how? Aly set out bacon on trays, whisked eggs together with milk and cheese. She didn't want to bother with biscuits, so she arranged bread on a cookie sheet to make a batch of toast. She focused on cooking, the only thing that kept her mind from racing.

It didn't surprise her that Landon returned from his morning chores before the other three appeared. He'd had maybe one drink last night. She also didn't think Nate had indulged much, though they'd pretended to.

Sam and Cal and her, on the other hand? They'd had their fill. She didn't know if she should draw any conclusions from that or not.

Aly poured Landon a mug of coffee while he shed his jacket and hung it on the hook outside the kitchen. He greeted her with a quick kiss on the cheek before lifting the mug.

It was their routine. It was a nice routine.

"Weird question. You didn't happen to take my key-chain off my keys, did you?"

Aly frowned at him. "No. Why would I do that?"

"I don't know, but it's missing. Not sure how it could have come off, but I guess it must have."

Before either of them could dwell on that, a voice interrupted.

"Do I smell bacon?" Cal's voice from the stairs made her smile.

When he appeared, he was freshly showered and dressed for the day. Well, *a* day, certainly not a ranch day in his pressed pants and button up shirt.

She heard Landon's sigh and was about to smooth everything over before Landon could make a comment, but Sam appeared next.

She stopped a little short at the three people already in the kitchen, then gave a wan smile. "Thanks for the place to crash, Aly. I should probably head out."

Aly studied Sam. She was a little pale, a little glassy eyed. Definitely not feeling well.

"You'll sit and eat first," Aly said with a nod, pointing at the table.

She turned back to the food prep, not expecting to be disobeyed. She finished everything she was making, heard Nate enter, and the low rumble of conversation in the dining room. A full house. Yes, that felt good. Positive.

She had everyone load up their plates, then they all sat at the dining room table and ate. But what they avoided last night with alcohol crept into the room. The reason they were all *here* crept into the room.

Aly was tempted to ignore it, but that felt like backpedaling. She wanted progress. Something productive to come out of yesterday. "So. In regard to Janie Turner, where do we go from here?"

Everyone sort of looked down at their plates, except Sam. After studying Nate for a beat, she glanced at Aly.

Then she spoke. "I think, like it or not, the next sensible step to go along with all the others is for Aly to sit down with Janie. Just you and her. Sort of."

"What do you mean sort of?" Landon demanded.

But Sam didn't look at Landon. She kept her attention on Aly. "I think it should be in a public place, and I think someone should be there to keep an eye on things. Not one of us, though. Someone Janie wouldn't recognize as a person who'd be looking out for you. We want Janie to be as honest as she might be, so we want it to seem like it's just you and her. What about Jill?"

"Jill. You want me to get Jill involved?" Panic was fluttering low in her stomach.

And not at the idea of getting Jill involved. No, this was all about facing Janie, *her mother*, and all the uncomfortable truths Aly flat out didn't want.

Secrets. Not just truths. *Secrets.* Didn't she need to be brave enough to rip them out, no matter the cost?

"Jill's just like … a support person," Sam explained. "And if she sits close enough, she can hear your conversation and fill in any blanks. You meet with Janie. You tell her you've needed time to wrap your head around everything. To grieve your dad again. Not untrue."

"No, not untrue," Aly murmured.

Did she feel sick to her stomach from drinking too much last night? Or the fact Sam was right, and Aly didn't want her to be?

"You want to hear her side of the story, because your dad didn't give you one. Then, you just let her talk. Then we look into whatever she says, see if it's true or not. If she gets pushy, like she did yesterday, Jill—or whoever—swoops in. But she's not going to speak freely if a Bennet is there, and now that I've thrown myself into the fray, probably not me either."

Aly didn't know what to say. Clearly Sam had given this some thought, and it was clear since no one else was arguing with her, that the Bennet boys all agreed.

Landon's hand came over hers. "You don't have to, Aly." He squeezed her hand and looked right at her.

He would never want her to do something she didn't want, but it was clear he knew as well as she did, whether she wanted to or not, this was the only way.

So, no, she didn't *have* to. But… "How are we going to know anything if I don't do this?"

"We're still investigating the other potential fathers," Nate said. "We'll be trying to talk to more than just Shawn Harrington. Collecting stories, information. Then we spread out, try to find friends, associates, old neighbors. It'll take time, but we'll get a better picture of her and maybe go from there."

Aly nodded along, though she knew the maybe was emphasized to show her just how long and drawn out that process would be. "I don't want to talk to her. I don't want to deal with this. But I don't want to sit around and wait for everyone else to deal with it for me either." Her gaze moved to Sam. "You were right yesterday. About the truth. Sometimes you have to pay the cost for the truth, but … it's better than these secrets. These lies. They've ruined lives. The truth hasn't."

Sam looked down at her plate. "Well, I wouldn't go that far."

But it was true. Maybe the truth didn't always yield positive results, maybe it didn't always make things *better*, but it didn't destroy. Not long-term.

"I'll call Jill, see when she can get away." Aly looked around. "After everyone eats their breakfast."

Chapter Eighteen

The Harrington Cabin

C AL SAT IN the passenger side of Aly's truck and wondered how he'd gotten roped into this.

By coming to Montana at all.

Always a mistake. Maybe he should book a flight back to Texas. Maybe he should return his boss's calls.

Instead, he was going to babysit Glenda Harrington while Jill went into town with Aly to sit down with Janie Turner.

For all her reticence, Aly hadn't wasted any time. It wasn't in her nature, Cal supposed. She'd called Jill, then contacted Janie.

Janie had agreed to meet Aly immediately, so things had snowballed quickly. And while Landon had chores, and Sam and Nate had investigative work to do, Cal was left as the only one without a responsibility.

So now he had to spend the afternoon with a ghost story. Luckily, breakfast and some aspirin had dulled the edges of the hangover from this morning. Definitely indulged a little too much last night.

Though *indulged* didn't seem the right word. *Drowned sorrows* seemed more apt. Except drowning them never killed them, did it? "I didn't do any online shopping last night that you know of, did I?" he asked Aly conversationally.

"No. Why?"

"I misplaced one of my credit cards. Usually keep it in my laptop bag, but I couldn't seem to find it this morning when I was looking into booking a flight back to Texas."

"I'll keep an eye out for it when I clean later," she assured him. "Are you going back soon?"

"We'll see," he hedged, as Aly pulled in front of the Harrington cabin.

"I appreciate this, Cal. I know it's ... odd," Aly said as she pushed her truck into park.

"Not much hasn't been odd around here lately, Al."

"I know," Aly agreed, watching the door as Jill stepped out. "I appreciate it."

Cal just grunted and hopped out of the truck. Jill would be driving her own down into town so if Janie was paying attention, she wouldn't see Aly and Jill arrive together.

Cal paused for a second, looked up at Aly in the driver's seat. She was a little pale. Nervous, clearly. Cal knew a thing or two about visiting with a parent you didn't want to deal with.

"Just let her talk, Aly. That's all you've got to do."

Aly smiled, misery at the edges of said smile. "Unfortunately, I have a bad feeling I'm not going to like any of what she talks about."

No, not likely. "Just remember, none of it's the truth until we corroborate it."

Jill came up behind him. "I'll be right behind you, Aly. I'll park next door like we talked about, go in and get the closest table to you guys as I can. Just like we planned."

Aly nodded. Cal and Jill offered her good luck then Cal closed the door and stepped away so Aly could back out of the drive.

Which left Cal to deal with Jill.

"I appreciate this," Jill said, echoing Aly's earlier sentiment.

But she was wringing her hands together. Cal didn't think her nerves were about Aly meeting Janie though.

They were about leaving her grandmother.

"She's easy," Jill said, looking at where Glenda stood in the cabin's doorway. "She'll garden or bake. Maybe take a nap. Or a walk. She really only needs someone around as a precaution. There shouldn't be any issues."

"No worries. Old ladies love me."

Jill looked from Cal to Glenda, who was frowning at him. "Uh-huh," she muttered. "Anyway, I'll be back as soon as Aly's done."

"No rush. Look after Aly. That's what's important."

"I will," she said solemnly. Then she got into her own truck and left.

So it was just him and the elderly woman currently staring at him in that way she had that felt like she could see through him, unearth any unknown secrets still hiding in his brain.

Not exactly a comfortable feeling, so he dealt with it how he often dealt with discomfort. A broad smile and a joke meant to poke. "So, Glenda. How's it going? Feast on any children's souls lately?"

Her mouth curved ever so slightly, those eerie eyes twinkling with a kind of mischief that didn't feel *threatening*.

Exactly.

She disappeared inside, so Cal followed. He got a quick look around the cabin that he hadn't had the presence of mind to take the last time he'd been inside. The night he'd remembered. The night that had … changed everything.

And yet, here he was, feeling mostly unchanged.

It wasn't *quite* as small as it looked from the outside. The front room was a kind of living room, complete with couch and an old-fashioned looking cookstove. A large watercolor that gave the impression of the mountains at sunrise or sunset dominated one wall. On the other wall hung an intricate looking quilt that almost seemed to mimic the watercolor.

Through the archway was the kitchen. Tiny and cramped what with the table shoved into the corner and all the other appliances lining the opposite wall. Everything was neat and tidy, and Cal couldn't deny there was a certain coziness to the whole thing.

Beyond the table was a dim hallway. No doubt where the bedrooms were.

But Glenda didn't stop in any of these places. She walked through the cabin, straight to the back door. It wasn't very many steps at all. Cal didn't know what else to do, so he followed her outside.

Even with fall encroaching, her garden was a showpiece. Beds spread out all around him. Some with neat rows of what were no doubt produce, winding vines trained on trellises. Some wild patches of blooms—many that Cal recognized from his childhood, so they must be at least a little wild. The air smelled like earth and summer despite the chill in the air.

Glenda moved about, gathering tools. Cal stood in the afternoon sun with that creeping feeling of dread inching up his spine, into his neck. He swallowed, blinked against the nausea, the dizziness. All the physical indicators of a memory he didn't want trying to reach him.

His therapist had told him to breathe through these moments, relax. Let them in. *Feel* them, she'd said to him, and hadn't flinched when he'd laughed at her.

Feel the memory of his father killing his mother? Not high on his list of things to do. But this memory didn't slam through him like that repressed one.

It was just his mother, the sun shining off her dark hair, bent over her plants. She was humming a song, some old lullaby he remembered her singing a lot, especially to Nate. He didn't remember the words, just the lilting melody, in his mother's voice.

And that was all the memory was. Nothing sinister. Nothing bloody.

He wasn't sure why he'd repressed what seemed the most innocuous memory of all time, but he somehow wasn't shocked. His brain was a mess.

Glenda approached him, head cocked as if by studying him she could see he was remembering things he hadn't in a long time.

She pushed the rake to his chest, then pointed to a big pile of mulch and a bed that was clearly the intended recipient of the mulch.

He hadn't exactly dressed for manual labor, but he figured that was likely his own fault. Besides, doing something physical sounded better than standing here and having some kind of unnecessary panic attack over a memory that didn't mean anything.

So, he rolled up his sleeves and got to work. He raked mulch, got his knees dirty when she pointed him to some pea plants and showed him how to snap off pods and drop them into a bucket. He raked pine needles along her meandering paths.

It was kind of enjoyable. Hard work, but something identifiable. If he spread mulch, it was spread. If he raked needles, they were gone. The basket full of peas was a clear testament to the work he'd put in.

Yeah, there was some kind of satisfaction in that. Something he hadn't felt in a long, long time. He stood back to survey his work, then stopped and looked around. There was a noise. A … melody.

He realized it was coming from Glenda.

She was making noise. Not talking, but Cal was under the impression she never made *any* noise. But she was standing there, working away, *humming*.

And maybe that wouldn't have been as notable if she wasn't humming the same tune from the memory.

Cal stopped what he was doing and just stared at her. She glanced over from where she was snapping off dying blooms from a big plant with deep purple blooms. She brought a finger to her lips in a kind of *be quiet* motion, then went back to working.

And humming, but this time, a different song.

Like he'd imagined the first tune anyway. Which he probably had.

But his shoulders didn't relax the rest of the afternoon.

Chapter Nineteen

Main Street Diner

A LY HAD GOTTEN to the diner a few minutes before Jill. She'd wanted to wait to go inside until Jill was there, as Landon and Cal had both told her to do, but she could see Janie Turner and her red hair sitting in one of the booths along the window, clearly watching the parking lot and waiting for her.

So Aly got out of the truck, though she took her time to settle her purse, lock the car doors, walk to the front of the diner. She kept an eye on the street and relaxed a little when Jill's truck passed.

It wouldn't take Jill more than a few minutes to park next door then walk over. Besides, what was Janie going to do to Aly in public? She shouldn't feel as nervous and sick to her stomach as she did.

This was just a conversation. Just *listening* as Cal had re-iterated when she'd dropped him off.

Slowly, swallowing at the ball of nerves trying to choke her, Aly approached the table Janie was sitting at. Habit of being raised to be polite had her trying to smile, but as Janie stood and smiled brightly at her, Aly thought *fuck that*.

She didn't smile. She sat across from Janie and said nothing.

Janie sat back down, but her smile didn't die. "I'm so glad you decided to meet me." Janie reached across the table and tried to take Aly's hand, but Aly kept her hands under the table.

"It seemed a better alternative than you continuing to show up at the ranch uninvited."

Some of that smile dimmed, though Janie kept it in place. Aly watched every inch of the woman's expression. Partly to try and get to the bottom of whatever Janie was after, but partly to see if any of it reflected her own face. Did her eyes narrow like that when she was annoyed? Did her mouth curve at just that angle when she was trying to smile through something?

The bell on the door jingled, and Janie's eyes tracked over to it, but Aly kept her gaze on her target. No doubt it was Jill. So she watched Janie's face. Even as she saw the shape of someone pass their booth out of her periphery vision.

But a few seconds later, Jill sat in the booth directly behind Janie. Which meant Aly could look right at her if she needed to. It was … solidifying. Not just Jill's presence, but what that represented.

All these people who wanted to help her and protect her. It reminded her that she wasn't alone, no matter what things happened with Janie.

She looked the woman right in the eyes—blue eyes, just like her own. "You wanted to talk to me. And here I am."

"Why don't we order something?" Janie waved at a waitress.

"I'm not hungry."

"Well, I am." Janie smiled big and bright at the waitress when she arrived. "Can I get a rancher's breakfast and an orange juice?"

"Of course. And you?"

"Nothing," Aly said.

"You sure? Not even some coffee?"

Thinking it would get rid of the waitress quicker, Aly relented. "Sure. Coffee. That'll be fine."

She left with their orders, and then Aly looked across the table at Janie. Who just smiled at her and said nothing.

It was such a waste of time. This whole thing a complete waste, if Janie wasn't going to *talk*. "What do you want from me? Why am I here?"

"I thought maybe you'd want to know your mother."

It took everything in Aly not to say *well, you're wrong*. Mostly she didn't say it because it wasn't true. She *did* want to know. But a part of her, the smart part probably, didn't.

Still, that wasn't why they'd arranged this. She had to find out why Benjamin Bennet had allegedly paid Janie to leave Marietta. She had to figure out if Tripp was even her father. She had questions and she deserved answers.

"It's been nearly thirty-two years. Why now?"

Janie sighed heavily. She toyed with the napkin on the table. "I'm not sure I have a good answer for that. You get older, you look back, you start to have regrets. I do have regrets, Aly."

Aly didn't want to soften to this woman, but that simple sentence was trying to wriggle under her defenses.

"I was young," she continued. "I was scared. Tripp … he had a job. He had stability. He wanted you. Maybe he didn't have much in the way of blood family, but he had the Bennet ranch family. I suppose you know that it meant something. You're still there."

It felt like an accusation, which made Aly angry all over again. "The Bennets were kind enough to keep me. I would have been turned over to the state if they hadn't intervened."

"I didn't know. It never occurred to me ... he was so young. How ... how did it happen?"

"It was a heart attack." Which she'd already told Janie, but to point that out wasn't *letting Janie talk*.

Aly studied the woman across from her and wondered if she outlined exactly how her father had died, exactly how Aly had been the one to find him, exactly how that awful memory still haunted her in the occasional nightmare, would Janie care? Feel guilt? Apologize?

Aly sat here and wanted ... none of those responses. So she didn't elaborate.

Instead, she asked the question that was really weighing on her. "Was Tripp really my father?"

Janie's eyes narrowed, the lines on her face that pointed to a hard life seemed more pronounced. "Who else would be?"

"According to what I've ... uncovered, Shawn Harrington, Brad Johnson, and some guy named Jim were some of the options." Maybe she should have kept her cards closer to her vest, but everything Sam had said about secrets yesterday kept playing in her head. She didn't know how to be smart and strategic when she was just damn tired of everything hurting.

"Who told you that?"

Aly shook her head. "It doesn't matter."

"It matters to me."

Was this why Dad had never told her about her mother? Because Janie Turner wasn't a woman she would want to know, let alone be her mother.

Or was it because she wasn't really his and he knew that was a possibility? But why would he hide that? Why would he take her?

All the answers sucked, and it just made her *mad*.

"You may be shocked to find I don't care what matters to *you* at the moment," Aly said, working hard to keep herself sounding calm even if she didn't feel it. "You left me. Over thirty years ago. You never contacted me. You never came back. My father never spoke your name, refused to answer all my questions, as did everyone else. I know nothing about you, but you've shown up out of the blue acting like I should just … want to know you. I'm fully grown and don't need you. So why? Why are you here? If you're not going to answer my questions, what's the point of this? What do you want?"

"I want to know my daughter."

Aly's heart twisted. God, she wished that were true. She really did.

But she just didn't know how it could be. "I don't believe you."

"The Bennets poisoned you against me." She shook her head in disgust. "Just like they poisoned your father against me. All because I wouldn't take Ben Bennet up on his insulting offer."

Aly wanted to rub at the sharp pain in her chest, but

found she couldn't move. She had to clear her throat to speak. "And what was that?"

The waitress arrived with Janie's breakfast. Janie sent her a brilliant smile. She was a good actress. Aly needed to remember that.

Janie dove into her food like a starving woman. "Look, I was no saint." She shoved a bite of eggs into her mouth. "I liked men. Still do." She smirked. "But that Bennet asshole your father was so enamored of gave me the flat-out creeps, and I listen to my gut. It's how I survived as long as I have in a world dead set against me."

"So, you took his money and left." Aly didn't have it in her to feel surprise anymore.

"Yeah. Maybe everyone else fell for his nice guy routine, but I knew he'd make his threats reality if I stuck around. I took the money while it was on the table. I left, until I happened to hear he was in jail. I thought maybe I'd come back, talk to Tripp … and you. See what was what."

"You're afraid of Benjamin Bennet?"

"I think any woman in their right woman should be. And look? Weren't my instincts right? Murdered his wife and everything."

Aly waited. For Janie to ask her how she'd felt, having her surrogate family be torn apart that way.

Instead, she just ate her food. "So, what is it you do up there? Ranch hand like your dad? Some kind of live-in maid? Mistress of the manor? That one Bennet boy looked awfully … protective. Looks a lot like his daddy, though." She pointed her fork in Aly's direction. "Wouldn't trust him, sweetheart."

For a full minute, Aly could not speak. Not trust *Landon*. Landon who had … been the one stable, dependable thing in her life all these years. And this woman who'd just waltzed back into her life told her *not to trust him*.

"Look, Aly," Janie said while Aly was still speechless with rage. Janie didn't seem to notice. She was way too focused on her food. "I wasn't ready to be a mother. So, I left. I basically did you a favor. If I'd kept you, you would have bounced around like my mom bounced me around, and trust me, that's no way to grow up."

Janie looked up from her food, seemed to notice *something* on Aly's face. "I really thought you'd be happy to see me."

Was the woman insane? Or just a complete self-absorbed narcissist? Maybe Aly would never really know.

But there was one thing she *had* to know. "Was Tripp my father?"

Janie sighed, placed down her fork. "Look, maybe I told a few stories back then. Worked up a few guys." She shrugged, unbothered. "They all deserved a little working up. But timing wise, it was Tripp. You want to take one of those DNA test type things, be my guest, but it was Tripp."

Could she really believe this woman? Tears burned in her eyes and words stuck in her throat. What was the point of this?

"He was a good man, your father. I knew I'd left you in good hands. Better hands than mine. I would have stayed away. I had no reason to come back to my way of thinking, but then I saw the thing about Bennet on the news. Killing his wife? Didn't surprise me. But it reminded me. Of this place. Of you. Of everything he told me to leave. And why should I have?"

"He gave you money to."

"Yeah, because otherwise Tripp was going to follow me. An affair or money—leave or break poor Tripp's heart. *Bennet* didn't care that I was seventeen. Bothered your father some when he found out, but the deal had already been done."

The relief was a heady thing. Maybe this woman was nothing but a liar, but Aly needed something to hold onto. Something to believe.

"I don't know why I came, Aly. I don't know what I expected. I hate my mother. But I didn't do anything to you. Not like she did to me."

"You abandoned me."

Again, she gave a nonchalant shrug. "Not how I look at it. Better than the way I had it, trust me."

"It's how *I* look at it." When Janie didn't respond to that, clearly didn't know *how* to respond to that, Aly finally understood that maybe Janie wasn't evil. Maybe she was. But she was never going to be the kind of woman who knew how to put someone else's needs or feelings even on par with her own.

Maybe Janie was right. Maybe she had done Aly a favor. Maybe Benjamin Bennet's gross ultimatum had saved Aly— even if she'd never give him credit for being so gross.

Aly supposed it didn't matter. She had confirmation Ben had paid Janie off. Confirmation, or close to it, that Tripp was her father.

And she had no desire to have a relationship with this

woman. Aly got to her feet, noted the way Janie frowned.

"I don't want to see you. I don't want anything to do with you."

"Now, Aly—"

"No, I'm serious. I don't want to see you. I don't want you at the ranch. I don't want to run into you. I want you gone."

Janie's eyes narrowed. Her expression got really hard. "The Bennets sure got their claws in you, but you can't run me out of town. No one's doing that to me again."

Maybe she couldn't. Maybe she shouldn't.

But maybe she could and should. "We'll see." And with that, Aly turned on a heel and stalked out of the diner.

JILL WANTED TO immediately scurry out of the diner when Aly got up and stalked out, but that would probably blow her cover. Maybe it didn't matter, but Jill found she agreed with the Bennet brothers on this one thing.

She did not trust Janie Turner. Especially when the woman called the waitress over, began to cry, not exactly quietly, that her daughter had invited her out to breakfast then stuck her with a bill she couldn't afford to pay.

Yeah, definitely not a trustworthy person. So, Jill left a generous tip for her waitress, slid out of her booth, and tried to walk at a normal pace, not hurrying her exit. She glanced back once through the window, saw Janie sipping her coffee, happy as you please. No, she didn't like that woman.

Once out of view of the window, Jill hurried. She jogged

down to where she'd left her truck.

Aly was parked in the spot next to Jill's. She was out of her truck, staring at Jill's, hand covering her mouth. It only took Jill a few more steps to see why.

Someone had spraypainted her truck this time. Aly saw her, reached out a hand, and Jill took it, still not fully understanding what she was seeing.

The same kind of messaging that had been used on Aly's truck was used on Jill's. Yellow paint. Nasty words. Jill was rooted to the spot for a moment. It just … didn't make any sense.

"Call the police, Jill," Aly said. She gave Jill's hand a gentle squeeze, but her words were hard. "We'll talk to them together. Because it connects to Janie Turner. It has to."

Chapter Twenty

S AM FELT MORE herself back in her office, at her desk, researching the life of Jim Gary. Yesterday—the whole of it—morning to night had been an aberration. Best pushed aside and treated like some weird fever dream.

She glanced at Nate sitting at his desk. He was looking back through Janie's past addresses, compiling a list of neighbors or associates or potential friends they could interview about Janie.

His eyebrows were drawn together, his mouth downcast in a serious frown as he typed away at his keyboard. Sam resolutely did *not* think about last night or their hallway conversation or how close he'd stood and said her name because that part was *especially* a weird, complex fever dream that didn't do thinking about.

She focused back on her screen and tapped away at her keyboard, looking into what she could find via legal means about Jim's past. She found a resume on a recruitment site, but it didn't list anything prior to his foray into working at grocery stores, which started about five years after Janie left town.

She changed gears, started looking into the history of the rec center, noting names she might be able to talk to about

Jim's potential employment, but then she found a random webpage that had maybe at one time been part of the rec center's page, but been taken off their menu or something.

It had a year-end summary for every year, reaching back the past thirty-five years. Sam immediately started at the year Shawn Harrington said he worked there, searched the document for the name Jim Gary, then skimmed it for good measure when none came up.

Methodically, she went through every year. Then hit paydirt three years later. Jim Gary, rec center night manager, had left for a position elsewhere. After five years of working for the rec center.

Which meant he had indeed worked there at the time Janie and Shawn Harrington had.

"Jackpot," Sam said, motioning Nate over.

She angled her computer monitor toward him so he could read the old newsletter about rec center manager, Jim Gary, being replaced.

He stood behind her, reading the screen over her shoulder. "When was this published?"

"About three years after Janie Turner left Marietta, but it says he's worked there for five years." She pointed to the corresponding sentence on the screen. "It puts him at the rec center at the same time."

"Yeah, I'd say that's a jackpot."

"Well, half of a jackpot anyway. We still have to figure out if they've had any connection recently." Sam leaned back in her chair, investigative gears turning. "Let's wait to hear what Aly has to report about her meeting with Janie before we jump to do anything on that front."

"Sure, but … what's the plan? Go talk to him? Bring up his connection?"

"I think so. Insist he must know Janie, which means he's hiding something about the vandalism." Sam shook her head. "Vandalism in plain sight. But no one saw anything. Janie Turner popping up out of nowhere. It's got to connect and maybe Jim knows how."

"Maybe. But I also can't think of a reason for Janie vandalizing Aly's car. Or Jim. What happened when Aly was born had fuck all to do with Aly herself."

Sam agreed, but tried to play devil's advocate, tried to find *something* that would prompt the vandalism. "But there's a Bennet connection, apparently, if your dad did pay off Janie to leave. Maybe it's less about Aly herself, and more about that connection."

"Then why not target Landon? He's the head Bennet these days, keeping the ranch going and what not."

"Anyone who knows Landon knows Aly'd be the target to go after there."

"Yeah, but who knows Landon that might be involved in this? Janie Turner didn't."

"That's the question," Sam muttered, drumming her fingers on her desk. She couldn't think of a damn person. But she looked at her computer screen. "You should go talk to Landon, see if he has any connection to Jim Gary."

Nate considered that, then nodded. "Yeah, not a bad next step."

Before they could discuss it farther, the phone on Sam's desk rang. "You go ahead. Just make sure you ask for *anything*. Not just stuff that seems weird. Any interactions he's had."

Nate nodded and began to gather his things while Sam answered the phone. "Honor's Edge Investigations. Samantha Price speaking."

"Price. Detective Hayes."

Sam sat up a little straighter. Detective Hayes had worked on her father's case, but she hadn't had much contact with him since this summer. "Hello. How can I help you, detective?"

"This isn't a professional call, exactly. More a professional courtesy. I thought you might like to know that Aly Cartwright and Jill Harrington are down here at the station."

Sam got to her feet, covered the receiver with her hand. "Nate. Wait."

Nate stopped halfway out the door, looked over his shoulder at her. She held up a hand while Detective Hayes spoke. When she hung up, she was already swiping her keys. "Change of plans. We're headed to the police station."

"Why?"

"Jill's truck was vandalized in the exact same way as Aly's. While she and Aly were in the diner with Janie Turner."

Nate swore, which just about summed it up.

NATE SAT, UNCOMFORTABLY, in Sam's car. "You ever think about buying a car suitable for a normal-sized human being?" he grumbled.

She slid him a quick glance. "I'm a normal-sized human being."

"You're tiny."

"Maybe you're just a giant. Next time, you let me drive your truck. Then you can have all that manly room."

"You're not driving my truck. You drive like a maniac."

As if to prove his point, she blew through a yellow light, smirked. "You're just a big baby."

It felt normal. Back on their even keel, a little good-natured ribbing. He didn't know what *she* thought about their strange conversation in the hallway of the Bennet ranch house last night, but it had kept him awake. Not the conversation. The *what-ifs*.

If Cal hadn't come out, what would he have said? Or worse, done?

It felt like a crisis narrowly averted, and yet relief wasn't the predominate feeling needling him—last night or even this morning. It was something closer to regret.

But he could hardly regret a nonevent. He could hardly regret making something messy when … he was a stranger to himself, and every interaction with his family, the Bennet Ranch, Marietta beyond the bounds of investigating, and so on, only reminded him of that simple fact.

He liked to think this job was something. A seed, maybe, that over time would sprout, and he'd figure out the person he was without the army, having dealt with childhood trauma and war trauma in some sort of fashion that allowed him to feel … real? Whole? Solid?

Something other than this … whatever this was. Like sometimes he was simply a soul floating around outside a body, watching it go through the motions.

"Janie was in the restaurant talking to Aly when it happened," Sam was saying, purposefully driving recklessly no doubt. "So, it absolves her of the crime itself. But it's suspicious. The timing. Both times, the timing is damn suspicious."

"I agree. Which points to, if Janie is involved, someone else is too."

"Exactly."

Nate studied her profile for a second. He shouldn't ask, but… "Your friend give you the tip?"

"My friend? Oh." She snorted. "No. Had to stop tapping that source. Brian didn't seem to understand the situation, and I was tired of explaining it to him."

Nate had noted much the same this summer. Officer Brian Matthews had been a pushy, whiny asshole. But Sam put up with a lot of crap if she thought it might help her business.

"It was that detective. Hayes? You probably ran into him some on your dad's case."

Nate had. A no-nonsense kind of guy. Nate hadn't had much opinion on him one way or another. "Why'd he call you?"

Sam shrugged, eyes on the road. "I guess Aly told him we've been looking into it."

"Doesn't explain why he'd call you."

"He said it was a professional courtesy."

Nate had never known any detective to offer information out of the blue out of professional courtesy. And that low-level feeling of something being *off* continued when they walked into the station. Jill and Aly were standing in the lobby area, talking to a man Nate recognized as Detective

Hayes. Nate hadn't had any strong feelings about him one way or another when the stuff with his dad was going down, but when the man spotted Sam, excused himself from Aly and Jill, Nate couldn't help but have … some odd negative reaction.

The detective took a few certain strides toward them. Nate noted the man didn't once glance his way. He held out his hand to Sam.

"Ms. Price."

"Call me Sam, detective."

"Sam. I heard you were looking into the first vandalism. I was wondering if you'd have time to sit down and discuss your investigation."

"We can discuss it, but I'm not handing over information for nothing," Sam replied pointedly.

The detective smiled at her. Nate frowned.

"Let's see what we can come to terms with. I've got an office. If you've got time now?"

Sam looked up at Nate. "Detective Hayes, you've met Nate Bennet."

"Sure." The detective smiled, but it was that cop smile. Polite, but not warm.

He'd given Sam a different smile.

Still, the detective held out a hand to shake. "Benjamin Bennet's son. You work for Sam, right?"

The *for* was pronounced. Correct, but pronounced. Bringing up Dad felt a bit pointed, but then again, maybe Nate couldn't blame him for that.

"Nate's an investigator for Honor's Edge," Sam said, both agreement and subtle correction. "We've been handling this particular case in conjunction with another one, so we work together a lot."

"Ah." Before he said anything else, Aly approached.

She gave Sam and Nate a wry kind of smile before turning to the detective. "Detective, Jill's answering a few more questions from your officer. Once he's done, are we good to leave? I'd like to get back to the ranch."

"I'm afraid Ms. Harrington will need to leave her truck for the time being, but you two are free to go." He turned to Sam. "Sam, if you'd like to come back to my office, Nate can wait out here with Ms. Cartwright and Ms. Harrington. Get caught up on their side of things."

Sam didn't agree right away, but Nate knew she wanted whatever information Hayes was dangling. Still, he wasn't about to be cut out.

Except Aly was watching *him*. His reaction. And it felt like if he argued somehow, it would mean something to Aly that it shouldn't.

So, he ignored Sam's look and turned to Aly. "Did you call Landon?"

"No, I think I better tell him in person." She glanced at Jill who was talking to an officer who was taking notes. "They wanted to ask Jill a few more questions first."

"I can wait with Jill and give her a ride back up, pick up Cal. I just have to walk back to the office, grab my truck."

"You don't have to do that," Aly said.

"No trouble. That way Landon doesn't hear it from someone else first." He glanced at Sam. "And Sam and Detective Hayes can have their little meeting." He forced his mouth to curve upward.

"Okay. Let me see if Jill's okay with that." Aly moved over to Jill.

"I'll be back at the office when I'm done," Nate told Sam. "You can fill me in on the meeting over dinner. Detective. Nice to see you again." Then he left them.

And the police station. To walk back to Honor's Edge and collect his truck.

And not think about Detective Hayes and Sam's *meeting*.

Chapter Twenty-One

The Harrington Cabin

WHEN CAL HEARD the rumble of an engine, he was quick to move to the front of the cabin. Though Glenda had long since stopped humming, it still stuck with him. Hung over him like a nightmare he couldn't shake.

Or worse, one of those nightmares he'd had that had turned out to be reality.

But Cal had convinced himself as the day had worn on that he'd talk to Jill about it once she got back. She would no doubt tell him Glenda always hummed and then it wouldn't ... settle in his chest like one of those disassociated memories he couldn't quite bring to the forefront of his brain.

Didn't want to.

Cal came to a stop in confusion as it was Nate's truck that came up the drive rather than Jill's or Aly's. Jill was in the passenger seat of Nate's truck, but Cal didn't see Aly with them. Already strung tight nerves vibrated.

When they both got out of the truck, Cal approached, trying to sound calm and only vaguely concerned.

"Everything okay? Where's Aly?"

"Everything's all right, except Jill's truck," Nate replied.

"Aly's at the ranch. I'll fill you in on everything on the ride over."

"Thanks for keeping an eye on her," Jill said. Cal thought maybe she was trying to offer a friendly smile, but it didn't quite reach her eyes. "I know Aly appreciates both of you helping her out with this mom stuff, and now I do too."

"Come on, Cal. I'll drive you back to the ranch."

But Cal ignored Nate for the time being. He followed Jill.

"Hey, your grandmother … I know she doesn't talk, but she makes sounds and stuff, right?"

Jill stopped at the door, turned to face him. "Every now and then. A sigh, or a grunt," Jill agreed. "Why?"

"Oh, that must be it then. I guess I just figured she wouldn't make any noise, so when she started humming, I was a little surprised."

Jill's entire demeanor changed. Color seemed to leech from her face. "I'm sorry. What?" she asked on a whisper.

This was not the reaction he'd been hoping for, but he could hardly backtrack now. "While we worked in the garden. She was … humming. That's normal. Right?" He could tell it wasn't, and still he just … wanted her to agree with him.

Even if it was a lie.

"I've never heard her … You're sure? She was humming?" Jill looked at the cabin and then back to him.

He saw it, the flash of doubt. Like he was making it up. Or he'd imagined it. Like he was *crazy*.

"You're sure?"

Since he was a little afraid he *was* crazy, he didn't get too

196

pissed off. Or tried not to. "I recognized the tune. An old lullaby."

"Maybe she wasn't aware she was doing it," Nate suggested from behind Cal. "She was focused on the task, so the humming came naturally. Doing something you enjoy can relax your brain." When Jill and Cal both glanced at him, Nate shrugged. "I know a lot of guys with PTSD. I ended up learning a lot about the brain and trauma."

Cal might have pondered that, and how likely the *guys* he knew were just Nate himself, but he couldn't get the image of Glenda lifting her finger to her lips.

That woman had been very aware of what she'd been doing. But he didn't know how to express that to Jill without making this…

Worse.

"Yeah, that could be," Jill said, her eyebrows furrowed, her gaze on the cabin. "That must be it. I've just never … you don't think…" She shook her head again, looked back at Nate. "I better go talk to her. Thanks for the ride."

"No problem."

But Cal just couldn't let it go. "I've only heard my mother sing that lullaby. I've never heard it anywhere else."

Jill blinked. "That's not so strange, is it? Your mother and my grandmother are from the same area. Do you listen to a lot of lullabies in Texas? I'm sure it's just a Marietta thing," Jill said firmly, jerking the door open, clearly irritated that he'd pushed it.

She didn't know what parts he hadn't pushed. Still. "Yeah," he said, even though he didn't agree.

Even though that connection left him feeling edgy. And

terrified there were more bad memories just waiting to come forward. But Jill went inside likely no longer grateful at all that he'd been the one to help.

"Come on," Nate said, walking back to his truck.

Cal followed, got into the passenger seat.

"What point were you trying to make?" Nate asked about halfway through the drive back to the ranch.

"I wasn't trying to make a point. I just … something about it is unsettling."

"What the fuck isn't right now?" Nate muttered.

And he wasn't wrong.

JILL WATCHED NATE'S truck disappear through the window. Her heart was racing, and she couldn't seem to calm it.

Humming. Humming rare lullabies. No. They weren't *rare*. It wasn't weird. It was just what Nate had said. Grandma's mind had been calmed or something, and she'd hummed.

No big deal.

Jill wanted to think it was progress, but there'd been so many times in her first year here where she'd determined something meant her grandmother was making progress only for it to never be true. Only for her father to chastise her, once and for all, that thirty some years of being psychologically mute weren't magically going to be cured just because her granddaughter had moved in.

It still hurt, the unusually harsh words from her father. Mostly because he'd been right, and she'd been foolish.

So, she couldn't go back to thinking everything was a damn *sign*. In fact, Cal Bennet wasn't exactly the most reliable source. Sure, he seemed to be a nice enough guy, but he had his problems. Maybe he'd imagined the whole thing.

And that wasn't fair at *all*.

She walked through the house. She could see Grandma outside the window, armed with her clippers, creating a pile of freshly cut flowers. When Jill stepped out, she was met with silence.

No humming. No sound except the wind and the *snip* of Grandma's clippers.

Grandma looked back at her. Smiled. She pointed to the pile of flowers, a sign she wanted Jill to pick them up.

Blinking back tears she didn't fully understand, Jill went over to do her grandmother's bidding. Hefted the pile of flowers Grandma would no doubt stick in vases and pitchers and little glasses all over the cabin. One last floral hurrah before winter crept in.

Jill straightened, looked at her grandmother. A woman she loved, but didn't understand. At *all*.

As if sensing Jill's turmoil, or maybe just knowing Cal would have told her about the humming, Grandma sighed heavily. She slowly straightened, then put her hands on Jill's cheeks.

Grandma's hands were cool and soft and smelled like dirt and plants and this glorious garden she'd built over years and years of tending. She studied Jill with eyes that reminded Jill of her father, and it made her feel homesick. Not for Boston, but for … being a kid again. The one who didn't have to shoulder all these confusing responsibilities.

Then Grandma kissed her forehead, like she'd done when Jill was a little girl, leaving to head back to Boston, a piece of her heart always back in this cabin. Back with this woman she didn't understand but loved with her whole heart.

That piece of her heart was feeling a bit bruised lately, because she was coming to accept that her grandmother had secrets.

And wanted to keep them.

Chapter Twenty-Two

The Bennet Ranch

L ANDON WALKED BACK toward the house, sweaty from hard work, irritated from arguing with Skinny over some inconsistencies with the inventory.

Usually Aly's arena, but Landon had been hoping to take care of a few things so she didn't have to think about them when she got back.

He shouldn't have. Not his area of expertise. "Which is why we make a damn good team," Landon muttered.

He came up short at the sight of Aly's truck in front of the house. Why hadn't she come to find him?

Frowning, he moved toward the house quickly, only to find her sitting on the porch swing. Her head was tilted back, and her eyes were closed. He was torn between the desire to let her sleep, and the driving *need* to find out what had happened.

But as though she'd sensed him there even though he hadn't moved, her eyes blinked open. Her mouth curved in greeting.

"You're back," he said, fairly lamely as he walked up to the porch.

"Yeah."

"How'd it go?" He didn't ask where Cal was.

She'd fill him in once she gave him the rundown of what had happened at the diner.

She stood up from the swing, gave him a rueful smile. "Shitty. Want some coffee?"

But before she could move past him, start *doing* something, he stopped her. "Al."

She lifted her chin. "I'm not going to cry. I'm done crying about this."

But there were tears shining in her eyes. He pulled her into his chest. "All right. How about a nice lean?"

She let out a sound, almost a laugh, and did just that. Leaned. He rubbed a hand up and down her back. A good team. Yeah, they were.

"I guess it accomplished what we wanted to. She confirmed Ben paid her off. It was either that or sleep with him and piss my dad off so Dad would kick her to the curb, I guess? I didn't ask for details. And I'm not sure that's the full story, but it's close enough, I think. Ben interfered, got her to leave."

"I'm sorry, Aly."

She shook her head, but she still leaned. "She would have left anyway, or maybe not. Maybe she would have stayed, but that would have been bad. She has no interest in me. It's just clear."

He didn't know what to say to that. He had his own childhood traumas, his own issues with his horrible father, but his parents had been *interested*. For good or for ill.

"The thing is … I never expected her to come back," Aly continued. "I never had a fantasy that she … the thing is, *she* left. My dad was great, and he didn't mention her. Didn't try to make her out to be good. Or bad for that matter. I just knew there wasn't a story there where she was the hero, and she'd sweep in and make it okay. Maybe sometimes I *wished* it, but I never believed it."

"But you hoped maybe she'd changed, when she showed up here."

Aly sighed against his chest. "I guess, yeah, I hoped. Not that we could fix the past, but that we could build something from here on out. That's not in the cards. She's ... she just ... it was hard to sit there and try to talk to her, reason with her. Everything was about her, you know? *She* didn't look at it as abandoning me. *She* thought I would be happy to see her. There was just no real attempt to put herself in my shoes, to think about *me*. So, whatever hope I had, it's long gone."

"I'm sorry, Aly."

"Yeah, me too. But it wasn't for nothing. I think the thing that worried me most with her coming back, with all these little threads was that ... that it all meant my father wasn't who I thought he was. That he was..."

"Like my father," Landon finished for her.

She winced a little at that, but it couldn't be denied. "Janie didn't say anything bad about my father. I don't know that I'd have believed it if she had, but everything she said about him matched with the man I knew. I think I have to choose to believe that. He was who I thought he was."

"I think so."

"That means something. It does." Her shoulders relaxed even more. "She warned me off you."

"Why?"

"She said you can't trust a Bennet."

"I can blame her for a lot of things, but I'm not sure I can blame her for that sentiment."

"Well, I can," Aly said firmly, pulling back enough to look up at him. "You're the only steady thing in my life, you and the ranch, ever since Dad died. She had no right to say anything about you." Aly shook her head. "I'm glad she said it though. It made it easy to realize and accept I don't want anything to do with her."

"Then you don't have to."

"I told her that. I don't know if she'll listen."

"We'll make sure she does. You've got a lot of people looking out for you, Al."

"I know. I think that's why ... it was freeing, in a weird way, to just accept she's not a good person. But this is a long-winded way of trying to get around telling you the next part."

Landon listened as she described what had happened to Jill's truck.

"Janie's involved in the vandalism," Landon concluded grimly.

"I think she has to be. What kind of coincidence is that if she's not? And the way the police seemed to take this a little more seriously ... something is there. Sam was talking to the detective privately. I'm not sure what about, but I'm hoping Nate will fill us in."

"I'll make sure of it."

"You'll make sure of everything." But she didn't say it in a bad way. She put her palm against his cheek, her mouth not quite curved into a smile but certainly closer than it needed to be. "I always felt lucky that I had this place, the Bennets, you. I don't know if it's luck. I don't know, but I can't … it hurts, that she is the way she is, that that's my mother. But like you said, I've got a lot of people looking out for me, and that matters."

"It does," he agreed solemnly. Like a vow. Because he would always make sure she was okay. He would always… "Aly."

She looked back at him, and she looked more settled. Less miserable. Like he'd actually done some comforting and helping, which he wouldn't say was a talent of his. A good team. A good … everything. She'd made him a better man, even back when friends was all he'd allowed them to be. These past few months had only added to that.

There'd probably be a better time, a more settled time, except everything had been so relentlessly *unsettled* for almost a year now that it seemed almost impossible. Certainly too long to wait.

"I don't suppose you'd want to get married."

ALY FELT LIKE her heart was riding a rollercoaster. One of those awful ones that went upside down ten times in a row. The only explanation for what he'd just said was that she'd had a stress-induced stroke, and this was a very realistic feeling hallucination.

"Aly?"

She tried to laugh, but the sound that escaped her mouth sounded far more deranged than jovial. "Funny," she managed to croak.

"I wasn't joking. I was asking."

"Asking if I want to get married? To you?" She shook her head.

It wasn't a funny joke, but it was a *joke*, because this was Landon and he didn't just … randomly and abruptly propose out of nowhere. Not Landon Bennet.

"Yeah. I'm asking you to marry me."

Panic filtered through her limbs, making them feel odd and heavy. Making it hard to breathe. Because … it was impossible.

"You're not on one knee, and this is a weird joke. I don't like it."

"I can get on one knee if you need me to, because I'm not joking."

"You just blurted that out and … you don't mean it. You haven't even thought it through."

He thought *everything* through. So, he couldn't possibly surprise her. Not like this. Not … spontaneously.

"I do mean it." His gaze never left hers. He didn't backtrack or step away. He just kept looking at her with that same quiet, determined, intense expression he always used when he said he loved her. "I haven't *not* thought it through."

She could only stare at him, and it took her a few seconds and spots appearing in her vision to realize she needed to breathe. She tried to move away from him, but he held her firm.

"Landon. I love you." The next words were hard, but they were damn necessary. "I hope … I hope marriage is in our future, but you don't need to pity propose."

His expression hardened. "It's not pity."

"You don't even have a ring."

He didn't agree or disagree with that, but when he took her hand and pulled her inside her heart jumped to her throat.

There was no way … there was…

"Landon." She thought she sounded quite firm, but he didn't drop her hand, didn't stop pulling. Through the living room and to the back room that acted as the ranch office. *She* spent most of her time here, not him.

But he pulled her right along until he got to the ancient floor safe that had sat in the corner for as long as she could remember. She'd never once seen anyone open it, mention it, consider it.

On occasion she'd wondered what Bennet treasures might be in there, then she'd remind herself Benjamin and Landon were the most practical men on the planet and the most fanciful thing that might be in that safe was a will and testament or a land deed. Probably from a hundred years ago.

But Landon did get on one knee then, not to propose, but to twist the knob and enter a combination. When the door opened, it squeaked loudly in the quiet room. But Landon must have done this before, because he unerringly reached in and pulled out something.

He straightened, little box in his hand. He flipped the lid. To a ring. An old ring, but a ring. A gold band, with a tiny little diamond set in the center.

It felt as though her entire throat had dissolved, and that

she didn't have feet. This was a dream. It was too surreal not to be a dream.

"It was my grandmother's," he said. "My mother's mother. I don't know if you remember her. She died when we were teenagers, but she only visited a few times. She didn't get along with my father." He paused for a second, brow furrowing. "She didn't get along with my father. She must have … known. Or if not known…" He shook his head. "It doesn't matter. She died just a few months before Mom, and I didn't know her well, but I know my mom loved her, respected her. I know she was part of why my mom was a good person. So Mom kept this ring, and Dad never cared about it at all. It just sat here."

She couldn't seem to catch her breath, but everything stilled when Landon looked from the ring to her. That dark, solid gaze. That *certainty* he brought to everything he did. Maybe it was spontaneous, impulsive, but that didn't mean he didn't *mean* it.

"You are also the most stable thing in my life, Aly. The ranch and you. But you and you alone are the *best* thing in my life. And we make a good team, a damn good team. Let's be a team. Legally, spiritually, whatever the hell."

"Whatever the hell," she echoed, wanting to laugh, but it got caught somewhere in her throat.

Because he was *serious* somehow. Landon, the most plodding, methodical, careful man alive was … seriously asking her to marry him.

Without any planning. Any… "We've never talked about … about important things. What the future looks like. I don't even know if you want kids."

"Do you?"

It legitimately felt like her brain was in a pool, swimming around, without a clue as to how to get to shore. *Kids?* "I don't know. I…"

"Then I figure that's something we can decide together, just like we do everything else."

"But what if we don't decide the same thing? What if—"

"You can say no, Aly. That's all right. But I love you, and I'm asking, so you're not going to talk me out of it. It's a yes, or not right now. That's okay."

"Landon, I love you. I want to marry you. It's just…"

"We can set it aside. Come back to it on a better day. I was impulsive and that never gets me anywhere."

"You were. Impulsive. You're never impulsive. You're never…" The first tear slipped over.

She just couldn't stop it. But for the first time in a long time, it wasn't a sad tear. Still, she wiped it away, and let all this ridiculous worry just…

She never had to worry when it came to Landon. Not like this. "Yeah. Yes, let's … let's get married and figure it out. A team."

His smile bloomed, that rare one that showed off the hint of a dimple. True, real, rare joy. Just for her. He took her hand—hers shook. His didn't. He slid the ring on her finger.

Aly could only stare at it for a full moment. This new, foreign weight.

But… "It fits. Perfectly."

"Yeah, it does."

NATE STOPPED HIS truck in front of the ranch. He pushed the vehicle into park, but he didn't immediately move to turn the ignition off.

Cal studied him. "You coming in? I imagine Landon will want to hear your take on things."

His take. Landon would want to hear *his* take.

And what Nate wanted was to call Sam. See what Detective Hayes had to say. She said she'd keep him in the loop, but he hadn't heard from her. Surely she was done with her *meeting*.

If she wasn't ... well, it damn well didn't matter if she wasn't. She'd tell him when she told him. So why shouldn't Nate go inside and tell Landon his *take*?

"Sure," Nate said to Cal. He turned off the truck, hopped out.

"You look pissed about something."

Nate looked at Cal. "No, I don't."

"Yeah, you do. You're pretty good at being Mr. Stoic, but when you're really worked up, you start clenching your fists."

Nate looked down at his hands, which were indeed clenched into fists.

He released them, scowled at Cal. "That some underhanded lawyer trick?"

"Hardly a trick. It's just basic observation. Good in a courtroom and when you're dealing with taciturn brothers, I've found."

Nate wanted to sneer, which was a strange impulse these

days. That emotional reaction. These *feelings*. All things he'd spent a hell of a lot of time turning off. Turning them back on was no easy feat for a wide variety of reasons. He supposed he should be happy when emotional responses bled through. Wasn't that something he was grappling with? Feeling like some emotionless observer to his own life?

But mostly it left him feeling exposed and uncomfortable and like some weird combination of the kid he'd been and the man he'd become. He hated it.

So he changed the subject. "Why did Glenda's humming freak you out so much?"

"I don't know." Cal looked back out over the mountains, in the vague direction of the Harrington cabin. "Just felt weird and wrong and … pointed. And like another damn thing I can't remember."

"Maybe she really is a witch."

Cal laughed, but the haunted look didn't quite leave his eyes. Nate supposed that Dad could be in jail for eons, and they'd still all be battling their internal demons.

Cal didn't knock, and Nate knew he shouldn't feel uncomfortable about that. Cal hadn't left like Nate had. Maybe he didn't *live* here, but he'd visited, stayed part of the family.

Nate had cut it all off.

Nate stepped through the threshold then grimaced at the sight in the living room. Aly and Landon wrapped up in each other.

Cal flung a dramatic arm over his eyes. "Jesus. Look, I never thought I'd have to say this with Landon the Prude, but absolutely no PDA in common areas while I'm around."

Nate glanced up, noticed they barely moved. Aly looked

like she'd been crying, but they were grinning at each other. They'd put some air between their mouths, but they weren't letting each other go.

"Hi, guys," Aly said. "You're just in time to celebrate."

"I don't think I want to know what we're celebrating," Nate muttered, earning a snicker from Cal.

But Aly finally detangled herself from Landon, stepped toward them and held out her hand as she wiggled her fingers a little. Nate didn't understand the meaning behind it until Landon said the words.

"Aly and I are getting married."

"Christ," Nate muttered at the same time Cal said, "No shit?"

"Did he tell you I told him to do it?" Cal demanded, but he was grinning. Happy.

Nate knew he needed to find some happy too.

Aly looked up at Landon, who rolled his eyes and shook his head. "He didn't tell me to do it," Landon said disapprovingly.

Cal moved over to Aly, hugged her tight. Nate stood, making sure not to fist his hands. Because he wasn't angry. He was just damn uncomfortable.

Especially when Aly turned to him. Her eyes were shiny and happy and for a moment it was like he could actually remember a time, long ago, when everything hadn't been so fucked up. Mom had been here. Maybe Dad had been a monster then too, but they hadn't known that yet. And maybe Nate had never felt particularly or especially *close* to his brothers—Dad had made sure of that—but they'd been … a family. Messed up, weird, sure. But a family.

Aly had been a part of that.

So he offered a *very* awkward hug, and meant it when he said, "Congratulations, Aly."

She stepped back, still grinning. "Thank you, Nate."

He turned to Landon, shook his brother's hand. "More congratulations for you, obviously."

"Obviously," Landon replied. With an actual *smile*.

Nate wanted to feel good about it. Maybe eventually he'd be able to get there, but right now it felt like some kind of blinding light on everything about his life that was just … standing still, running in place. Sure, he'd stayed in Marietta, gotten a license to be a private investigator, but he was still just going through the motions.

It was a sinking discomfort. Life moved on. Even in the midst of questions, vandalism. Landon and Aly were going to get married. In spite of all the shit their parents had left them, they were going to be brave and live.

"I better go," Nate said, hoping it didn't sound as abrupt as it felt. "Still got a vandalizer out there on the loose. Even if Janie Turner is connected, she wasn't the one spray painting Jill's car, so we've got to figure out … sorry to bring it back up."

"No, it's all right," Landon said, as though he actually meant it. "You'll let us know what Hayes said to Sam?"

"Yeah, when I hear, I'll … let you know." He forced his mouth to curve upward, hoped it seemed more like a smile than it felt. "Congrats again."

"When this is all over, we'll have a real family celebration," Aly said firmly.

Over. Would it ever all be over? That felt like a hope

Nate wasn't sure he knew how to have. He stepped outside. The day had turned gray, putting a new autumnal chill in the air. Nate shoved his hands into his pockets—still not fisted.

But as he reached his truck, he couldn't help but look back at the house. The Bennet Ranch.

He'd spent the first sixteen years of his life thinking of it as home. Ignoring all the cracks or running away from them.

Just like he'd done fifteen years ago.

But he was back now. He'd made the conscious decision to be back. Landon of all people moving forward with *life* seemed like a pretty clear sign that Nate couldn't just settle for that decision to stay anymore.

He had to … find a way back into himself. Into being a person instead of soldier. A brother instead of an empty space at the table.

His thoughts turned to Sam. He didn't have any good answers there either. Just questions, discomfort, things he wanted to avoid lest they get … complicated.

But maybe that was the point. He'd decided to stop running away. To stay put. To see if roots could plant in the place he'd once ripped them out of.

He couldn't expect them to grow if he was *avoiding*. If he was still running away every time something got to be a little too … much.

So he headed back to Honor's Edge, wondering what staying put really looked like.

Chapter Twenty-Three

Honor's Edge Investigations Office

S AM LET HERSELF into the back of the office. She was happy Nate's truck wasn't here, because it meant *he* wasn't here. And since he hadn't responded to her text about the meeting being over, he was probably either busy talking to Landon or driving.

It gave her time to sort through whatever that meeting with Detective Hayes had been.

Sure, he'd given her some information about what little the police had found regarding the damage to Aly's truck. He'd been interested to hear Sam's thoughts on how Janie Turner might connect.

He'd also been flirting. It wasn't like Brian either. The old friend who'd become a cop and often would slip her information on a case—who'd then struggled to take *not interested* for an answer.

No, she didn't get that feeling from Detective Hayes—*Jake.* He'd asked her out, essentially, and hadn't been anything but relaxed and decidedly *unpushy* about her uncertain answer.

It would be smart to say yes. For her own mental well-being. An interested party over ... whatever her brain thought it was doing when it came to Nate.

Hayes was a good-looking guy. A little old for her, but hell, what was ten years when one person was in their thirties and one person was in their forties? He seemed to have his life together, and wasn't that a step in the right direction?

But when Nate came into the office a little while later, she knew what had caused her reticence.

Detective Hayes might be attractive, interested, and have his life together, but her heart didn't do the little weird stutter step it did when she saw that lost look in Nate's eyes, hidden under a million layers of stoicism.

She could tell herself it was some warped adult trauma bonding, and she probably wasn't wrong, but it didn't change anything. And that was her fucked up cross to bear.

"Get Jill and Cal dropped off okay?" she asked.

"Yeah." He stared at his desk, and that lost look didn't fade. "Yeah … Aly and Landon are engaged."

Sam blinked at him, not making full sense of the words for maybe a minute or two. "No shit?"

"You and Cal are on the same wavelength there." He dropped into the chair of his desk. "Landon had a ring and everything."

"Well, I should hope so." Sam tried to wrap her around this turn of events. "I think she always loved him. Even in high school when she claimed to have a thing for Keith Jones, but it was always Landon."

"Yeah, he was definitely it for her."

"That's sweet. I hope they're happy."

"Yeah, me too."

Silence settled, an odd weight around them. Partly because it didn't *feel* particularly happy, even though she had no reason not to be happy for them.

Well, maybe Landon had been an asshole to her a lot, and there were times Aly hadn't been much better, but *still*. They'd had a shit road to walk, too. Seemed like someone should get something good.

"Well, what was the meeting with the detective like?" Nate asked, shaking off the weird silence and booting up his computer.

Sam hesitated, not sure what to include and what to leave out. "There was nothing in the footage of the Bennet utility shed, but they did talk to a cashier at Wraiths—a store which apparently sells a small selection of spray paint. One of the cashiers remembers someone checking out with it, so they have a description, but it's pretty generic and not much to go on. I asked about footage from the store, and he got a little cagey. They'll look at the security cameras from where Jill was parked, but they were unlikely to have picked up the parking lot as it was more pointed at the entrance of the building. My take is they don't have much more to go on than we do."

Nate was quiet a few seconds before he looked up at her. "That was a hell of a long meeting for information we mostly already knew."

An uncomfortable heat started to bloom in her cheeks, which was ridiculous. She was never embarrassed, and it was hardly like Nate knew she'd spent some of the meeting discussing personal things. "Did you talk to Landon about Jim Gary?"

"No, kind of seemed like the wrong time. They were all happy and stuff."

Right. Engaged. "Guess you're right. I can do some more digging on his past since he left the rec center. And figure out if there's some paper trail tie to Janie beyond that."

"Why are you avoiding my question?"

She looked up at him again, his gaze intense. "What question?"

"That was a hell of a long meeting."

"That's not a question, Nate," she replied evenly. "That's a statement."

"And that's still avoiding."

Sam rolled her eyes, tried to behave far more casually than she felt. "We talked a little about my dad's case, Ben's. He said he admired my work and my tenacity." She shrugged, and it felt jerky and awkward, definitely not the calm, unbothered demeanor she was going for. Nate didn't need to know the rest.

She repeated that thought to herself at least three times before the truth tumbled out. "He asked me out."

Nate didn't react right away, and when he spoke it was in that emotionless way he had that drove her crazy. She liked to think she'd developed a pretty tough outer layer, kept all those emotions deep under it when she worked. But she had nothing on him.

"Did you say yes?" he asked.

"What's it to you?"

Nate didn't answer right away, and the way he was studying her had those flutters starting. *Nerves.* "I thought we were friends. Figured it was the polite thing to do to ask."

Polite. She wanted to punch him. And since that was ridiculous, she answered the question instead. "I didn't give him an answer right away. Seems like a no brainer though. He's hot. We're in a similar line of work, so we'll have stuff in common. I don't have to explain my dad's a psycho killer. Pluses all around."

"He's old."

"He's *forty*." Well, forty-two. "That's not that old."

Nate leaned back in his chair. He wasn't studying her anymore. He was looking past her to some spot on the wall.

"I guess, you should do whatever you want, but if you're on the fence … You should probably decide what it is you want before you say yes. Out of fairness."

"Gee, thanks for the love life advice I didn't ask for."

His eyes came back to hers. "Friends, right?"

She had no idea why she just wanted to cry. "Right."

Nate looked back at his computer, for about thirty seconds, then pushed away from his desk and stood. "I can't sit around here poking at old newsletters on computers again."

She could feel that restless energy pumping off him. If he had any flaws as an investigator, it was that. He could be the most patient, stoic guy in the world, but when he wanted to be *doing*, he didn't have much patience for the wait.

"We could go down to Wraiths again," she suggested. "See if we can get Jim to talk about Janie. Maybe if we're direct this time, he can't run away. Or we could find him at home, instead of at work."

"We could. Yeah, you know … at home. That's what we're missing, isn't it?" He didn't pace exactly, and there was no restless movement from Nate, no there was still too much soldier in him. She wondered if he'd do better if he *did* let himself pace. "What if instead of talking to him, or Janie we follow one of them? Or both of them?"

It was action. And as patient as she could be, it did sound a hell of a lot better than sitting around searching for some needle-in-a-haystack post-rec-center connection on the internet.

Especially right now.

"I don't see as there's much point following Jim. We want to prove a connection to Janie, and that only works if they connect. But following Janie? That might give us something."

She thought maybe she'd surprised him by agreeing. But he jumped on it quick enough. "First, I guess we need to figure out where she's staying."

"Hayes said after talking to Aly and Jill he was sending an officer out to talk to some of the people at the motel she was staying at. There aren't that many motels around here. We start at the closest, move out."

"How'd he know she was staying at a motel? They weren't looking into Janie about the first vandalism before Jill and Aly went in this morning."

"I didn't ask, but it's information. Are we going to take it and use it or question the hows and whys? We know what kind of car she's driving, thanks to Aly. We'll check out all the motel parking lots as a first step."

He scowled, but he headed for the door, Sam at his heels. "We'll take my truck. It's going to blend in more than your junk pile."

"Hey, that's no way to talk about my baby."

He snorted.

They got in his truck and Sam gave him directions to the

Rosebud. A few miles out of town, it would make the most sense for Janie, especially if she was planning on going up to the Bennet Ranch a lot.

They were silent. Sam figured they were both thinking about next steps—what happened if they spotted her car, what happened if they didn't. But when Nate spoke, it wasn't about Janie Turner at all.

"You know you should do whatever you want, right? With Hayes."

She had *no* idea why he'd brought it up again. She slid him a look. His brow was furrowed, his jaw tight, and one hand tight around the wheel, the other clenched in a fist resting on his thigh. She didn't know what to make of it, of the sentence, of *him*.

And since she didn't, the only response she had was just bald honesty. "I don't know what I want, Nate."

"Then I guess we're in the same damn boat," he muttered.

Chapter Twenty-Four

The Bennet Ranch

L ANDON WAS ON horseback when his phone rang. Normally, he'd wait until he got to where he was going, but with everything going on lately, he figured he better check the display. He slowed the horse to a stop, pulled out his phone.

It was just Skinny. He was on his way to the stables anyway, to put the horse away for the night and head back inside. Skinny should be in the vicinity right now. He'd just talk to him when he got there.

But the ringing stopped ... then immediately started again.

Landon cursed, answered the phone.

"I need you to come out to the creek," Skinny said without any preamble. "Out by the ... old barn."

Just from the way Skinny said *old barn*, Landon knew he was referring to the barn that had burned down ... with his mother's murdered body in it.

"What's wrong, Skinny?"

"I'm not sure. I'd like you to come take a look rather than try to explain it."

Landon sighed. "All right. I'm on my way." It'd be easier

to ride the horse out than stable her then get a UTV or his truck.

He considered calling Aly as he urged his horse into a trot. She was supposed to be finishing up the inventory, then she was going to make them a nice dinner. He'd suggested going out to celebrate, even though he didn't *want* to. But he wanted her to know … he'd do whatever made her happy if he could.

It had been her insistence to stay home. To have a meal—just the two of them and celebrate accordingly.

Would whatever Skinny wanted him to see ruin that?

Landon wanted to believe he wouldn't let it, but he'd seen too much, been through too much this year to have that kind of confidence.

When the lot where the barn used to sit came into view, Landon didn't see anything except Skinny and another hand standing next to each other, hands in their pockets. They both turned to face him at the same time, their hats shadowing their faces so Landon couldn't see their expressions.

Once he was close, Landon pulled the horse to a stop and swung off. He fastened the reins to a young tree then moved over to Skinny and Deke.

He saw why he was here before they said anything. On trees, on the dirt and grass that made up this area of the ground between where the barn used to be and the creek that marked the boundary between Bennet and Harrington land, someone had taken spray-paint and had a field day.

It was the same yellow color that had been on Aly and Jill's truck. The same crude words. So, it had to be the same perpetrator.

Janie Turner or whoever her accomplice was. That would have been frustrating enough, but the location was a concern. This wasn't a well-traveled part of the ranch, and this vandalism wasn't exactly destructive considering it was done to natural things like trees and grass and dirt. It was just annoying.

And, he supposed, that was what made it feel more sinister. This wasn't destruction. This was an attempt at ... what? Intimidation? Fear? From the start, Aly had wanted to believe it was a prank, but Landon had always felt it was more threatening than that.

And Sam had agreed. Called it *personal*—from the jump. So he wasn't being unreasonable or overprotective. Maybe the paint itself was harmless, but there was something deeper here. Something *concerning*.

Landon looked from the paint to the creek, and then back to the where the barn had been. He wanted it to be coincidence, his imagination or faulty memory, but it just seemed impossible.

All of this graffiti, essentially, was exactly halfway between where his mother had been found and Sandy McCoy had been found. Both murdered by different men, but all that violence and horror stemming from one place. One man.

Landon sighed. Yeah, this was going to ruin his and Aly's night. He pulled his phone out of his pocket. "Let's stay put, Skinny. I'm going to call the cops."

CAL WAS GETTING the hell out of dodge. He was going to spend a few nights with Nate. He hadn't been able to get a hold of Nate to tell him so, but like hell Cal was going to stay in the house with a newly engaged couple.

Maybe it was no different than the way Aly and Landon had been shacking up as of late, but it *felt* different. At least tonight. Let the happy couple have a night to themselves to celebrate. He might enjoy irritating the hell out of Landon, but playing third wheel at *this* serious juncture?

Nah. It made him itchy.

The thought of going back to Austin, or even just calling his boss back, crossed his mind, but he rejected it as he hopped in his rental car. He needed to have a clear head to deal with his life back in Texas, and he just … didn't right now.

Maybe he'd call his therapist. Set up one of those video sessions. He still didn't think therapy was *helping* all that much. He felt more off-balance than he'd ever felt in his entire damn life.

He wasn't sure why Landon and Aly's engagement had only exacerbated that feeling. He wasn't sure he wanted to know why.

Right now, all he wanted was some peace and quiet, and maybe to get a little drunk. But he drew the line at doing that alone, so he'd hunt up Nate first. Based on Nate's hasty exit earlier, Cal figured he'd be up for it.

Cal drove off the ranch, down the mountain and closer to town. When he stopped at the sign before turning onto the highway, he heard an odd *clank* from the backseat. He glanced behind him and saw something on the floor. He reached back and picked what had rolled out from under the seat.

He immediately dropped it when he realized what it was. A bottle of spray paint.

Yellow spray paint.

For a minute, he was frozen. There was an odd buzzing in his ears. He didn't … he wouldn't have any cans of paint. Yellow paint. In *his* rental car. It couldn't be a coincidence, but what did that mean?

He wanted to pretend like he'd never seen it.

Instead, he pulled off the road, put the car in park, and called the police.

It didn't take long for someone to arrive on the scene, but Cal wasn't too happy with who got out of the marked police car. His impression of Officer Brian Mathews was not a positive one after dealing with him in the spring. Brian had a terrible bedside manner and struck Cal as … one of those guys constantly on a power trip, because he and his life were just plain sad.

People in glass houses shouldn't throw stones.

His mother had loved that saying.

Cal struggled to breathe through the tingle of a panic attack or unwanted memory or whatever the hell was wrong with him. He thought he could have handled Brian, would have and easily, but the unmarked car parked behind Brian's made him leery.

He supposed there was a reason for Detective Hayes to be here. He was investigating the vandalism of Aly's and Jill's trucks. And now he'd have to investigate who would have hidden one of the tools used in said case in Cal's rental car.

"Thanks for coming, gentleman," Cal greeted. He wasn't sure the lawyerly smile he'd fixed on his face was doing its job, but he tried. "I pulled to a stop and the can rolled out from under my seat. Obviously, it's not mine." Cal opened the back door, pointed at the back seat where the paint lay. "And obviously, I know what this looks like."

"Why don't you walk us through exactly what happened?"

"That is exactly what happened," Cal replied to Officer Mathews. He struggled to keep his voice neutral.

"And why is your bag in the back?" Detective Hayes asked. "Headed back to Texas?"

Cal knew these two had every reason to know he lived in Texas, but the personal detail irked. "No. I was going to go bunk with Nate for a few days."

"Trouble at the ranch?"

One of those pointed cop questions that were meant to poke, to stir up. Effective because they worked. But Cal breathed through his anger and flashed that lawyer smile. It was still here.

He was still *him* somewhere at the center of all this *other* stuff. "Quite the opposite, actually. My brother got engaged. Thought I'd leave him and his fiancée to enjoy their celebration without his brother hanging around."

"And about what time would you say you left the ranch?"

"Around four, if I had to guess, but I wasn't really concerned with the time so much as heading out before Aly and Landon were done with their afternoon chores. Give the lovebirds some space."

"Meeting absent mothers in the morning, getting engaged after, then chores in the afternoon? Quite the day."

Cal kept the smile in place, if only by picturing plowing his fist into the guy's gut. "That's ranch life for you, detective."

For a minute, they all just stood there, silent and observing each other. But Cal was tired, not just of this but in general. Tired of *all* this. Why had he come back home? At the moment, he'd rather be facing his bosses' disapproval.

"The can is not mine. It rolled forward when I came to a stop. I picked it up. That's when I realized what it was, and I dropped it." Cal struggled not to say more. He shouldn't be telling them anything if they were considering him a suspect.

But he wasn't a damn suspect, and they needed to find whoever was doing this and framing him of all damn people.

"And if we got prints off it, and they're only yours, will your story stay the same?" Hayes asked. Conversationally. *Casually.*

Cal changed the picture in his head from a gut punch to hitting the guy right in the nose. He shoved his hands into his pockets. "It's not *mine*. That's why I called the police. I'm not going around vandalizing trucks of people I *like* and then calling the police when there's the same kind of paint in my car. Doesn't quite add up, does it, detective?"

The detective nodded along as Brian collected the can and put it into an evidence bag.

"I worked your father's case," the detective in that same casual manner, as if anything about this was casual.

"I'm aware."

"His trial is going to hinge on you, isn't it? And the idea

you suffered from…" He furrowed his brow as if he didn't know for sure. "Forgetting … something or other?"

"It's called dissociative amnesia," Cal muttered. He needed to start thinking about this like a lawyer. Not like an offended victim who was being framed. "A condition caused by trauma. You know, like seeing your mother killed. Not fun, turns out."

"Right." Hayes studied the car, then him. "Is it possible you still suffer from it?"

It took Cal a minute to get the implication. That he might be doing these things and then … forgetting them? Or he was using that as an excuse? Cal wanted to be furious.

Instead, he was momentarily frozen by terror. Luckily, a sweep of anger followed soon enough, heating all that ice with rage. "Are you going to arrest me? Because I can assure you, that's not going to go well for you."

"It's not going to go well for me if I arrest a man who is in possession of the item used in three different vandalism cases?"

"You'll need to do tests to prove that. You'll also need to get prints off it. You'll have to build a case, detective. And as there *is* no case, because if I was going to be a criminal, I'd be a damn better one."

"*If.* But who needs to be a better criminal when you're pretty good at worming out of those kinds of cases? Gotten a few criminals off in your day, haven't you?"

"I'm not just pretty good at it, I'm the fucking best," Cal retorted, the fury slipping through. "Now, I'll repeat the question. Are you going to arrest me?"

Hayes didn't directly answer that question. "I'll be in

touch, Mr. Bennet. Stay in town, won't you?"

Cal narrowly bit off telling him to go to hell. Hayes ambled away like he had all the time in the world and Cal wanted to hurl something at him, but some of the fury ebbed.

He hadn't even been in town when Aly's truck vandalism had occurred. He could prove that. He'd been at Glenda's cabin when Jill's had happened. He could probably prove that too, even if Glenda didn't speak. Had Hayes said three vandalism cases? What the hell was he talking about besides those two?

Cal got behind the wheel of his rental, stared at the way his hands shook. Anger. Just the aftereffects of anger.

But there was the tiniest little seed of doubt and worry. He knew he wasn't right.

Was he this bad off?

It was ridiculous. Of *course* he hadn't done it. He wasn't even *here* when the first one had happened.

But the worry chased him all the way out to Nate's place.

Chapter Twenty-Five

The Harrington Cabin

JILL DIDN'T FULLY recognize the sound on the door as a knock for she wasn't sure how long. She was deep in the scene and had tuned most of her surroundings out.

The writing had been going well. Turned out she'd much rather deal with a fictional mystery she got to control than deal with the real, complicated mystery of her grandmother.

Speaking of. Where was Grandma? Jill looked up, recognized the sound that she'd been ignoring was indeed a knock, and her heart jumped to her throat even as she jumped to her feet.

Had something happened? Had she been so deep in it she'd completely lost track of her grandmother and something had happened?

She jerked the door open to find Aly standing on the porch. Though she didn't look panicked, Jill *felt* panic.

"Aly. I … Is everything okay?"

"Yeah, everything's fine. I just wanted to tell you something. Nothing bad."

She didn't look upset. More … excited, Jill realized.

"Come inside. Just give me a second." Jill moved through the house, looking for signs of Grandma. She let out a long breath of relief when she saw her through the window, fussing with her birdfeeders.

Jill tried to shake all that sudden worry out of her limbs and fix a smile on her face when she turned back to the living room and Aly.

"Sorry. I was deep in the story and out of it. What's up? You want some tea?"

"I didn't mean to interrupt. I should have called."

Jill waved that away. "Don't be silly. I clearly needed a break. There is such a thing as *too deep* and forgetting that you're responsible for an elderly woman. I could use some coffee though. You want a mug?"

"Sure."

Jill set about making the coffee, getting out mugs and cream. She set everything on the table while the coffee brewed, trying to get her thoughts back in order. Move from fictional worlds to real ones.

And that's when she noticed it. Aly was sitting at the table, hands over the surface, her left settled over her right. The ring was new. Aly never wore jewelry. So it stood out. Simple, an antique if Jill had to guess. Her mom loved jewelry, so Jill had an eye for certain things.

But it wasn't just the ring. It was the finger it was on. "Aly … Oh my *God*. It's beautiful. It's…" She threw her arms around Aly and squeezed. "Oh, I'm so happy for you."

Aly squeezed right back. "It's nice to have something to be happy about."

"It's *amazing* to have something to be happy about." Jill squeezed her again. Then jumped up and down. "Oh my God, we get to plan a wedding!"

Aly laughed. "I can't stay long. I want to make this big elaborate celebration dinner, but I had to tell somebody."

"Why are you making your own engagement dinner?" Jill gave her a friendly shake. "You should go out!"

"That's what Landon said." She laughed, staring at the ring again. "I don't want to go out. I don't want … ever since everything happened with Ben, people … look at us differently. Even in Livingston. It was too big a story and I hate having to wonder if everyone staring is … thinking about *that*."

"Well, that's fair. If I was even half as good a cook as you, I'd offer to make something to take off your plate."

"It's all good. I know you don't believe me, but I *like* the cooking and cleaning."

"I could accept the cooking, but the cleaning?" Jill shook her head. "I want to do *something*. What can I do?"

"We're not exactly the same size, but I thought maybe I could borrow something to wear. Landon's seen all my clothes a million times, and they're all meant for ranch work. Maybe you have a dress that wouldn't be crazy short on me or … something? At least then it would kind of feel celebratory or different than our usual night in."

"Come on. We'll figure something out." She grabbed Aly's hand and pulled her back to her room. "It's too bad I didn't have room in the cabin for my entire wardrobe. I bet I've got a million things in a storage unit back in Boston."

She made Aly try on a bunch of different things. Aly was taller than her, slimmer, and didn't have much in the way of curves. Their coloring was almost opposite, so a lot of the colors Jill favored didn't do much for Aly's skin tone.

Jill was close to giving up when Glenda appeared in her room, holding a folded piece of fabric. She held it out to Aly. Aly took it uncertainly, but Glenda made a hurry up motion.

"What is it?" Jill supplied.

Aly let the fabric unfurl into a pretty sundress. A little summery, but it was a cream color with tiny delicate roses printed on the fabric.

Grandma pointed at Aly, and the mirror.

"She wants you to try it on."

"Oh. Well…" Clearly Aly didn't know what to make of it, but she took the dress and dutifully tried it on. It fit better than most of Jill's things, but it was still a little short.

Grandma studied the dress, then motioned for Aly to take it off again. When Aly did, Grandma took it and disappeared.

"What was that about?" Aly asked.

Jill shrugged. She wasn't going to ruin the good mood by complaining about how little she understood her grandmother.

"Well, you could take the green dress and wear it like a baggy shirt with some leggings."

Aly laughed. "It's still better than jeans and flannel. I better get back if I'm going to get started on time."

They walked back out to the living room.

"You need to set a date ASAP so we can start planning. I mean it. Rings mean dates," Jill said, because Aly seemed to be getting a kick out of having an overbearing planning friend.

"I'll see what I can do. Jill … it's really nice to have a friend to share this with. Maybe … everything happens when it's supposed to."

"I like to think so," Jill said.

Jill moved to the door with Aly, but Grandma bustled in. She held the dress again, pushed it at Aly.

"Oh, but…"

Grandma held out the edge of the dress, pointed to the stitching.

"I think she let out the hem. Made it longer for you," Jill explained, studying where Grandma pointed.

"That's…" Aly blinked rapidly, eyes suspiciously shiny. "That's really kind of you, Glenda. Thank you."

They waved their goodbyes, Jill shouted one more insistence on having a date by the end of the week, or at least the month, then closed the door.

She looked at her grandmother, who seemed oddly sentimental about the whole thing.

"That was a really nice thing to do, Grandma. Was it your dress?"

Grandma nodded slowly. Then she turned and walked away.

Jill sighed. Well, at least Grandma had answered. Jill settled herself back on the couch, looked at her computer. She tried to remember where she was, but the flow had been interrupted and now she felt a bit at sea.

Then Grandma came back in the room. She held out a small piece of paper to Jill.

Except it wasn't paper. It was a picture of a couple. The woman wore a dress identical to the one Grandma had given Aly. The man, tall and handsome, and young. They were both so young.

And so happy.

Jill tried to think if she'd ever seen a picture of the grand-father she'd never known, aside from the military one that still sat on Grandma's nightstand to this day. Dad didn't like to talk about the father he'd lost suddenly when he'd been away at med school, and Glenda didn't talk, period.

Grandma motioned for her to flip over the picture, so Jill did and read what was written on the back.

Glenda Small and William Harrington. Engagement. 1964.

"You both look happy," Jill said, blinking back the tears in her eyes.

Grandma nodded. She took the picture back, traced her arthritic finger over the man's face.

This time when she left the room, she didn't return.

And Jill's heart ached for a woman who'd lost too much.

ALY SAID GOODBYE to Jill and Glenda with the pretty dress tucked under her arm.

She never wore dresses. There just wasn't a place for it on the ranch, and she hadn't been shopping for fun in years. She bought all her clothes for ranch work off the internet.

It had been beyond kind for Glenda to alter this on the spot for her. To offer a dress that had to have been hers.

Landon would be beyond surprised. Aly grinned as she drove down the curving bumpy lane. He'd surprised her with an engagement, now she got to have a little surprise of her own. Maybe it was small, but she *liked* small. Small was happy.

Humming to herself, she was determined to hold onto all that happy.

Halfway back to the ranch, she caught something out of the corner of her eye. An incongruence to the very normal landscape on her very normal drive. An oddly colored ... lump half hidden by a boulder and a swell of land. She might not have thought anything of it, but when she glanced in the rearview the lump moved, and at a really weird angle.

Heart in her throat, Aly hit the brake. Maybe it was just a wounded animal. Or a trick of the eye. She should just keep driving.

But the way her heart slammed against her chest made those things hard to believe, and her conscious wouldn't let her keep driving, not if there was something ... in trouble. She moved the truck into reverse, crept back, swallowing at the tightness in her throat.

But it only increased, along with that pounding heart, especially as the truck moved back, and she could see through the trees that lined this side of the road and beyond the rock enough to make out the shape of the moving lump. Not moving anymore, but definitely not an animal or a trick of the eye.

It was a woman.

With red hair.

Chapter Twenty-Six

The Tik-Tok Motel outside Livingston, Montana

NATE WAS FRUSTRATED, but at least now it was in part due to trying to track down Janie Turner, and not all his own … whatever the hell was wrong with him.

"If she's not here…"

"We'll try again in the morning. Look farther out," Sam supplied, holding the door of the shitty motel office open for him. "Or we'll move on to Jim Gary. We'll figure it out. One step at a time."

He hated how *rational* she could be when he wanted to pound something in frustration. Especially when she was right. Even in his short time as a private investigator he understood that he couldn't *make* things happen. He could only do what she said—take things one step at a time.

Finding where Janie was staying was an irritatingly difficult step. At least the TikTok motel seemed about the type of place Janie Turner, accessory to vandalism, might stay, he'd give her that. The main office was dimly lit, the floors had a vague sticky quality, and the woman behind the counter staring at her phone was smoking a cigarette.

Which she quickly hid, if halfheartedly, when the bell on the door sounded.

She looked up at them, narrowed her eyes. "Help you?"

Sam gave him a nudge, a clear sign she wanted him to take the lead. Which was a bit of a surprise, since she tended to take lead to herself without thinking twice about it.

But Nate stepped up to the counter, smiled politely at the woman who sized him up. Whatever her conclusion was, Nate wasn't sure. "We're looking for someone who might be staying here."

"What's it to me?"

"We're hoping you could tell us if she's staying here and answer a few questions about her stay."

"That's not the kind of place we run."

"Then what kind of place do you run?"

The lady smirked. "A place for the weary traveler to rest their head."

"Well, we're just looking for one of those weary travelers," Sam said. "No cops. No fuss. Her name is Janie Turner. Does she have a room here?"

The woman studied Sam, then Nate. "I don't have anyone by that name."

But Nate didn't like the way she phrased that, said that. Almost like there was more behind that *name*. "Okay, how about a woman. Redhead, blue eyes, about five-seven. Mid-fifties, though she tries to pass for younger. Anyone who fits that description?"

"Maybe. If she's in trouble, I don't want it around my place."

"She's not in trouble. We just want information. If you know she's staying here, have had any interactions with her, we just want to ask you a few questions." Nate slid a twenty across the counter.

"You think I can be bought?"

At the way the woman was staring at the twenty, he could only respond with the truth. "Yeah."

She cracked a smile. "Well, you ain't wrong, are you?" She tucked the twenty into her pocket. "Okay, what's your question?"

"Is she staying there alone? And if she is alone, has anyone stopped by, even just for a brief chat?"

"She's alone, far as I know. Only one visitor that I've seen, but I'm not spending my days spying on my guests."

Sam and Nate exchanged a glance. Maybe a visitor didn't *have* to be her accomplice, but it was a step.

"Male? Female?" Nate asked.

"Male. I remember because he was kind of a handsome looking guy. Now, I'm not judging. To each their own. Just seemed a bit young for the lady." She shrugged. "Definitely not a trucker. That's our usual clientele. Had one of those work trucks—guy in construction or something, if you ask me. You spend enough years behind this desk, you start being able to judge people based on what they drive. We got a whole game about it." She grinned. "I'm almost never wrong."

Nate glanced at Sam. That definitely didn't describe Jim Gary, who was neither young, handsome, nor drove a construction truck.

Before he could think of another question, his phone rang. He checked the screen. It was an unknown number, but didn't register as a spam call. Nate knew he could let it go to voicemail, but with everything going on, it felt smarter to take it. He motioned for Sam to talk to the woman at the desk, then he took a step back from the counter. "Hello?"

"Bennet, right?"

Nate didn't recognize the voice. Still, it was a waste to hedge. "Yeah."

"Brody McCoy."

Interesting. He motioned to Sam that he was going to step outside to take the call. She nodded before turning her attention to the woman behind the counter.

Nate stepped outside. "What can I do for you, Mr. McCoy?"

"I want to talk. In person."

"About what?"

"About Sandy."

Nate waited for more details, but Brody stayed silent. "Sandy's murder was solved, Brody. The man responsible confessed and will go to sentencing soon. Not sure what reason I've got to talk to you about Sandy."

Brody's silence stretched out. "You're the ones who came to me. Now I'm willing to come to you."

"So this is about the vandalism? The vandalism you said had nothing to do with you and didn't connect to you in any way?"

Brody didn't respond.

Nate bit back a sigh. "Okay, you want to talk? You've got the address for Honor's Edge. Come on by."

"I'm not meeting with that bitch whose dad killed my sister," Brody said with a certain kind of fervor Nate didn't like.

It also didn't quite make sense. Brody hadn't been cooperative, but he hadn't lashed out at Sam when they'd questioned him before. He hadn't singled her out for her father's crimes. Maybe he'd been that ignorant, but Nate doubted it.

So why was Sam suddenly a bitch he didn't want to be around?

Nate glanced at Sam through the grimy glass of the door. She was still talking to the woman behind the counter, the woman growing more animated. Hopefully getting somewhere.

"Then why do you want to meet with me?" Nate asked. "I work for her."

"Someone's gotta handle this, and it's not the cops. Fuck the cops." Brody's disgust rang in every word.

Nate had a lot of patience, he liked to think. He handled his frustration well, more or less, these days. He'd had to learn. Learn or die.

So he didn't know why he felt like snapping this guy's head off. "Handle what?" he demanded.

"Meet me. We can do it at your family ranch, if that makes you comfortable. But I need to talk to you somewhere private. No Price. Not that shitty office. Just you."

Nate took a page out of Brody's book and let silence settle while he considered. With Janie Turner's connection to the vandalism all but proved, he didn't know why he'd bother to deal with Brody right now.

But this was weird, and it didn't quite add up. "I need more information."

"Well, you're not getting it. You meet me on the road up to the Bennet Ranch in about an hour. You're not there in two..." Brody trailed off. Never finished his sentence. Just hung up.

Nate frowned at the phone. When Sam stepped outside, he explained the conversation to her from start to finish.

"Something doesn't add up," Nate said, frowning at the horizon. The sun was starting to set. It'd be dark in two hours. "Something doesn't feel right."

Sam studied him. "Then you shouldn't go alone."

He was leaning toward agreeing with her, but at the same time... "Handled men who wanted to kill me before. I don't think this is that."

"Wow, you don't think he wants to *kill* you. Comforting." She rolled her eyes. "You're not going alone. It goes against policy."

"You made the policy."

"Yeah, and I'm the boss. So you have to follow the policy."

They walked to his truck in tandem. "Why would he want to meet with me? And he left it on a vague threat. We're just supposed to ignore that?"

"I thought you just said you weren't afraid of..." Sam stopped walking. "Wait. While you were on the phone, I asked her about the truck. The work truck this visitor had? A black Ford F-150, wasn't sure on year, and she claims she didn't get a plate, though I wonder if that camera might have." She pointed to the camera fixed over the front door that pointed out toward the parking lot, though at that angle Nate wasn't sure how much of the actual lot would be in the picture.

"I'd love to say that narrows it down, but do you know how many trucks fit that description in Marietta, let alone Livingston and surrounding areas? Even a partial plate isn't going to give us much. *If* she'd give us the footage."

"The point is, Nate, what kind of truck does Brody McCoy drive?" Sam asked him, patiently, like he was a student and she was a tutor. It grated.

"It was a red Silverado when we met up with him. So, not close to black or a Ford."

"Okay, now extrapolate. Maybe Brody McCoy doesn't have a truck who matches that description, but you know who does?"

Nate frowned, thinking back to everyone they were looking into. Not Jim Gary. Not—

"It's my good friend Denver McCoy." She grinned up at him.

But Nate wasn't grinning. "It's a reach," he murmured. "It's a common truck." But he understood what she was getting at, especially with a weird ass call from Brody. If the McCoys connected to Janie Turner…

It made things feel more dangerous. Because vandalism might be harmless, but anything connected to murder—even a solved one—wasn't.

"Thought you told me Denver was harmless."

"I think he is," Sam agreed. "But Brody's not. And if Brody and Denver have a good relationship—which I don't know one way or another—they might share trucks. They might even share crimes."

"But we know Janie Turner connects."

"Yeah, and if that was Denver's truck here … I'd say our next step is to see how Janie Turner might connect to the McCoys."

"What if it's a wild goose chase?"

"Then we end up with some wild goose. You can't be guaranteed every thread you follow is a good one, Nate. Haven't you learned that by now?"

He had, or he thought he had, but everything about this left him feeling edgy. It reminded him too much of tracking a target in those final days when he'd been deployed. He'd known everything was going to hell, but he hadn't been able to figure out how or why.

Worse, how to stop it. So, he'd gotten blown to hell instead.

"I should go meet him. It might give us a lead."

"Okay, we'll do that first," Sam said.

She wasn't one of his men. She wasn't his responsibility. And still … he didn't want her mixed up in whatever was so very wrong. "He was very clear that he didn't want you there."

"Who says he has to know I'm there? We head up now to the ranch, you drop me off. Maybe I round up Cal for backup. You come back to town. We'll wait closer to the two-hour mark, just to make him squirm. You come up from Marietta. I come down from the ranch. Stay out of sight, until I don't."

"So you can piss him off?"

"Sure. Emotions lead people to lose control. And when people lose control, sometimes they let things slip that implicate them in some crimes."

"Yeah, and sometimes when people lose control, they pick up weapons, Sam. And use them."

"Sure," she said again, so damn cavalier about *hurt*. "Sometimes you risk a little hurt for some answers, Nate.

That's the job."

The job. "Then let me go alone." *That* was an acceptable risk. She wasn't.

Now she scowled at him. "No. We do this together. Risks are part of the job, but we don't have to take unnecessary, *stupid* ones. Now, let's go so you can get me to the ranch before he gets there."

He didn't want to. Damn, he didn't want to. He wanted to handle this all on his own. That was better, safer.

Or so he'd spent the past fifteen years thinking. But he was trying to … change or heal or grow the fuck up or something. He supposed that meant ignoring the isolation tendencies he preferred. That felt safe.

But he'd never been safe. Not in his whole damn life, except maybe up on that mountain in Tennessee. But even then, there'd been a danger lurking, even if only in his own mind.

And then Sam had found him.

Anyway, this was a *job*, not his childhood, not the army. This was investigating. The point wasn't to save everyone else. It was to find answers.

"Fine," he muttered, not liking it, but… "You're the boss."

Chapter Twenty-Seven

The Bennet Ranch

LANDON CAME HOME to an empty house. He walked into the kitchen and frowned. Empty. No sign of cooking. No sign of Aly, period.

Worry started, just a little flutter low in his gut. Hadn't she said she was going to make something?

Maybe she'd changed her mind and wanted to go out. He'd been relieved when she'd said she wanted to stay in, but he'd take her out. Hell, he'd do whatever she wanted. Whatever would make Aly happy. That was the goal.

Especially considering he had to tell her about this new vandalism and its location.

He went upstairs, and poked his head into every room, calling her name. He even went into her old set of rooms off the kitchen, but she was nowhere. The house eerily still and quiet.

Maybe she'd gone into town to pick something up. But wouldn't she have told him?

Unless whoever had been on the property vandalizing trees had also been *here*. Unease settled deeper in his gut, the kind he couldn't talk himself out of now. He checked his phone again. She hadn't texted him back. He tried to call, but it just went straight to voicemail.

Her truck. Was it here? If it wasn't, she'd gone somewhere of her own volition, and she was ... okay. She had to be okay. Since he was in a room that looked out over the front door, he raced to it.

No truck in the drive. She wasn't here. She'd just gone somewhere and hadn't told him. He took a careful breath.

She wasn't answering his call or text because she was driving. Probably driving home. Maybe she'd just run into town to grab an ingredient for dinner, and here he was, overreacting.

He shook his head, then moved back to his and Aly's room. He'd get washed up. Then he could help her with dinner when she got back or convince her they could just eat leftovers and celebrate in other ways.

He could always tell her about the ranch vandalism in the morning.

But before he could get to the shower, he heard the faint thud of a knock at the front door.

A knock. So not Aly. Not Cal.

More cops? More bad news? Wouldn't that be exactly what he deserved for trying to hold onto a little happy? A little positive? Bennets weren't meant for that, were they?

The knock sounded again, louder this time. Not a cop knock. Landon was all too familiar with those. He shook himself out of the fear, or at least the paralyzing part of it, and moved down the stairs and across the room to open the door.

Only to find Nate and Sam on the porch, which didn't ease his concern any.

"What are you guys doing here?"

"IT'S A LONG story," Nate said grimly. "We'll fill you in when we can. Right now, we need Cal."

"He's not here. I came back from chores and the house was empty. I don't know where anyone is. I haven't even…" He realized he had to be the only one who knew about the vandalism. He hadn't had a chance to tell anyone else. "You guys don't know."

"Don't know what?"

"They found more graffiti. Here on the ranch. Near where … well, in between the two murder scenes. The police were here, taking pictures."

Sam and Nate exchanged a look Landon couldn't read, but Landon looked out to where Aly's truck wasn't and should be. He checked his phone one more time. Maybe he should go look for her.

He blew out a breath. Everything felt wrong, but she'd left and gone somewhere she wanted to. Somewhere … well, she didn't have service because her phone was going straight to voicemail. Unless her battery had died, or she'd turned off her phone. Neither were things Aly would do. So…

"Listen, Landon," Nate said. "We're meeting Brody McCoy on the road between the ranch and the highway. If Aly's in town, we need to stop her from coming back up for a while. We've got to keep the road clear so he doesn't bolt."

Landon's sense of unease and just *wrong* didn't lighten any. "I can leave her a message, but she's not answering her phone. I'm not altogether sure where she went."

"Call Jill," Sam suggested.

Landon frowned at her. "Why?"

"Because Aly probably at least called her to tell her about the whole engagement thing. Aly would want to tell someone, and Jill's about all she's got in that department that isn't a Bennet. Maybe she mentioned to Jill what she was planning on. It'll give you an idea of where she is and if we need to stop her from coming back up for a while."

Landon didn't have time to be surprised that the suggestion was a good one. "Yeah, okay." He didn't have Jill's number in his phone, but he knew Aly had it written down in her little notebook inside.

"Stay off the road for right now," Nate told him. "Call Cal if you need someone to look for Aly in town. If he's not here, he's probably there."

Landon didn't really respond. If he needed to go to town to find Aly, he'd damn well go to town, Brody McCoy and whatever the hell Sam and Nate were up to be damned.

He jogged back to the house, made a mess looking for Aly's book of phone numbers. When he finally found it, he punched Jill's number into the landline phone.

"Hey, Aly. What's up?"

"It's not Aly," Landon said, relieved Jill answered right away. "I'm looking for Aly. I don't know where she went, and she isn't answering her phone."

Jill's pause iced his gut. "She was here. She left a while ago though, and I thought she was headed back to the ranch. She'd be there by now."

"She didn't say anything about going into town or running an errand?"

"No, Landon, and you're worrying me. She was going

back to the ranch. To make you guys dinner. She should have been back ages ago. I'll go look for her. I'll—"

"Just stay put. I'll handle it."

"Landon."

"Sam and Nate are here. We'll handle it. I'll call you when I find her, okay?" He didn't wait for Jill to agree or disagree. He hung up and ran.

SAM AND NATE stood at the top of the road next to Nate's truck after Landon ran inside going over their plan.

"I'll walk up toward the Harrington place," Sam said. She didn't know the area *that* well, but she could figure it out. She had good spatial recognition and a compass on her phone. "Then cut across in the woods, so Brody won't see or suspect someone is coming."

"It's not an easy hike, and if dark falls, you could get lost," Nate said, that scowl so deep on his face it was a wonder it wasn't permanent. "You should have backup," Nate said firmly.

"So should you," she replied. "But it's this way, where he at least thinks you're on your own, or we go together."

Nate was squinting up at the ever-lowering sun. "I don't like any of this. Something is wrong."

"So, let's put it to rights. I'm armed, Nate. You're not. You should be."

"I've got hand-to-hand combat experience, Sam."

"So you keep saying." She knew he owned a gun. Knew he was licensed to carry one. But for the most part, he refused to carry, and he wouldn't explain why.

She didn't like it on a good day. Which wasn't today, because she agreed with him, something wasn't right. More than just Janie's possible connection to the McCoy brothers. They were missing a step. She could *feel* it, but she couldn't *find* it.

So they just had to keep moving forward. Armed or not.

"Drive, Nate. If he catches you driving down, he might bolt too." *Or worse.* Sam understood they both worried that Brody was up to something much worse. Gut feelings over anything from evidence though.

But, damn, Sam had learned to listen to her gut.

Nate turned to her then, those dark eyes intense and … something. Not that usual stoic of his. Maybe this was worry?

"Sam…" He paused for a long time. A long enough time, standing this close to him, that her heart started doing that fluttery thing that couldn't be trusted. Or worried about in the middle of all this.

In the end, all he said was, "Be careful."

"You too," she said with a nod, then purposefully turned away from him. She had a lot of walking ahead of her. She refused to look back to watch Nate drive away, but she listened for his truck. Let out a long breath of relief when she heard it move away.

Down the road.

Toward possible danger.

Yeah, maybe, but she'd be there. She'd damn well be there, if she had to run up this damn road.

"Sam! Wait!"

Sam turned to find Landon jogging over to her. He had a grim expression that looked just like Nate when he got it in his head something needed to be done, his way or the highway.

Not comforting. But she waited.

"I called Jill," Landon said on his approach. "She said Aly left the cabin a while ago—at least a half hour—and she was supposed to come here. If you're going up that road, I'm going with you."

"She could have gone to town." But if Brody was expecting to meet Nate on this road, if there'd been graffiti up at the north side of the property ... it was possible Aly had run into Brody, and if he was up to any of the no good she was starting to suspect him of, that meant Aly was in the crosshairs.

"Aly told Jill she was coming right back, and she should be here by now. When I try to call her, her phone goes straight to voicemail. You know Aly. Her phone doesn't die. She's in a dead spot. I know exactly where the dead spot between Jill's and here is, and if she stopped for some reason—"

Yeah, *some* reason sounded bad. And Sam was going up there anyway, wasn't she? Besides, this was the backup Nate had wanted her to have. Now she just had to pray he'd handle himself. "Come on," she said to Landon. "Let's go."

But Landon grabbed her arm before she could start striding up the road again. "We'll take my truck. Faster."

Sam glanced where Nate had driven down the road. If Brody was meeting him on the road *before* the Bennet Ranch, driving the road beyond it shouldn't matter.

NICOLE HELM

"Okay, yeah, we'll take your truck." It might have been funny.

Landon Bennet and Sam Price going to help someone together.

But nothing felt too funny right now.

254

Chapter Twenty-Eight

The road between the Harrington Cabin and the Bennet Ranch

ALY HAD LEAPT from her truck and hurried over to the body. Janie. It was definitely Janie, though her face was ... Aly swallowed at everything that wanted to rise up.

Janie was bleeding, bruising was forming on her face and neck. Someone had hurt her, badly.

"Janie?"

The woman didn't move. Didn't answer. She was so still. But she was breathing. Aly could see the faint rise and fall of her chest. So she was breathing. Alive.

She'd been beaten up pretty bad, but she was *breathing*. With shaking hands, Aly pulled the cell phone from her pocket.

"It's going to be okay, Janie. Just hold on." She'd call an ambulance and ... Aly's heart sank when she realized she was in the dead spot between the Harrington Cabin and Bennet Ranch. She couldn't call for help from here.

For a moment, she was frozen with indecision. Leave Janie, broken and bleeding, to go make the phone call, or...

"Or what?" Aly muttered out loud to herself. There was no damn *or*. She could administer basic first aid, but she couldn't fix *this*, and she'd likely do more damage trying to drag Janie to her truck to drive her to the hospital herself.

"Janie, if you can hear me..." Aly reached out with a shaking hand, placed it against Janie's shoulder. "I'm just going to go get some cell service. Call for help. I'll only be gone for a few minutes. I promise. Just ... hold on."

She ran now to her truck. She knew just where on the old road that her cell service would kick back up. Maybe five minutes of driving, if that. She didn't bother with a seatbelt, just jammed her key and turned the engine over. She shoved the truck into drive, but when she looked up ahead of her, someone was standing in the road.

Aly froze. She recognized the man. Sandy's brother. The one who'd come for her things. What was his name? Brody? What was he doing standing on the road...

With a gun.

Pointed at her.

"Get out of the truck," he shouted. She only barely heard him over the motor and through the windows, but she saw each word enunciated clear as day.

Aly tried to breathe through the fear. Had to think. She considered just hitting the gas. Could he really get a shot off before she ran him over? If she just bulldozed forward...

But the aim of his gun changed. From the truck ... to Janie on the ground.

Aly didn't have to hear whatever he was shouting to get the gist. If she didn't get out of the truck, he was going to shoot Janie.

Aly didn't love her mother. She didn't have one positive feeling about Janie Turner. And who even knew if Janie would survive whatever had happened to her.

But Aly couldn't stand the idea she might be the reason

the woman was shot. She just … couldn't.

How many women had to be murdered on this land before it was enough?

And she could not run Brody over before he got *that* shot off. So, not knowing what else to do, Aly pushed the truck into park, turned off the engine. Still, she hesitated before getting out. He had a gun. Hers was locked up in the bed of the truck. She couldn't call anyone. And poor Janie was unconscious and bloody on the side of the road.

Was there a way to save her? Was there a way to save herself? Aly was starting to worry the answer to both was no.

Brody was stalking toward her truck. He never pointed the gun anywhere other than in Janie's direction. Aly stayed where she was, watching him, trying to come up with some plan.

If he came up to the door, she could shove it into him. Knock him over and run.

Except, unless it knocked the gun out of his hands and *she* got a hold of the gun, he'd still be able to shoot Janie.

Or her.

It didn't matter, because he stood next to the door but far enough away that even if she swung it open with all her might, it wouldn't touch him. He kept the gun trained on Janie and motioned Aly to get out of the truck with his other hand.

Aly didn't know what else to do but comply. She opened the door, then waited.

"You weren't supposed to be here," he said to her.

"Then you should probably let me drive on." She flicked a glance at Janie. They were losing daylight, so it was hard to determine if she was still breathing.

Brody shook his head. "No. No, the Bennets have to pay. Get out."

Aly swallowed. "I'm not a Bennet." It was both the truth and a lie, but Aly was ready to say whatever she needed to say to get out of this.

"Bad enoughBad enough. Get out. Now."

Not knowing what else to do, Aly carefully got out of the truck. She considered angles. Maybe she was no expert at fighting, but she was tall, and she was strong. She just had to find a way to knock the gun out of his hands.

"Did you do that to her?"

Brody flicked a quick glance at Janie, but not quick enough for Aly to make a move.

"We were supposed to work together." He shook his head. "Your mother's a liar. It was going to be a little revenge. It didn't have to end like this. She messed everything up."

Aly forced herself to breathe through the panic. If she could stay calm, they could get through this. She had to believe that. She fixed things. It was what she did. "Okay, so how can we fix it?"

"We can't." He was shaking his head. He was sweating, even though with the falling light the air was cold. "Where the hell is he?" Brody used his free hand to wipe at the sweat on his upper lip. Then he pulled a phone out of his pocket.

"There's no cell service here," Aly told him.

He looked up at her. She saw something like defeat in his eyes. "Then I guess I don't have a choice."

JILL HAD WANTED to listen to Landon. She even had … for all of one minute. But her worry got the best of her. She'd told Grandma to stay put, prayed that the woman would, and then grabbed the gun Grandma had taught her how to use.

Maybe it was an overreaction. Aly could have had some truck trouble. There could be a perfectly reasonable explanation for just not going home.

But Jill couldn't think of one. Not when Aly had been so excited. She'd wanted to make the dinner and wear the dress. She wouldn't have stopped, and if she'd gone to town, she'd respond to *someone*.

Jill walked down the road. She knew her imagination was getting the better of her. This wasn't one of her books. It wasn't nefarious.

Who would hurt Aly? The people who'd been doing murdering around these parts were both in jail. Even if that vandalism was personal and targeted, it was still petty. It didn't actually hurt anyone.

Unless whoever was doing it was ready to escalate. Unless Aly walking out on Janie in that diner had pissed Janie off. Unless…

Jill shook her head as she continued to walk, gun carefully gripped tightly in her hand. The worst-case scenario was that Aly'd had some kind of car accident. And it would have been far more sensible for Jill to take her damn truck. Not a gun. Not a quiet approach.

But her truck was still in town, getting inspected by the

police. So she kept walking, kept following that gut inclination that this was the right thing to do.

If she was a fool, so be it. If this was wrong and she was making whatever was going on with Aly worse, she'd feel guilty for the rest of her life.

Before she could decide which was worse, she spotted the telltale silver of Aly's truck. Parked in the middle of the road. From her vantage point, it didn't look like an accident, but she couldn't see the front. Maybe she'd hit an animal?

Jill almost rushed forward, but she saw Aly off to the side of the road. Well, mostly just her red hair. She was standing, so she had to be okay. She opened her mouth to call out Aly's name, but then she saw a man near Aly.

A man Jill didn't recognize, but she saw the gun in his hand. It was pointed toward the ground, not at Aly, so that was something.

Not at Aly, Jill repeated in her head, trying to focus on that over the panic that had her limbs starting to feel like jelly. She could shoot him. He didn't see her, clearly. She could shoot him.

But she wasn't a good enough shot. Especially with Aly standing so close. And he wasn't pointing his gun at Aly, so maybe … she shouldn't jump to terrible conclusions. She shouldn't…

She adjusted the gun in her hand so she actually had her finger around the trigger. She left the safety on for now. For now.

She needed to get closer. Needed a better idea of what was happening. If she got closer, maybe she could help.

Unless this is just your overactive imagination, Jill. But as she crept closer to Aly's truck, to get a better view of the full scene, she realized the man's gun wasn't pointed at the *ground*, it was pointed at a red-haired woman on the ground.

Janie? It had to be. Hurt. Janie was hurt. The man had a gun. And Aly was standing there, all alone, with no protection.

Jill blew out a careful breath, meant to calm. Well, *she* had a gun, and sort of knew how to use it. And she could use Aly's truck as a kind of … shield, if she angled herself the right way.

She had to help. She had to.

She took one step, only one, before she was jerked back.

She didn't have a chance to scream—someone's hand was over her mouth before she sucked in a breath.

LANDON DIDN'T KNOW what kind of joke the universe was playing on him to have Sam Price sitting in the passenger seat of his truck, but these days it just about figured.

He wanted to speed forward, but Sam kept telling him to slow down, and something about the focused confident way she spoke, moved, acted, had him doing just that.

Listening to Sam Price against all desire to do the opposite. Life was a hell of a ride.

"Stop."

Landon hit the brake. "What is it?"

"You see that?" she asked, pointing at the trees. They were shrouded in the shadow of approaching night. He didn't see anything. At first. But he stared long enough, saw a strange glint of silver, then started to make out the shape of a truck.

"It's a truck. A black truck. I don't recognize it from here, but it might be…"

"It's Denver McCoy's truck. I'm almost dead sure of it," Sam said.

She was halfway out of the truck before those words penetrated.

"McCoy. One of Sandy's brothers?" Landon shoved the truck into park and killed the engine.

He jumped out of the truck and jogged after Sam who was walking right into the woods and toward the truck.

"You got a gun?" she asked him, without looking back at him.

"No." But now he wished he'd brought one. With all the murder business, he'd gotten in the habit of keeping all the guns locked up, which didn't make for ease of grabbing unless he was home.

"Sam, what the hell is going on?" Landon demanded.

"Look, I think there's a connection between the McCoys and Janie. I don't know what or why, and Nate thinks I'm reaching, I know he does, but … the truck, the timing of his phone call."

"Whose phone call?"

Sam shook her head. She wasn't really talking to him. She was talking through whatever her and Nate had been investigating. "You don't have a gun, so I'm going to need you to just stay behind me, follow me."

"Sam." He didn't know what he wanted to say.

Only that this was fucked up.

"Listen, Landon. We want the same thing, right?" She looked up at him. Eyes direct and focused. There wasn't disgust or hate or even suspicion in her gaze—the things he'd become accustomed to when he had to interact with Sam.

"We don't want anyone to get hurt," she said calmly, reasonably. "I've got the weapon. You stay behind me. Do what I say. You can do that no matter how much you hate me, right?"

He couldn't say that hate was the predominate feeling inside of him right now. He was too worried about Aly to give even a little shit about who helped him make sure she was safe.

"We want the same thing," he repeated.

He didn't trust Sam Price. Hadn't for fifteen years.

But she'd been right about his father all along. And she was a private investigator. She knew what she was doing.

So he had to trust her. Follow her.

She took maybe ten steps down the hill, away from the Harrington cabin and where Aly *had* to be. He didn't want to go the wrong way. He didn't like this at all. "Sam…"

"Brody wanted to meet Nate. Alone. On the road between the ranch and the highway. Now his truck is hiding in these trees?" She shook her head. "Nate was right. None of this adds up. We have to go find Nate."

"I thought you said this was Denver's truck."

"It's complicated. That's the problem. It's too damn complicated. Wrapped up in Janie Turner *and* Sandy's murder, but I don't know *how*." Sam kept walking down— she would end up on the road between the highway and the ranch. But Aly, as far as he knew, had never passed the ranch on her way down from the Harrington's.

He looked up in the direction he *wanted* to go. "Sam, we'll split up. I'll go up. Find Aly. You deal with this."

"You don't have a gun."

"If you think Denver or Brody or whoever the hell is down there, lying in wait for Nate, you take the gun. I'll handle whatever stopped Aly."

Before Sam could respond, a gunshot went off. Somewhere ... up. Landon was sure it was up the mountain. And since Sam turned in the same direction, he didn't stop and think.

He just ran.

Chapter Twenty-Nine

Nate's Rental Cabin

CAL SAT ON the porch of Nate's rental cabin, wondering where the hell everyone was. Nate wasn't returning texts or calls, and no one had been at Honor's Edge when he'd driven over there. He wasn't about to bother Landon and Aly, but at this rate, he'd have to go into town and get a hotel room for the night.

But for now, he sat on the porch, brooding, as night started to fall. Until he heard the sound of a truck engine getting closer. Cal stood, squinting out at the road. It took a minute to realize the truck wasn't coming from the entrance to the rental properties, but from the opposite direction.

Must be someone staying at one of the other rentals headed into town. Cal sat back down assuming it'd pass him by on its way, but instead the cherry red truck turned into the little lane that would bring it up to Nate's.

A young man hopped out. No more than a kid. Early twenties at most. Cal didn't recognize him, though he catalogued a description, because something about this had unease settling in his gut.

The kid walked right up to him. "I need your help."

Cal had enough experience with people who struggled with addiction to note the signs all over this kid. The wild eyes, occasional twitch or jerk, an edginess in his movements, in the way he spoke.

"Do I know you?"

"You're that lawyer, right? The Bennet who's a lawyer."

Cal considered lying, but in the end, he didn't think that'd get him anywhere. "Yeah."

"I need your help," the kid repeated.

There was a desperation to him, but … Cal had helped a lot of people in his time. He understood the different layers of fear, desperation, and need. He understood, to an extent, the effect drugs had on all those things.

He also had a lot of experience with criminals. The lies they told other people, and themselves, to achieve whatever it was they thought was necessary. Whatever might get them the next high.

If he was asked to lay bets, he'd lay his bet on this kid leaning far more criminal, but that didn't mean he didn't need help.

"I'm going to need a lot more information than that before I do anything. What's your name, kid?"

"You have to come with me. You have to."

"That's not an answer. Why'd you come to where my brother is staying if you were looking for me?"

The kid stilled, blinked. He offered no explanation, as if caught in a lie.

"Add to that, why'd you come from the opposite direction of the highway? Like you were somewhere on this ranch already?"

The kid blinked some more, looked over his shoulder at the direction he'd come from, then beyond. Like he was looking up at the mountains.

A mountain where the Bennet Ranch was tucked into—on the other side.

"What do you really want, kid?" Cal asked.

The kid opened his mouth, but didn't offer anything. Before he could, Cal's cell rang. He glanced at the screen. Nate. "Let me take this." He swiped the screen to answer the call, held it up to his ear. "Nate?"

"Hey, I just got your messages. I've got maybe five minutes I can swing by and let you in if you're still in the area, but then I've got to go."

"I'm still here. Got a visitor, in fact. Some kid driving a red Chev—"

The kid shook his head. He lifted the edge of his shirt, showing off that he was armed. A clear threat. Cal didn't say anything else.

"A red Chevy Silverado?" Nate demanded in his ear.

Cal watched the guy's hand curl around the butt of the weapon. He wanted to say yes, but he was afraid that'd give this guy a reason to shoot. "Never mind about all that. I'll handle it. You go on and do what you need to do."

"It's Denver McCoy. I'm on my way."

Cal kept his eyes steady and alert on the guy. Could Denver hear Nate's side of the conversation? Cal hoped not. "See you later," Cal said. He ended the call, smiled genially at Denver. McCoy. One of Sandy's siblings.

And clearly a problem if Nate's tone of voice was anything to go by. Add the weapon, the clear drug usage, yeah, this was a problem.

"He's coming, isn't he?" Denver asked, that hand still

dangerously on the gun.

"Now, Denver," Cal said, calmly and making sure to maintain eye contact. "Why don't we talk this through."

"He's not supposed to come here. He's supposed to…" Denver shook his head. His grip on the gun tightened. His lips twisted into a sneer. "It's time for the Bennets to have a little bit of a reckoning, don't you think?"

"This may come as a shock, but I find myself disagreeing. What with being a Bennet and all." Cal didn't waste any more time.

He knew he didn't have more than seconds to tackle the kid before he got that gun out of his pants.

So he just leapt. Crashed right into the kid. Denver was tall, but gangly. Cal had figured it'd be easy enough to take him. Now he realized the mental load of the past few months had affected him physically. The weight had fallen off of him, and he didn't have quite the bulk and strength he'd once been used to. This kid was young, wiry, and aided by the high of whatever drugs he was on.

They both struggled against each other. Cal managed to get a hand on the gun's barrel, but Denver still had a grasp on the handle. They jerked, back and forth, neither quite capable of shaking the other.

Dimly, somewhere in the background, Cal heard an engine approach, but he couldn't concentrate on that. Not when his grip on the gun was slipping.

He was so focused on the gun, he missed the elbow— which crashed right into his nose. Stars exploded behind his eyes, and he fell back, losing his grip entirely.

He scrambled back, bracing for impact of a bullet and

hoping like hell he could somehow get out of this. But once he could see clearly, he saw Denver's attention had moved.

To a dark truck, and the man getting out of it. *Nate.*

Denver shot at Nate, but he must have missed because Nate kept coming. Cal watched in a kind of horrified fascination as Nate didn't seem to fear *bullets* coming toward him, like he thought he was Superman or something.

But Cal knew well enough Nate wasn't invincible even if he thought he might be. So before Denver could get another shot off at Nate, Cal dove at the kid's legs. The gun went off again, but Cal couldn't focus on where the bullet might have landed. He crawled on top of Denver, locking the guy's legs with his own. Denver struggled, but then Nate was there.

With an ease that must have shocked both Cal *and* Denver, Nate had pushed Cal out of the way, jerked Denver's arms behind his back, and tied them tightly with some kind of rope. He did the same to Denver's ankles, while Cal sat on the ground and watched, his brain scrambling to make sense of *anything* that had just happened.

Once done, Nate turned to Cal, helped him to his feet. "I already called the cops. They should be on their way."

"Well, shit, they're not fans of me right now."

"It doesn't matter. We've got to go." Nate jogged to the cabin door, shoved his way inside.

Cal scrambled after him. "Go? You can't leave the scene of a crime. That's a bad look, and I've already got a few of those."

Nate crossed the living room and disappeared into his room without saying a word. When he returned, he had a gun. But that was not why Cal came up short.

Nate's shirt was torn at his shoulder, and blood bloomed in its spot. But he didn't say a word. Acted like he didn't notice.

"Shit, Nate. You've been shot."

"It's just a scratch," Nate said, in a determined way that nearly convinced Cal he was right. Especially when Nate grabbed him by the arm and started pulling. "We need to get up to the ranch. Find Landon and Sam. And Brody fucking McCoy."

Chapter Thirty

The road between the Harrington Cabin and Bennet Ranch

ALY NERVOUSLY GLANCED at the sky, and the ever-darkening shadows around them. Then Janie. Was she still breathing? It was getting harder to tell.

She stood in the exact same spot, while Brody paced. He kept the gun on Janie for the most part but occasionally raised it to point it at Aly herself. He was sweating, mumbling. Sometimes he'd pull out his phone and check it, then mumble and pace some more.

Aly stood where she was, tracking his every movement, waiting for some kind of ... moment. A weakness. A distraction. Brody was bigger and stronger than her, but he didn't seem ... right.

Maybe ... maybe she could talk him out of whatever this was. Keep him talking, pacing, and someone would ... someone would have to come help. Landon would be looking for her, at the very least.

And what if he drove up and Brody used his gun and...

No, she had to *do* something. Not just wait. She couldn't risk anyone she loved coming to save her.

"It wasn't supposed to be like this," Brody was muttering.

"How was it supposed to be?" Aly asked, trying for gentle, placating.

She risked taking a tiny step toward him.

"Not murder," Brody said, glancing at Janie. "Not ...It was just going to be some trouble. She was going to help us cause some trouble for the lawyer, for *you*. She was on our side, then she flips?" His eyes went hard, and he held the gun so still, pointed in Janie's direction, Aly thought for sure he'd pull the trigger.

But after a moment, he stopped himself. "She just kept talking and I had to shut her up, and I hadn't had a hit in a while and she's yapping about more money? Like I've got that. I had to shut her up. Once I did ... Denver ... it was his idea. Make it look like the Bennets had hurt her. That would be the real punishment."

"Denver. That's one of your brothers, right?" Had Sam or Nate mentioned him? Aly couldn't remember for sure.

"Yeah, my brother. My *brother*." Brody was staring at her now, some of that wild desperation sharpening into a direct focus on *her*. "We knew it was wrong. It wasn't just fucking Ben Bennet who killed her. You all are responsible. Your fucking lawyer. You in that big house, looking down your nose at Sandy."

Aly's heart was beating overtime, but she tried to remain calm. Calm to his anger and his fury. If she was calm, she could think her way out of this. *Please God.* "I didn't kill Sandy. Ben didn't kill Sandy."

"You hated her." He sneered at her, and Aly's pulse pounded so hard in her neck it actually *hurt*. "You don't think she told me? You all hated her."

Aly could deny it, but she didn't think lying was going to

get her anywhere with a gun pointed at her. She *had* kind of hated Sandy, but she'd tried to be kind. Or at least ambivalent.

She hated to think ill of the dead, the unfairly murdered, but Sandy had been someone who would have complained to her brothers that everyone hated her, that everyone was mean to her, even if Aly had tried to be her best friend.

"Maybe that other guy *killed* her, but it's still your fault. The Bennets' fault. She'd be alive if not for the fucking Bennets." With a shaky hand, he lifted the gun and pointed it at her. "And you."

Aly's legs felt like jelly, and tears filled her eyes, but she worked so hard to keep her voice calm. "So you want to be like us and kill me?"

Brody shook his head. "It was just going to be messes y'all had to clean up. Spend some of that money that Sandy should be alive to spend. It was just going to be … but then she came along." He whirled the gun towards Janie.

He was losing it, Aly could tell. Whatever tether he'd had on control, it was fraying completely.

"She lied."

"How?" Aly demanded, wanting both answers and Brody to keep his attention on her.

"She was going to get money out of you. Out of that asshole Bennet. If we kept you guys distracted with the vandalism, she was going to bleed you dry and share the profits. Then she flips the script. She wants money from *us*? Bitch."

For a minute, Aly was stunned into silence. It wasn't like she'd expected her mother to have been involved with the

McCoys for any kind of good ... but just for money? And not just from her, but from Landon? It was so ... gross. So pointless.

But Brody had a gun, and Aly had to get out of this. She couldn't think about her hurt. She had to think about living. "So what happened? Why'd you hurt her?"

"She lied." Brody shook his head. "She wasn't supposed to be in that diner while we were painting your friend's car. She was supposed to leave you hanging. She wasn't supposed to throw the blame to us. She wasn't supposed to demand money from *me*." The gun was pointed at Janie again, shaky and volatile. "She lied and lied and lied." He was crying now. He even wiped his running nose with the back of his sleeve. "She ruined everything. Everything."

He was going to shoot Janie. And Aly didn't think he'd stop there.

Aly didn't want to die. But she couldn't, just couldn't, let Janie die either. And she couldn't wait any longer. She had to act.

So she raced forward.

JILL FOUGHT AGAINST the hold on her mouth, but it was more panic than skill. Her assailant made a kind of noise, an odd humming grunt that reminded Jill of ... she stopped fighting the hold, and the hand on her mouth slid away.

She whirled around. "Grandma?"

Grandma held a finger up to her lips. She took the gun from Jill's hand. Then stepped in front of Jill.

Shock and confusion had Jill forgetting they needed to be quiet. "What are you *doing*?"

Grandma held the free hand to her mouth again, the silent *shh*. Then she moved closer and closer to the truck bed. Jill followed. It gave them a better angle to see the man and Aly. A better angle, Jill realized, to shoot the man.

Which was clearly Grandma's intention. Glenda lifted the gun, rested it on the wall of the bed of the truck, and aimed.

Jill's heart leapt to her throat. She couldn't get a sound out. Was Grandma just going to shoot him?

Before Grandma did anything, Aly moved. She rushed forward and crashed right into the man just as his gun went off.

And then Grandma's gun went off too.

LANDON'S LUNGS WERE burning, but he didn't stop. Sam was somewhere behind him. She was fast, but on much longer legs, he was a lot faster.

He should have taken her gun. But there was no room in his body for feelings of regret. Another gunshot had followed the first, and terror was the only thing he felt.

He ran toward the noise—someone groaning, the frantic murmuring of voices. He saw people moving and burst onto a scene of chaos—three people laying on the ground, two people swarming around them.

Chaos. Chaos. And in the midst of all that chaos, all Landon could care about was Aly.

He saw red hair, matted and dirty, crumpled on the ground. His heart positively stopped before his brain engaged enough to realize and accept it was Janie.

But Aly was also on the ground. Except she was moving. She pushed to her knees, swiping her hair out of her face. He rushed over to her. Pulled her into his arms, then thought better of it, pulling her back. What if she was hurt? What if—

"I'm okay. I'm okay." She held onto him, sturdy and strong.

She was shaking, but when he got her to her feet, she stayed there. And they just held onto each other.

"It was Brody McCoy," she said breathlessly. "He hurt Janie. I just stumbled upon … Janie and it … I don't know. We need police. An ambulance."

Landon glanced over at Janie. Sam was crouched next to her, clearly trying to find a pulse.

She met his gaze. "Aly's right. We need an ambulance. Quickly."

"I'll go," Jill said. "I'll run down the road until I get service."

No one argued with her, and she took off. Glenda crouched next to Sam, gently moving some of Janie's hair out of Janie's bruised face. Landon just held onto Aly's shaking body.

"We'll just stay put until the police get here," he managed to say. "That's best, right?" He looked at Sam for confirmation.

She nodded, then frowned. Her gaze moved from him to the other body on the ground. Brody McCoy.

Who was moving. Reaching behind him.

He had another gun.

Landon pushed Aly behind him, and Sam shouted, lunging toward Brody, but she was too far away. And that gun was pointed right at him.

It was too late.

But someone wasn't.

Footsteps thundered from behind Landon—the shot went off, aimed right at him blocking Aly—but though he braced for some kind of impact, using his body to shield Aly's, nothing happened.

Except the footsteps ending in a large thud. Right there at Landon's feet.

Cal.

On an oath, and Aly's shriek of distress, they both fell to their knees next to Cal. A nasty bloom of red was evident on his shirt.

A frozen kind of terror stole through Landon. Cal had … appeared from nowhere to take the bullet for him.

"Fuck," Cal gritted out, writhing there on the ground.

What the hell did he do? Landon looked up and saw Nate. Nate's expression was grim, but he'd wrestled Brody onto his stomach. Brody was moaning now, writhing in pain, Landon assumed. The previous gunshots had hit Brody.

Sam rushed over to Nate, and they switched places, so Nate came and knelt next to Cal. Who was doing some moaning and writhing of his own. Landon did the only thing he could think to do. He grabbed Cal's hand and held on.

"Jill's calling an ambulance," Aly said. "It'll be okay. It'll be okay."

He wasn't sure who she was talking to. Her babbling was just a strange distant buzzing in his ears.

Glenda handed Nate a scarf. And Nate seemed to know what he was doing. Landon was frozen. The only thing he could seem to do was hold tight to Cal's hand, while Nate pushed the scarf to the wound.

"Guess you're lucky I've got some battlefield first aid experience since you wanted to play hero," Nate said, moving with quick efficient movements.

"Lucky," Cal choked out still writhing even as Nate and Landon tried to hold him still. "Some luck."

Sirens sounded in the distance while Nate continued to put pressure on and wrap the wound with whatever Glenda scrounged up and handed him.

"See?" Aly said, sounding hysterical. "That was fast. It'll be all right."

"It better fucking be," Cal gritted out.

"See, he's just fine," Nate said, trying to smile at Aly, but Landon saw the cracks in it.

And the worry when Nate glanced back at the road, as if willing the ambulance to hurry.

Chapter Thirty-One

Marietta Regional Hospital

NATE RODE IN the ambulance with Cal. Janie and Brody
got their own ambulance and a police escort. It left
Sam with Jill, Glenda, Landon, and Aly.

It made sense. Nate was family to Cal. Aly was beside
herself and needed Landon, not to ride in an ambulance with
a mother who'd … done all that.

Sam was, as always, the odd man out, but it gave her a
role at least. Tell everyone what to do. Organize things.

They'd had to answer questions from the police before
being given clearance to drive to the hospital, where they'd
no doubt have to answer more questions.

Sam went through it all in a rote kind of fog. Landon
and Jill fussed over Aly. Glenda was her usual silent self,
though she signed to Jill on occasion—clearly giving her
instructions to do something for Aly or Landon.

Once everyone was situated in the waiting room of the
hospital, Sam slipped out of the room. It wasn't her place to
sit around and wait to hear how Cal was. Or Janie Turner or
even Brody McCoy. Maybe this had been her case, but boy
had she fucked that up.

Sam had a lot of hope and belief Cal would come out all
right. He was a healthy enough seeming guy. He'd been

swearing up a storm into the ambulance. Nate had that battlefield first aid experience—which gave her a full body chill that Nate might have had to have done that before. Lots of times before, even.

Point was, Cal would be okay.

She wanted to believe it, so she told herself it was the truth as she wound her way through the hospital.

Denver McCoy was apparently fine enough to be taken into the jail—despite whatever punches Nate had landed at his place before Cal and Nate had come rushing in to be saviors. Brody McCoy's injuries weren't serious. Two gunshot grazes and a knock on the head from a rock when Aly had crashed into him.

Janie ... Sam wasn't so sure Janie would pull through. She'd been beat up pretty badly, and the sheer length of time she'd been unconscious wasn't good.

Sam's heart twisted. Not for Janie Turner, but for Aly. Maybe there was no relationship there, but if Janie didn't pull through, Sam knew that it would always leave a question mark on Aly's life. A what-if.

She had a lot of what-ifs of her own, though she'd loved her mother. Maybe that made a difference.

Sam stepped out of the main doors of the hospital and into the cold night. She didn't belong here, but she didn't know if the police would have a few more questions for her, so she didn't feel right about leaving. It was freezing out here in the middle of the night, but it felt good. Grounding. Chilled some of that fog away.

There was a bench, off the main pathway a little bit, almost hidden completely in shadow. She moved for it, lowered herself onto the cold metal.

Without anything to do, she had to come to grips with the whole mess of a day.

She'd failed.

She closed her eyes, let her head fall back. She'd told Nate that Denver McCoy was harmless—she'd believed he was. Maybe she'd had suspicions about Brody, but she'd been so focused on Jim Gary, she had let the whole McCoy thing slide.

What if she'd stayed focused on them instead? What if she'd trusted Nate's instincts about Denver? What if … what if…

So many fucking what-ifs. And the end result was a terrible woman hurt. A good man shot. A handful of other injuries. Pain and suffering because she couldn't solve a simple vandalism case in time.

Just like her father's case all over again. Would she ever succeed when it mattered?

"What are you doing out here?"

Sam opened her eyes to find Nate standing in front of her. He hadn't cleaned up any. There were streaks of blood across his clothes. His hair was a mess.

She didn't bother to answer his question. "Any word on Cal?"

"Getting stitched up. Didn't hit any major organs. He'll be okay. Recovery will be a bit of a bitch, but he'll be okay."

Sam wondered if he knew he'd said it twice, like he was reassuring himself. "Good. Good."

Silence settled around them. After a few moments when Sam didn't know what to say, Nate settled into the bench next to her. Close enough she could feel warmth on her side instead of the cold air.

"Sam, why are you out here alone?" he asked, in a low voice that belied a gentleness she just ... couldn't possibly deserve.

"I'd head home, but I didn't know if the police would have a few more questions for me."

"Sam, you know what I mean. Why aren't you inside?"

She shook her head, knowing she should maintain her silence. Knowing she should keep her failure to herself, but exhaustion or *something* meant it all just kind of ... fell out.

"I failed. I said Denver McCoy was harmless and he was the fucking ringleader."

Nate didn't say anything at first, because she was right. What the hell was she doing with her life aside from failing? Maybe she should just hand Honor's Edge over to him. She could move to ... somewhere. Do ... something.

"The ringleader of some petty vandalism. Brody's the one who hurt Janie. And Janie's the one who made the plan about money. She upped the stakes."

"And Denver's bright idea was to frame you guys for it."

"Okay, they both suck."

She almost, *almost* laughed. And she so desperately wanted to lean on that sturdy shoulder of his, but she'd ... failed. "I should have..." She swallowed. It felt like her father all over again.

When it mattered, when people were in danger, she couldn't solve the case in time.

"Sam, you made the connection," Nate said, in that steady, stoic way of his. "The trucks? I didn't make that connection, and if we hadn't had that conversation, who knows what Denver would have done with Cal out at my place. Cal and I even made it to the mountain because of the connection *you* made."

She looked at him, wanting to believe that some little connection she'd considered might have helped. But people were still hurt.

"So, still my fault Cal got shot. Because if you hadn't made it to the mountain—"

"What? Landon's shot instead?"

Sam blinked. She didn't quite know how to argue that. Cal had been shot jumping in front of Landon or Aly or wherever the bullet would have landed instead. Still...

Nate sighed. "There's no fault here. There's just a shitshow to get through. And we did."

She glanced at him. The blood on his shirt. The exhaustion written into his face. Her heart twisted again. All for him. "It's not war, Nate."

"Isn't it?" he muttered, shaking his head as he looked out into the dark of night. He blew out a breath and looked down at his hands. He must have realized he hadn't cleaned up, because he turned them, palms up, where there were smudges of dried blood.

She wanted to do something, fix something, help him in some way. "Nate..." She reached out, put her arm around his shoulders, though it was an awkward angle for her. She gave him a little squeeze.

It wasn't war. It was their lives. It was a good reminder, for her—but only if she could extend it to him. The man who'd *actually* seen war, after dealing with his mother being murdered, his father beating him up. War and now his brother shot in front of him.

She wrapped her other arm around him in a hug, because she just didn't know what else to do. He made an odd hissing noise, almost like he was in pain, but then his arms came around her, like maybe it hadn't been the wrong move. To offer comfort, a hug.

A *friendly* hug, here in the cold dark. She felt some of the tension in him ease. Something warm and satisfying swept through her. Maybe it wasn't all failure.

After a few moments, Nate pulled back. Except he didn't quite let her go. So they still had their arms touching, but he was looking down at her, studying her, with one of those inscrutable expressions.

She stared right back, wanting … a million conflicting things she couldn't detangle or make sense of.

"There you guys are."

Neither Sam nor Nate looked in the direction of Landon's voice at first, but Sam could hear his footsteps. Getting closer. Eventually she had to tear her gaze away from Nate and look up at Landon.

"The doctor just gave us the go ahead to see Cal. One at a time. Aly's in there now. You—shit, Nate, you need to get that stitched up."

"What stitched up?" Sam demanded.

In the pale light of the parking lot lights, she couldn't really make out anything, so she pulled out her phone and turned on the flashlight app. When the beam landed on his opposite shoulder, she made an involuntary sound of distress.

"What the hell happened?"

Nate scowled at Landon like this was his fault, but Sam couldn't look away from the bloody line on his shoulder, the tear in his shirt.

"Denver got a few shots off back at my place before we made it out to the ranch. It's nothing."

"You were *shot*?" she all but screeched.

He patted her leg companionably. "It's fine. Nothing. Trust me, I know nothing."

"Okay, well maybe we at least get that nothing cleaned up," Landon said firmly. "Come on, soldier." He jerked Nate up off the bench by the good arm.

"It's fi—"

"It could get infected. It could ... you absolutely need to have it looked at. What were you thinking?" Sam demanded, standing and fisting her arms on her hips.

Nate sighed irritably. "Fine. I'll have it looked at," he grumbled, which only *kind* of eased some of the fluttering worry inside of her.

Landon's gaze moved to Sam. She couldn't read his expression. He had a better stoic face than even Nate did.

"Could you do me a favor, Sam? If you're not busy." If he considered asking her for a favor momentous, like she did, he didn't show it. "Maybe you could go pick us up some food. Real food. Everybody should eat. Something decent. Not hospital stuff."

"Sure, yeah." She could be helpful. She wanted to be helpful. "If you make sure he gets that looked at, I'll be back as soon as I can." Most things close by would be closed at this hour, but she'd figure something out.

"I will," Landon agreed.

Since Sam itched to march Nate inside to a doctor herself, she turned to head toward her truck, but Landon called her name. She turned back.

"Pick up enough for yourself. I know Aly'd appreciate her friends hanging around."

Sam had been through the emotional gamut today, but that one about sent her over the edge. "Sure," she said, then turned on a heel.

Because if she let that sink in—the idea there were friends to be had here—she might come totally unglued, and hugging Nate had been bad enough.

She hurried into the parking lot, blinking back tears, then nearly ran into someone.

"Sam." A strong hand steadied her when she tried to shuffle step out of the way of running into the body.

She glanced back to find Jake there. His badge was hanging around his neck. She found herself staring at the shiny surface reflecting the parking lot lights. He was here to ask questions. To get to the bottom of things.

Things she hadn't been able to get to the bottom of in time ... but maybe she hadn't failed completely. Maybe Nate wasn't just being nice. Maybe...

She shook her head. She had to focus on the here and now. She managed a paltry smile up at Jake. "Detective. You, uh, still working?"

"Pretty much done. Just have a few more questions to tie up my report."

"For who?"

Jake studied her in silence for a few seconds, slowly released her arm and took a slight step away from her. "I bet you could use a drink after your day," he said, ignoring the question. Which was probably fair, since his investigation was not exactly her business.

A drink. Sam laughed in spite of herself. God knew what she could use.

"I'll buy you one. Down at the Wolf Den. Say an hour?"

She could. Bring back the food, then bow out. Maybe she even should. But Landon had called her one of Aly's friends, and she wasn't. She *wasn't*, but...

"I, uh, promised..." Sam trailed off.

Nate had been shot too. Landon had said Aly needed friends, as if she was one. Landon Bennet, of all people.

She blinked at the tears in her eyes. "I promised my friends I'd pick them up some food. Stick around for moral support."

"Some other time then?"

"Yeah, maybe."

CAL WAS GOING to be okay. Aly repeated this in her head, over and over again, while she switched places with Landon. Then Nate would get a turn. Everyone would talk to him and know that he was going to be okay.

She needed to go find Jill and Glenda and tell them they could go home. They should be home, resting. She and Landon would stay in the hospital, even if Cal had told her to go home.

She wouldn't. She just ... wouldn't. Landon would have

to, but Cal deserved...

If she thought about what he deserved, she'd relive him jumping in front of that bullet again, and then she'd just ... fall fully apart. And she couldn't. Not yet.

Outside Cal's room, she'd expected to find Nate. Instead, there was a face she vaguely recognized, though it took the badge hanging around his neck to put the puzzle pieces together.

"Detective."

"Ms. Cartwright. Do you have a few minutes?"

She wanted to tell him no, but she also wanted this over with.

"I told the police everything Brody McCoy said to me before they let me come to the hospital."

"Yes, and I appreciate it. It seems Denver McCoy's story mostly matches up, and we'll be collecting evidence to determine charges against both of them. And..."

"And my mother."

"She's a victim of a violent crime, but..." The detective hesitated, then pulled out a phone.

He held the screen toward her. On the screen was a picture of a bunch of items lined up on a white table. Aly blinked at the picture. Landon's keychain. A credit card. A little angel figurine from her apartment.

Some coins that reminded her of the coin collection Benjamin Bennet had amassed. "I don't understand."

"These items were found in Janie Turner's motel room. I was wondering if you recognized any of them."

Janie's ... motel room. But how? Aly looked at the picture even closer. That was definitely the crystal angel Mrs.

Bennet had given her years ago, Landon's keychain, and one of Benjamin Bennet's watches that Landon hadn't known what to do with after his father's arrest, so it had just sat in a drawer in Benjamin Bennet's unused room. The credit card...

Then she remembered Cal saying he couldn't find his.

Aly sighed, rubbing at her chest, where a pain and pressure duked it out for prominence. "Those all belong to me or Landon or Cal."

The detective nodded. "I assumed as much. I won't take up more of your time tonight then, and building the case against the McCoy brothers is going to take precedence, but this will be a secondary part of the case. I'll have to keep these things for the time being, and we'll eventually want some documentation of ownership and a few other things, but to get the ball rolling, I needed to know for sure."

"We'll ... help wherever we can, detective."

"I know it's delicate, Ms. Cartwright."

Aly shook her head. "Not as delicate as it should be." She tried to smile at him.

Failed. Then she excused herself. Landon had wanted her to stay put, wait for him to be done with Cal, but...

Aly needed to do something. She found a nurse, asked for Janie's room. Claimed distraught daughter status. She did the same thing with the police officer stationed outside Janie's room.

Once finally inside, Aly didn't know quite why she'd wanted to do this. Janie lay in the hospital bed, bruised and bandaged up, machines connected to her and beeping at various intervals.

But Janie opened her eyes, the same shade of blue as Aly's own.

Aly felt nothing. Except sad and wrung out. Maybe there was some pity, but it was faint. Maybe it'd bloom over time. Or maybe, once Janie healed up, it'd go away completely and all that would be left would be anger and betrayal.

Janie looked right back at her through puffy, swollen eyes.

Her cut lip curved slightly. "You saved me, my girl. How can I make it up to you?"

Maybe it made her a bad person, but this woman had actively tried to hurt her. Had stolen from her. Sure, Janie had paid a price for it, but that didn't mean Aly had to forgive her.

"There is something," Aly said.

And even as she thought it, she realized it lifted a weight that had been on her shoulders even long before Janie had made an appearance.

"I don't want you in my life. I will cooperate with law enforcement to make sure you do jail time. Whenever you get out, I never, ever want to see you again."

"What?"

"You stole from me. You plotted to steal from me and Landon. You worked with someone who *shot* a man I love like a brother. I don't want you in my life. Ever."

Janie's eyes went flinty.

She tried to sit up in her bed, but it clearly hurt her because she winced. "You have so much, and you're sending me away with nothing?"

Aly wanted to cry, but she wouldn't. Not in front of

Janie. "I would have given you so much. The chances I would have given you. But this? This is unforgivable."

"Maybe you're just selfish."

"Maybe," Aly agreed. "Maybe the apple doesn't fall far from the tree. This is my goodbye, Janie. Leave me and mine alone. For good." And with that, ignoring Janie's blustering replies, Aly turned on a heel and left the hospital room.

To find Landon waiting right outside the door for her. He didn't say anything, just pulled her into a hug. She leaned into him, letting him hug her close.

"Sam brought some food," he said, rubbing a hand up and down her back. "Let's go sit down and eat, huh?"

Aly managed a nod. But she couldn't quite let it go yet. "I don't ever want to see her again."

"Then you won't."

Aly let out a slow breath. She wasn't sure she believed that, but she knew Landon would do everything in his power to make sure of it.

And that was enough.

Chapter Thirty-Two

The Bennet Ranch

C AL DIDN'T LIKE the way the painkillers made him feel, but he figured that was better than being helped up the ranch stairs in all the pain he was in without them.

Being shot was no joke. He didn't relish it. Particularly when both his brothers were the ones helping him walk. Up the stairs, through the house, back to Aly's old apartment that was all set up to facilitate his recovery, which was apparently going to take at least a few weeks, much to his dismay.

While Nate and Landon helped him into the bed, Aly fluttered around, opening curtains, straightening different things, and chattering on about the welcome home meal she'd made.

Home.

Was he home?

Aly had certainly worked hard to make her old apartment off the back of the house feel less like some girly refuge and more like every other room in the house. She'd brought his bag from Nate's, unpacked it like he was going to stay.

Stay. Home. Give up everything he'd worked for. To do what?

He didn't know, but the time in the hospital had given

him a lot of time to think. The idea of returning to Austin was no longer a refuge he'd once sought. It didn't feel like home or a safe place.

It felt like cowardice. And therapy hadn't really helped at all, but maybe because at the end of the day, he had to deal with the source of everything. The source wasn't in Texas.

Landon and Nate left to deal with some ranch chores. Cal expected Aly to bustle off too. She no doubt was behind on a million things because of him and everything that had happened.

Instead, she settled onto the very edge of his bed. "We're going to take good care of you. And I won't hear a word about you going back to Texas until you're one hundred percent better."

He studied her. She was a little pale yet, but he could tell that the course of the case was easing some of her worries. Janie Turner was still in the hospital, and likely would be for a while yet. No doubt she wouldn't relax fully until Janie was behind bars.

"Maybe I just won't go back."

She paused, met his gaze. "We told you a while back you'd be welcome."

"And now you mean it?"

Aly smiled ruefully. "*I* always meant it. But now I owe you too."

"No, you don't." Cal didn't know why none of them seemed to get it. "He's my brother, Aly."

Her eyes filled at that, but she didn't let them fall. "I'm glad you're all starting to realize that."

He wanted to roll his eyes. Offer a sarcastic quip. Instead, he closed his eyes, settled into the pillow because he was fucking *exhausted* and fuzzy from the painkillers. "I'm glad too."

NATE STUCK AROUND for a few hours to help Landon with some ranch chores. He needed to get to Honor's Edge, but Landon and Aly were behind, even though he'd done his level best to handle most of what needed to be handled at the hospital for Cal.

Cal, who was recovering. Sometimes he had to mentally remind himself of that. That it wasn't *war* as Sam had reminded him. It was just … a shitty hand dealt in life. That they were all going to recover from.

"I've got to get to work," Nate told Landon as they walked back to the house around noon. "Sam's got her dad's sentencing in about an hour, so I'm on Honor's Edge duty."

"Invite Sam to dinner," Landon told Nate. "I'm sure she could use some company after a day like that."

"Yes," Aly agreed. "I'm making enough food to feed all of Marietta. And I made a cake for Cal being home. Tell her we won't take no for an answer."

Nate looked at Aly and Landon. Two people who had spent the last fifteen years at odds with Sam. They'd all hated each other and now were trying to find some … common ground.

Nate had figured putting Dad in jail was enough, uncovering the truth was enough, but all this stuff on the other side of that was hard. Painful. Fucking terrible.

But it was growth. It was healing. And Nate found he wanted that for all of them.

"I will. She'll come." With that assurance, he left the Bennet Ranch and headed into town. He was a little worried he'd miss Sam, but her car was still in the little back lot when he parked his truck.

He entered through the back, found her in the main room. She was dressed for court—black dress pants, high heels, and some kind of blouse that looked a lot more feminine than what she usually wore.

She stopped her pacing when he stepped into the room. "Oh. Hi. Hey." Nerves radiated off her, but her gaze moved to shoulder. "How's the arm?"

"Fine, just like the last few days you asked me."

She kind of grimaced, but she let it go. "You didn't have to ... *be* here. You've got the main email on your phone, right?" She tried to smile at him, but it didn't work. Didn't reach her eyes. Didn't hide any of the heavy weights holding her down.

"Yeah, but Cal's settled, and Aly's nervous bustling was exhausting. Figured being here would be a bit of a break."

She nodded, grabbing the purse off her desk. "I should get going." She moved for the exit, and Nate followed. "I'll be back when I can, but you can close up whenever you'd like."

"What if I close up now? Come with you?"

She stopped, but didn't turn around to face him. Just stood there still, gripping her purse strap. "I ... I'm good. I should handle this."

He didn't care for that answer, but he figured that was

her prerogative. "Then come to dinner at the ranch tonight, after the sentencing. Landon's invite. My insistence."

"I don't know." She slowly turned to face him with a very fake smile plastered on her face. "I think I'll probably just want to be alone tonight."

"Maybe, but you should be with friends. Besides, there'll be cake." He studied her. All the nerves and misery in her eyes even if she'd tried to school them out of her expression. "You've got friends, Sam."

She nodded. "Thanks. I … appreciate it. I'll … try to stop by."

"Good."

She inhaled deeply. Started to leave again, then stopped. Nate waited.

"I don't know if my aunt is going to be there. She never returned my calls. I guess she's still … blaming me."

"I'm sorry."

"Yeah, me too. I just don't get it." She shook her head, still not looking at him. "I don't get why … he killed that woman, and it doesn't excuse Brody and Denver, but it started this whole thing. Was I supposed to lie to protect him? Go against everything that I'd spent fifteen years fighting for just because it was *him*?" She swore quietly under her breath. "Never mind. I have to go," she muttered.

She started to leave, but he followed, gently taking her by the elbow and turning her around. "She's wrong to blame you. I know you know that, but that doesn't mean it doesn't hurt."

She swallowed hard, nodding. "Yeah. I have to…"

She'd given him a hug back at the hospital. It seemed the

thing to do—comfort, support. Maybe there were some complicated feelings lurking under that basic surface, but the fact of the matter was they were all still dealing with the fallout of their fathers' actions.

But it felt like an end was in sight. It felt like ... hope was within reach.

So he gave her a hug, held her close, tried to offer some of that support she'd offered him. She'd been a friend when he needed one. He wished she'd let him do the same in return.

When she let him hug her, when she even leaned against him, he thought maybe he was getting somewhere.

"Maybe I *could* use a friend," she mumbled into his chest.

"Then you've got one, Sam." He pulled her back, wrapped his arm around her shoulders to guide her out the door. "More than one."

The End

If you enjoyed *Dark Mountain Ambush*,
you'll love the other books in…

A Western Edge Mystery Series

Book 1: *Double-Edged Reckoning*

Book 2: *Dark Mountain Ambush*

Available now at your favorite online retailer!

More books by Nicole Helm

Bad Boys of Last Stand series

Book 1: *Homecoming for the Cowboy*
Book 2: *Christmas for the Deputy*

Big Sky Brides series

Book 2: *Bride for Keeps*

Firefighters of Montana series

Book 3: *Ignite*

The 77th Copper Mountain Rodeo series

Book 3: *Keep Me, Cowboy*

Montana Born Brides series

Book 3: *Bride by Mistake*

Available now at your favorite online retailer!

About the Author

Nicole Helm writes down-to-earth contemporary romance—from farmers to cowboys, midwest to *the* west, she writes stories about people finding themselves and finding love in the process. She lives in Missouri with her husband and two sons, surrounded by light sabers, video games, and a shared dream of someday owning a farm.

Thank you for reading

Dark Mountain Ambush

If you enjoyed this book, you can find more from all our great authors at TulePublishing.com, or from your favorite online retailer.

TULE
PUBLISHING